paperback ISBN: 978-1-66789-853-7

eBook ISBN: 978-1-66789-854-4

ABDUCTION
OF SCORPION 6

DAVID JONES

CHAPTER 1

8 October 1871
Egersund, Wisconsin

Both nervous and excited, Hanna sat in the chair while her younger sister laced up her sandals and her mother braided her hair. It was the right of every woman to look beautiful on the most important day of her life. She was dressed in soft colors that meshed with her desire to be one with nature. Her pale skin and blond hair reflected her Norwegian heritage and aided her natural yet elegant look. The braids of her hair were rolled around the top of her head forming a crown adorned with small flowers and ribbons. At just fourteen years old, she felt she was ready to take the next step in her faith.

"You look so beautiful," exclaimed her mother.

"Thank you," she replied, looking forward to her ceremony but not entirely sure of what to expect afterward.

A knock on the dressing room door let them know it was time for the ceremony to begin.

"Are you ready?" asked her mother.

Rising to her feet, Hanna took in a deep breath and exhaled. "Yes, Momma, I'm ready."

Her younger sister, with tears in her eyes, gave her one last embrace. "I don't want you to go, Hanna," she cried. At only ten years old, Thordis didn't fully understand the ceremony or its meaning. She only knew she would no longer share a bed with her older sister and spend every day with her.

Returning the embrace, Hanna said, "Don't be sad child, for this is a glorious day. I have been chosen."

Their mother pulled the young girl away saying, "Be careful not to wrinkle your sister's dress before her ceremony."

As the child continued to cry, her mother wiped her eyes and explained, "Sweet child, you are too young to understand the meaning of this special day. It is a huge honor for all of us that Hanna is the chosen one. Now let us go and wait outside with the ladies and children until the ceremony is over."

Hearing the organ music playing, her mother knew it was time to say goodbye to her oldest child. "I am so proud of you Hanna," she said, as she took one last look at her beautiful daughter in her special gown.

"I love you, Momma. I will see you in Valhalla." Hanna could see the love and warmth in her mother's eyes. She wondered how it was possible to be so sad yet so happy at the same time.

"Until Valhalla," replied her mother, giving her one last embrace before taking her younger sister outside as the women and children were not permitted to observe the holy ceremony.

Hearing another knock at the door, Hanna knew it was time for the ceremony to begin. As she opened the door, she could hear the organ music much more clearly. As she stepped out of the dressing room and into the large barn which had been adorned like a church, she could smell the strong aroma of sage and burning incense.

The incense had significant meaning to her religion. As it lingered in the air, the fragrance pleased the Norse Gods. During a ceremony such as this, the incense can also heighten individual awareness, focus thoughts and provide an opportunity for connection with Divine Spirits. The fact that it masked the otherwise putrid smells of the barn was an added benefit.

The makeshift temple was illuminated by dozens of candles strategically placed around the room. Benches were located on both sides of the aisle like pews in a church. Leaves and flowers decorated the pathway from the back of the room to the altar in the front. All thirty-four men of the small village of Egersund, Wisconsin were present, as was required by their leader.

Guenther, as he was called, was both the spiritual leader and de facto mayor of the group. His influence was paramount as their faith was intertwined with every aspect of their lives. Dressed in dark ceremonial clothes and a black cape, his attire was representative of their Scandinavian roots, but more importantly, their Norse-influenced religion. He wore an eye patch over his left eye from an injury he received while fighting in the American Civil War.

"Who gives this child as a sacrifice to the Norse God Odin?" asked Guenther.

"We do," spoke the entire congregation in unison.

"Come forward," requested Guenther, as Hanna slowly walked down the aisle while all looked on.

Once she reached the front of the room, she stepped up to the altar and turned to face the men in attendance. As she gently laid onto her back, she could feel the cold of the limestone altar emanating through the ceremonial gown. Swimming with anticipation, her thoughts transported her to a different place. While she could hear Guenther preaching his sermon, it sounded far off in the distance. She was very proud that she had been selected by the Norse God Odin, who had come to Guenther through one of his visions.

As she waited to feel the cold touch of the ceremonial blade on her throat, a growing sound drew her attention. The animals tied up outside were making a commotion as they pulled against their ropes. The unfamiliar sound grew louder and Hanna could hear the screams of the women and children in her clan outside the barn. One of the men in the congregation looked out the door and screamed, "The Gods have cast fire down upon us! Run!"

The fire was like no other they had seen before. A massive wall of flames was consuming everything in its path. Standing taller than the forest, it was closing on their town at an impossible speed. It was like a living beast sent to destroy them by the gods.

Panicking, the men fled the barn, desperately looking for safety. While some tried to outrun the impending doom, Guenther dropped to his knees and cried to the heavens. "Norse Gods of war, why do you smite me? What have I done to anger you? Odin, Thor, Tyr, please forgive me and deliver my people from peril!"

As he pleaded with the heavens, a tornado of flames was visible high in the sky. Guenther could feel a strong wind at his back as the massive flames drew in all the air and combustible materials from the small community to feed the growing vortex. The heat grew so intense, items not yet touched by the fire burst into flames. Within moments, the town of Egersund was no more.

CHAPTER 2

20 June 1955
45,000 feet above Lake Superior

Captain Glen Casper had a lot on his mind. Just before takeoff, his wife Becca informed him that they were expecting their first child. The couple had been trying to conceive, unsuccessfully, since his return from the Korean War three years earlier. While the news was an answer to his prayers, he now faced the difficult decision of continuing his military career or transitioning to civilian life.

He loved serving in the Air Force and his well-deserved promotion to the rank of major was only weeks away. If he accepted the promotion, he would incur an additional service commitment and would likely be reassigned to a base in Europe. While his wife was supportive of his service, he knew she preferred to return to civilian life and move back home to Alabama to be near their families. He would need to make a decision, and soon.

His thought process was interrupted by the sound of his radar operator calling over the intercom from the back seat.

"Ghost from Legend. You awake up there?"

"Ghost here. Yeah, I'm awake."

"We are drifting off course a bit. I thought maybe you were napping."

"No, I just have a lot on my mind. I'll correct course."

"Everything OK? I saw Becca stopped in to see you just before the mission briefing."

"It's good news, but it's not public just yet. Becca is expecting."

"Congratulations old man! If I got a girl pregnant, I suppose I would be flying off course too. Probably all the way to Canada," the confirmed bachelor said with a laugh.

"I'm sure you would," laughed Ghost.

"You thinking about punching out of the best job in the world to fly drunk tourists on Pan American Airways?"

"I'm considering all my options," he replied.

"Well think a little longer old buddy. You are about to pin on major and will have your own squadron soon enough. I think you would regret leaving the service at this point. You survived Korea. The rest is all downhill."

"I'll think about it. Ghost out."

"Roger that. Legend out."

A newer practice with fighter pilots was to assign a nickname or "callsign". This served two purposes. It provided a new layer of anonymity over radio communications as well as filled the need for comradery in the service. While some callsigns were innocent enough, others were based on mistakes or incidents during training. Glen was assigned the callsign "Ghost" simply because his last name was Casper like the cartoon character. His younger backseater, First Lieutenant Kelly Jensen, earned the callsign "Legend" because he was able to land a date with an attractive young woman who had a reputation for rejecting the advances of several other pilots.

Once back on course for their patrol, Casper tried to keep his mind focused on the mission. Protecting the nation's northern border from the growing Soviet aggression was about as important a job as one could have. Russia was rapidly increasing its iron grip on the globe and just a few weeks earlier established the Warsaw Pact in response to the allies' North Atlantic Treaty Organization (NATO). This new pact aligned East Germany, Czechoslovakia, Poland, Hungary, Romania, Albania, and Bulgaria with the growing Soviet Union.

With both sides possessing nuclear weapons, the world feared the escalating Cold War would soon turn hot...very hot. With the United States being geographically separated from Europe, the most likely means of a nuclear attack would be a Soviet long-range Tupolev bomber coming over the top of the globe and passing over Canada. To defend against this, the US and Canada established a defensive shield known as the North American Aerospace Defense Command (NORAD).

The American portion of NORAD was called the Air Defense Command (ADC). Capt. Casper and his aircraft were part of this elaborate team. The defensive trip wire consisted of various ground radar posts positioned across the northern border of the US. When an unidentified aircraft was detected, an Air Force fighter was dispatched to investigate and defend the nation against a nuclear attack.

Night patrols were always a little more mundane as visibility was limited. Tonight was especially dark with bad weather and storm clouds blocking the light of the moon. It was hard not to let your mind wander while sitting in the cockpit looking out into the dark abyss.

"Ghost from Legend," came his partner's voice once again over the intercom system.

"Go ahead."

"I heard the commander talking in the hallway this morning. He was telling someone that NORAD will now be tracking Santa Clause as he leaves the North Pole with our advanced early warning radar system. What is that all about?"

Laughing, Casper said, "Yeah, I know all about that. The Air Force is trying to make the best of an embarrassing situation.

"What embarrassing situation?"

"Sears put out a Christmas advertising gimmick telling kids to call Santa directly on the telephone. The advertisement had a typo and the phone number listed accidentally went to the NORAD watch desk. Kids kept calling wanting to tell Santa what they wanted for Christmas. The officer working the desk pretended to be Santa a couple of times. It grew out of hand as the calls kept coming in so the Air Force had to act like it was intentional to save embarrassment."

"Ha, that's a pretty good public relations stunt. That desk officer will probably end up getting himself a medal rather than a court martial."

"We should be back on course now," said Casper.

"Roger that. We are looking good from back here."

"Scorpion 6 from ADC," came over the radio as their aircraft was being contacted.

"Go for Scorpion 6," replied Casper.

"Scorpion 6, the ground intercept radar at Sault St. Marie, Michigan has identified an unusual target over Lake Superior, near the Soo Locks. It's about one hundred and twelve miles from your current location. Please proceed in that direction and see if you can see anything."

"Roger that ADC, we will adjust course to that heading and investigate. Please update as the location changes."

Casper adjusted their heading and the Wisconsin-based fighter jet was now on course for the upper peninsula of Michigan. With a cruising speed of six hundred miles per hour, it would only take about eleven minutes to be in the vicinity of the unidentified flying object. The highly advanced F-89C Scorpion was an all-weather, twin-engine interceptor aircraft and the backbone of the Air Defense Command. It was the nation's best hope of stopping the feared long-range Soviet bomber. The Scorpion carried new air-to-air missiles capable of shooting down sizable aircraft and had a radar capable of scanning targets up to fifty miles away.

"Ghost from Legend."

"Go ahead."

"Not to be superstitious, but this feels eerily similar to the situation where Felix and Robby went missing."

While Casper, as the ranking officer, didn't want to feed into his partner's paranoia, it did seem very familiar. On November 23rd, 1953 First Lieutenant Felix Moncla and Second Lieutenant Robert Wilson were on the same mission patrolling the northern border in a P-89C Scorpion. It was also a dark and stormy night when they were sent to respond to a UFO in restricted airspace near the Soo Locks, the Great Lakes' most vital commercial gateway. Those men would not return from their intercept mission.

While the official finding indicated they had responded to a Canadian Air Force C-47 that had flown thirty miles off course, there was widespread skepticism in the report. The investigation stated that the likely cause of the plane's disappearance was that the pilot experienced a case of vertigo and crashed into Lake Superior. The wreckage was never found. The official report was refuted by a former Marine aviator who published his book *The Flying Saucer Conspiracy*, just weeks earlier.

"I told you not to read that stupid book Legend. Let's just focus on our mission."

"Roger that."

As the two aviators closed in on Michigan air space, Legend was having a difficult time tracking the object on the Scorpion's short-range radar.

"ADC from Scorpion 6. I am having a very difficult time tracking the target. Can you vector us in with the ground radar?"

"Roger that Scorpion 6. The target is now over land just west of Marinette, Wisconsin. Adjust your heading to the west and you should have visibility very soon."

"Copy that ADC. I will advise when I have visual."

After three more minutes, ADC contacted them again, "You should be right on top of the object now Scorpion 6. Do you have a visual?"

"Negative ADC. We have no visual at this time. What altitude are you showing the object at?"

"I think we have a bad radar reading. Our radar is showing the object at an altitude of 60,000 feet."

Casper assumed the radar ping was not working properly as commercial airliners flew between 10,000 and 20,000 feet. Even his state-of-the-art P-89 Scorpion had a maximum ceiling of only 49,000 feet under the best of conditions. Nothing could be operating at 60,000 feet. Looking up to see if he could see anything in the sky, he saw a bright flash of light just above him.

"ADC from Scorpion 6. I have a very bright light directly above…"

"Scorpion 6, your transmission was cut off. Please repeat."

Ground Control had tracked the Scorpion and the unidentified object as two separate "blips" approaching one another on the radar screen. The two blips grew closer and closer until they seemed to merge. Assuming that the Scorpion had either flown above or below the unidentified object, Ground Control anticipated that moments later, the fighter and the unidentified object would once again appear as two separate blips on the screen. After a few moments, Ground Control feared the two objects had collided with one another, however, the unidentified blip continued on its previous course while Scorpion 6 was no longer on the radar screen.

"Scorpion 6 from ADC."

"Scorpion 6 from ADC."

"Scorpion 6 from ADC. Do you read me?"

CHAPTER 3

Truax AFB, Wisconsin

Hearing a knock on the front door of his base housing unit, Special Agent Don Golden was awakened from his sleep. Looking at the alarm clock next to his bed, it read four-thirty in the morning. As a member of the Air Force Office of Special Investigations (OSI), it was not uncommon to be woken at odd hours to investigate criminal or counterintelligence activities.

Putting on his bathrobe, he walked to the front of his small home without turning on the interior lights to protect his night vision. As he got to the front door, he turned on the porch light and peered through the peephole. Standing on his steps was the familiar face belonging to Master Sergeant Donovan Tratnyek, the combat-hardened Air Police flight chief.

Opening the door, he greeted the veteran police officer, "Good morning, Donovan. What brings you to my doorstep at this hour?"

"Good morning Agent Golden. Sorry to get you out of bed but Colonel Roberts sent me to request your attendance for a briefing at his office."

Smiling, Agent Golden asked, "Did Roberts demand I attend or request I attend?"

"Sir, that's above my pay grade. I was just sent to come and get you."

"Thanks, Donovan, but I have my car. You can tell the colonel that I will be there shortly."

"Yes, sir," said the sergeant with a grin.

After closing the front door, Agent Golden returned to his bedroom to get dressed for the meeting with the base commander. While he was certain it was important, he had been struggling with Colonel Roberts since getting assigned to Truax AFB four months earlier. The colonel was infuriated that the OSI agent was stationed on his base but did not fall under his command authority.

After the Air Force became a separate service in 1947, the need for an independent criminal investigation agency was highlighted by a Senate oversight committee looking into war profiteering by an Air Force General. Researchers determined the structure of the Army Criminal Investigative Division (CID) was not conducive to an unbiased investigation because the investigators reported directly to the base commander. Not wanting to duplicate the Army's flawed organizational structure, the civilian Secretary of the Air Force, Stuart Symington, consulted with the Director of the FBI, J. Edgar Hoover.

Director Hoover loaned his top agent, Joseph F. Carroll, to the Air Force to help create the agency that would become the OSI. Agent Carrol recommended a command structure that aligned all of the special agents under the civilian Secretary of the Air Force to avoid improper command influence by senior military officers. Impressed at the design, Secretary Symington requested FBI Agent Carroll to serve as the first OSI commander and appointed him directly to the rank of Brigadier General.

This didn't sit well with many senior Air Force officers who had grown up through the ranks during WWII. Additionally, some were outraged that they were going to have a new watchdog organization operating on their bases which they had no authority over. This was the case with Colonel Roberts.

As Agent Golden finished tying his tie, he put on the black coat of his business suit. OSI agents wore civilian attire and their actual military rank was confidential to prevent it from becoming an obstacle to their investigations. At thirty years old, it was obvious that his actual rank was well below that of the base commanders, however, his pay grade was irrelevant to his duties. Unfortunately, Colonel Roberts didn't see it that way.

As Agent Golden pulled his vehicle into the parking lot outside the base Headquarters building, the time on his watch read four-forty-five am. As he entered the building, there was a flurry of activity and several staff officers were milling about. It was unusual for this much activity so early in the morning so something big must have happened.

Lieutenant Spalding, the commander's aide, greeted him as he entered the command section.

"Good morning Special Agent Golden, the meeting is about to begin. Please take a seat at the briefing table."

As he entered the commander's briefing room, he observed there were about a dozen senior officers seated around a large wooden conference table. Golden took the last seat at the far end of the table next to Major Bob Gibson, the Air Police Squadron Commander, who reported directly to Colonel Roberts.

"What's going on Bob?" asked Agent Golden in a low tone.

Replying in a whisper, he said "A P-89 Scorpion went down somewhere in Northern Wisconsin. The boss thinks they were abducted by space aliens."

Rolling his eyes, Agent Golden said, "Never underestimate the influence of science fiction. It's been almost two years since the movie *War of the Worlds* came out and people are still looking for little green men all over the place. And that new book about the 1953 incident isn't helping anything either."

"Room, attention!" called Lt. Spalding as Colonel Roberts entered the briefing room.

"As you were. Thank you all for coming, now let's get down to business," said the colonel

Lt. Spalding closed the door to the conference room as the briefing was of a classified nature. Once it was closed, the colonel continued.

"At 0300 this morning, Ground Intercept Radar at Sault Sainte Marie, Michigan detected an unknown object traveling over restricted air space above Lake Superior moving south. A P-89 Scorpion was sent up to intercept the unidentified object. Radar indicated the Scorpion made contact with the object over Northern Wisconsin and simply disappeared from the radar screen. The unidentified object was at 60,000 feet and our fighter was at 45,000 feet. The pilot reported seeing a bright light above his location just before losing radio contact. We attempted to launch search and rescue teams, but due to the weather, we will need to wait a few hours. The unidentified object eventually turned around and proceeded north before disappearing from radar as well. There should have been no aircraft in that area, certainly nothing that could take down a P-89…and nothing human can survive at that altitude."

The colonel continued, "At 0800, I will again attempt to launch search aircraft to Marinette County. The area is heavily wooded and very sparsely populated. I will try to get one of the new helicopters brought up from Illinois to assist with the search, but it may take a few days to get one up here. Major Gibson dispatched a ground search team of Air Policemen about an hour ago. It's expected to take about six hours to drive up to that part of the state."

The colonel looked at Don, the only man wearing civilian attire in the meeting. "Agent Golden, I believe OSI has been charged with investigating matters such as this."

"No sir, the OSI is not charged with investigating plane crashes or aerial combat unless foul play is suspected," he replied.

"Don't toy with me, Golden. You know I'm talking about Project Blue Book."

"Sir, OSI does investigate UFO reports and unexplained phenomena under Project Blue Book. Are you suggesting some sort of extraterrestrial activity took place?"

"I'm not ruling anything out Golden!" said the colonel with a stern tone in his voice. "I expect you to contact your leadership and get a Blue Book agent up here today."

"I will make the request immediately after this meeting colonel."

"Good! I want some answers and I expect your agency to be completely forthcoming."

The staff meeting continued for another twenty minutes as the many logistical and technical aspects were coordinated to conduct a search operation. Once Colonel Roberts was satisfied that the group understood their assignments, he dismissed them.

"Meeting adjourned. You all have things to do so let's get to it."

Everyone in the room stood to attention while the commander exited. Once the colonel was gone, the officers in the room started to go about their duties. As everyone collected their papers and hustled about, Major Gibson and Agent Golden sat back down to coordinate their activities.

"How many guys did you send up to Marinette County for the search team?" asked Golden.

"Sixteen Air Policemen in two jeeps and two trucks. I have also requested manpower assistance from both the Wisconsin and Michigan National Guards as they are closer to the crash site."

Agent Golden asked, "So, are you thinking the plane crashed and wasn't abducted by space aliens?"

Major Gibson replied, "I prefer to focus on the most likely scenario," careful not to say anything disparaging against Colonel Roberts, who has a reputation for retribution.

"So, what is this Project Blue Book the boss was talking about?" asked Gibson.

Rolling his eyes, Agent Golden explained, "Project Blue Book is the code name for the study of Unidentified Flying Objects (UFOs). It started a couple of years ago in 1952 and it's based out of Wright-Patterson Air Force

Base, Ohio. There are a small handful of OSI special agents assigned to the program. It's pretty secretive, even within OSI."

"Interesting. Did that start as a result of the flying saucer people say crashed in Roswell, New Mexico?"

"In a roundabout sort of way, I suppose. The Roswell incident was a weather balloon, but that didn't stop conspiracy theorists and hack journalists from taking advantage. The Roswell incident was in 1947. Air Force General Nathan Twining was a believer in extraterrestrial entities and ordered "Project Saucer" with the goal to collect and evaluate UFO sightings on the premise they might represent a national security threat. It was changed shortly after to "Project Sign," then to "Project Grudge" in 1948, and finally "Project Blue Book" in 1952."

With a confused look on his face, Major Gibson asked, "Why so many name changes?"

Smiling, Agent Golden replied, "I don't know what the official answer is, but the rumor was it's because of influence from General Officers based on their view of the existence of extraterrestrial life. General Twining was a believer and designed the program with the goal of proving the existence of space aliens. Then General Vandenberg wasn't a believer and changed the project's goal to debunking UFO claims. In 1952, General Garland, who claimed to have witnessed a UFO, switched it to Blue Book. I wouldn't be surprised if it changes again when another four-star gets involved."

"So how did they come up with the name Blue Book?" asked the major.

Laughing, Don said, "Project Blue Book was named after those blue test booklets that colleges and universities use for their examinations. Some generals said the study of UFOs was at least as important as a college exam, so the project was dubbed Blue Book."

"I take it you are not a believer?" asked Major Gibson.

"Well, I'm not read in on Project Blue Book personally, but I have never seen anything that could not be reasonably explained through science."

"So, are you going to bring one of the Blue Book agents out to investigate?"

"That's above my pay grade but I will certainly make the request as Colonel Roberts wants them here. I guess I better go make the call before he flips his lid."

CHAPTER 4

Wright-Patterson AFB, Ohio

Special Agent Conner Price loved the wind in his hair as he rode his 1941 Harley Davidson knucklehead motorcycle to work. Like many American GIs returning home from WW2, it was challenging for him to integrate back into society. At a time when combat vets were expected to quickly forget the war and all the psychological trauma they experienced, motorcycles offered a sense of freedom. Riding with like-minded friends supplied the camaraderie and adrenaline rush the young men became accustomed to in the war. Unfortunately, thanks to the movie, *The Wild One*, which came out two years earlier starring Marlon Brando, motorcyclists were now starting to be viewed as misfits and outlaws.

Conner had served in the Army Air Force during the war as a fighter pilot. Flying a P-38 Lightning for the 95th Fighter Squadron, he fought in North Africa and Europe before getting shot down and serving the last few months of the war in a German Prisoner of War (POW) camp. Like many Army Air Force vets, he wore his old leather flying Jacket as protection while riding his motorcycle.

After WW2, he joined the new investigative agency known as OSI. His first assignment as a special agent was a felony crimes investigation at Lackland AFB, in San Antonio. His next assignment was counter-espionage and counter-intelligence in Europe. Operating in West Berlin, he was on the front line of the new Cold War. For the past two years, he has been assigned to the highly classified Project Blue Book.

As he approached the security gate at Wright-Patterson Air Force Base, he slowed and brought the bike to a stop. The Air Policeman exited the shack to verify his identification. Dressed in a khaki uniform with a white hat and gun belt, his blue arm band indicated he was a military police officer. Conner noticed the young man was wearing the newly issued Air Force stripes that had finally replaced the Army ranks after the Air Force became a separate and equal service. As an Airman 3rd Class, he wore a single stripe with a star on each sleeve. After examining his OSI credentials, the Air Policeman rendered a salute as he allowed Conner onto the base. While the law enforcement credentials did not identify a military rank other than a special agent, the young policeman saluted just to be safe.

Riding through the base toward the OSI office, Conner worked hard to maintain the designated speed limit. His motorcycle was loud and often drew the attention of young air policemen looking for an easy traffic stop. As he pulled into a parking spot in front of the nondescript building, he could see some of the OSI special agents assigned to the base criminal investigative detachment walking to their building next door. They all wore the typical black suit, black tie, white shirt, and black fedora…most carried a briefcase.

While Conner, assigned to the Project Blue Book office, was expected to wear similar "agent attire," he only did so when he had to interact with his leadership or other ranking officials. He kept a suit in his office for just such occasions. Being part of Project Blue Book, he typically worked assignments all over the country, and in many locations, the business suit made it impossible to blend in with the locals. Other agents assigned to Blue Book typically wore agent attire as directed, however, there was a growing conspiracy among the UFO crowds about "Men in Black" showing up after UFO sightings from some obscure government agency. Conner felt wearing the black suit to small backwater towns fed into this conspiracy and additionally hurt his ability to interact with the locals. Plus, small-town cops didn't always appreciate "G Men" poking around in their backyards either.

As Conner walked into the detachment he was greeted by Jan Green, the administrative assistant, whose desk was positioned behind bulletproof glass. As a civilian employee, she was the constant presence in the office as the field agents spent the majority of time on the road. The spunky thirty-three-year-old was the gatekeeper to the program commander, Special Agent Johnson.

"Good morning, Conner. You better go put your suit on because Agent Johnson wants to see you," she said with a grin as he was known for trying to avoid the boss when he was between investigations.

"What did I do this time?" asked Conner with an eye roll.

"There is a new case up on the Wisconsin/Michigan border. Boss wants you to take it because you went to school there."

"The University of Wisconsin is at the very bottom of the state, a good six-hour drive from the border with Michigan," replied Conner.

"Well, you can discuss the geography of the Midwestern United States with him," she said while giggling and buzzing him into the secure area of the detachment.

Conner had just returned from an investigation in Arizona the day prior and was looking forward to a couple of days off to relax and complete his report. He wasn't very excited about the idea of taking a twelve-hour road trip. Going to his office, he changed into his suit and placed the gold Special Agent badge on his belt, just forward of his service weapon.

OSI agents were issued the new .38 special, Smith & Wesson with a three-inch barrel. The small five-shot revolver was introduced in 1950 at the International Association of Chief of Police convention. Smith & Wesson allowed a vote for the new name of the revolver and the "Chief Special" was the winner. While adequate, Conner much preferred the heft and power of the old model 1911, 45-caliber pistols that he used during the war.

Looking like an agent, Conner walked down the series of hallways to the commander's office. Knocking once on the door frame, Special Agent Johnson shouted, "Get in here Conner and you better be dressed appropriately."

Conner entered the large office and took a seat in front of the desk.

"You wanted to see me boss?" asked Conner.

"What did you find down in Arizona?"

"It was another fake UFO photo hoax. A couple of drunk locals hurled a Buick hubcap into the air and took a photo of it. In the photo, it looked like a flying saucer from the movies. They showed it around in the bar and eventually, a couple of others claimed to have seen it also. By the time I got there, eight people claimed to have witnessed the thing. I eventually got the two original idiots to admit it was a hoax and turn over the hubcap they used. After that, the other six witnesses admitted they only saw the photograph."

"Typical," replied Agent Johnson. "You can write your Arizona report when you get back from Wisconsin."

Conner, attempting to hide his annoyed expression, asked "What's in Wisconsin?"

"Early this morning, radar found a strange blip over Lake Superior traveling south over Northern Wisconsin. A P-89 Scorpion was sent to investigate and seems to have disappeared. From the way it looked on radar, the plane collided with the object and disappeared."

Conner asked, "Couldn't the P-89 have just gone under or over the object, making it look like they collided on the radar screen?"

"Sure, it could. The radar operator thought the same thing and waited for the two blips to separate. But they never did. The unidentified object continued south while the P-89 disappeared from the screen. The object turned north and eventually disappeared from the screen as well."

"Did they find a crash site?" asked Conner.

"Not yet. Bad weather is slowing things down. A ground search team is driving up there but it's a six or seven-hour drive from their base. The area is heavily wooded with not too many folks and few roads. It will be hard to find a crash site up there unless we can spot it from the air."

"Isn't that the same location where that other P-89 Scorpion disappeared a couple of years ago?"

"Yes, same squadron and similar circumstances. That's got a lot of folks concerned. The base commander wants a Blue Book agent up there today and I have already received two phone calls from the Pentagon. Of course, they were not read into Project Blue Book so I couldn't tell them anything."

Conner looked up at the ceiling imagining all the UFO hysteria this could generate. "That's the same missing plane that the ex-Marine pilot wrote about in his book *Flying Saucers from Outer Space?*"

"Yup, the same. Major Donald Keyhoe has made a lot of money with his UFO books. It should be noted that he has been writing fiction books for thirty years, many of which revolve around extraterrestrials, superheroes, Extra Sensory Perception (ESP), and the Bermuda triangle. Now with his credentials as a WW1 pilot, he has transformed his science fiction writing into UFO books and articles. It's getting a lot of folks worked up but he is making big money at it. He uses real Air Force interviews, cherry-picks the information to make them sound ominous, then prints his perspective without all the facts. You will want to get this investigation closed out before he gets wind of it."

"I will do my best. Didn't the plane from two years ago crash into Lake Superior?"

"Yes, that's the theory, but as it went down over the water, we never found it. That fits into the conspiracy theory pretty well."

"Who is my contact in Wisconsin?" asked Conner.

"I want you to drive up to Truax AFB in Madison this morning. It's about a six-hour drive so you need to leave soon. It's another six or seven-hour drive beyond that to the location the plane went missing. You will meet up with the resident OSI agent at Truax, Special Agent Don Golden. He said the base commander, Colonel Roberts, is not a big fan of OSI but is a believer in extraterrestrials. He is the one who requested a Blue Book agent to respond personally."

"Can you reach out and confirm if the Air Force or Central Intelligence Agency (CIA) had any classified aircraft up there this morning? It wouldn't surprise me if it was a U-2 or another classified aircraft from Area 51."

"I reached out to the CIA at Langley and I'm waiting on a callback. It's still a bit early to reach anyone with Project Dragon Lady knowledge at Edwards AFB in California. By the time you get up there and have a look around I should know something. I'll dispatch a classified courier to you when I get some hard information."

"OK, I will sign out a car, run home to pack a bag, and head up there," said Conner.

As he was leaving the boss's office and entering the hallway, he could hear him shout, "And Conner, wear a suit when you talk with that colonel up there!"

Smiling to himself, he replied, "Roger that boss!"

CHAPTER 5

Returning to his office, Conner collected the clothes he wore on the ride to work and placed them into a paper bag. He then walked down the hall to the equipment area to pick out some investigative items to take with him. Picking out a camera kit with extra lenses and an OSI crime scene kit, he carried it all to the reception area to see what kind of duty car he could get from Jan.

"Hey Jan," he said with a flirtatious smile. "What duty cars are available for my trip?"

Smiling, she replied, "I have a nice 1948 Ford Super Deluxe for you."

"Come on Jan, it's June and I have a long drive ahead of me. What's the deal on that 1952 Chevy Bel Air parked out there? You know, the one with air conditioning."

Laughing, she said, "Tucker already called dibs on the Bel Air."

"Tucker can't call dibs on a duty car. It's first come first serve."

"Dems the breaks kid," she said with a laugh.

Knowing she could be bargained with, Conner persisted. "So, what would I need to do to get the Bel Air for my trip to Wisconsin?"

"Now that you ask, my cousin is coming to visit next month and I would like to set her up on a date while she is here."

Frowning, he replied, "The Ford will do just fine thank you."

Laughing out loud, she said, "Wait a minute, Conner. She is very attractive. Let me show you a photo." Jan pulled a photo out of her purse that was staged and ready to go.

Looking at the photo, he replied, "Yeah, she's gorgeous in this picture, but how long ago was it taken?"

"During the war."

"And just which war was that?" he asked with a sarcastic tone.

Jan held up the keys to the Bel Air and said, "Just one date Conner. It can even be a double with my husband and me."

Hesitating for a moment, Conner reached out and took the car keys.

"Just one date," he replied.

Smiling, she said "That's all I ask. Have a safe trip."

Wanting to get out of the building without Special Agent Tucker seeing him, Connor took his gear and left through the back door. Quietly loading his equipment into the Bel Air, he got in the driver's seat and closed the door as quietly as possible. Knowing that the car was parked just outside Special Agent Tucker's office window, Connor couldn't help but give the horn a short beep.

As Tucker looked up from his desk to see who had honked, his eyes met with Connors, who was sitting in the driver's seat of the Bel Air, smiling and waving as he pulled out of the lot. The two Blue Book agents were both friends and rivals, never missing a chance to pull a practical joke on the other.

Arriving at the small one-bedroom home he rented off base, he went inside to pack a bag. As he entered the front door, he couldn't help but notice that after living there for almost two years, the walls were still bare and only a couple of pieces of furniture occupied the dwelling. It was very apparent that he spent little time at home.

Walking into the bedroom, he considered switching clothes before his trip but thought better of it as he would be meeting Agent Golden and probably Colonel Roberts before he could check into the Visiting Officers Quarters (VAQ) and change back into his suit.

After packing a small suitcase with a couple of changes of clothes and some hygiene items, he went to his closet and pulled out a small canvas World War II aviator's bag. Conner always took the small bag with him when he traveled alone on an investigation. Opening the bag to inventory the contents, he pulled out a Government Model 1911, 45acp pistol. While it was not his duty weapon, he liked to keep it in the trunk of his car just in case he ran into trouble on the road. While his OSI issue 38 special could handle most situations, Conner had a knack for finding more trouble than the average agent. Next, he pulled out three magazines for the pistol, a USAF Pilot Survival Knife, a compass, a rain poncho, a first aid kit, twenty-five feet of cotton rope and other survival-related items. After being shot down over enemy territory and spending several days on the run before getting captured, Conner made it a point to be prepared for anything going forward.

With his suitcase and aviator's bag stowed in the trunk along with his investigative equipment, Conner closed the heavy lid with a slam. Walking through the well-manicured yard of the pink house next to his, he knocked on the door. After waiting a few moments, a middle-aged woman wearing an apron opened it.

"Hi, Conner. Did you have a good trip?"

"It was typical. I got back late last night."

"Yeah, I heard your motorcycle when you left for work this morning." Looking down at her watch, she said, "It's only nine o'clock in the morning. Are you taking the rest of the day off?"

"Unfortunately, no. I caught another case and I am on my way out again."

"Well that explains the suit," she said with a grin.

Smiling, he said, "Yeah, got to keep the boss happy."

"I hate to ask again already, but can you keep getting my mail and have Mike mow the grass while I'm gone? I'll make it up to you the first chance I get."

"Sure, not a problem. Be safe."

"Thanks, Amanda. Say hi to Mike for me."

Amanda and Mike were great neighbors to have. He was a biologist assigned to the civil engineering squadron on base and she looked after their three boys. While they knew he was an OSI agent and traveled often for his work, they knew not to ask too many questions about what he was working on. They were always willing to look after his place while he was away, which was the majority of the time.

Starting his six-hour road trip to Madison, he adjusted the air conditioning so it was blowing nice and cold. While it wasn't the same as having the wind in his face on his Harley, it was a welcomed luxury. He grinned to himself as he thought about Tucker having to take the old Ford with no air conditioning on his next assignment.

Conner tuned the radio dial until he came to a station without static. "Thanks for listening to WAVI, the Real Rhythm of the City." Conner continued to drive and let his mind wander to the sound of the Andrews Sisters singing a familiar song. It had been several years since he had been to Madison, Wisconsin. As an enlisted pilot during the war, he was promoted from Staff Sergeant to Flight Officer, the equivalent of a Warrant Officer. After the war, the Air Force had an abundance of pilots and Conner had a choice to revert back to a sergeant or complete the last two years of college and earn a commission as a second lieutenant. Conner opted to complete his degree at the University of Wisconsin, graduating in 1948.

While the college material was not challenging for him, what was difficult was trying to fit back into civilian life after experiencing years of combat and life as a POW. Much of the trivial things that traditional college students worried about seemed completely insignificant to him. It was hard for him to relate with his fellow students and professors as he was struggling with the memories and horrors of his past.

Thinking about his time at the university, his mind went to his favorite professor, Dr. Melvin Crane. A scientist and meteorologist, he was an expert in atmospheric phenomena. During the war, he was appointed as a Lieutenant Colonel with the Army Air Force and contributed heavily to the success of the allied landing on D-Day. Helping plan the invasion from a weather standpoint, it was critical to select the right day and time for the invasion. Many factors affected the conditions from the phases of the moon to the level of the tides. A full moon was desirable, as it would provide illumination for the aircraft pilots. The beach landing had to take place shortly before dawn, midway between low and high tide, with the tide coming in. This was critical to improving the visibility of obstacles on the beach while minimizing the amount of time soldiers would be exposed to machine gun fire in the open. It had to take place at a time with calm winds and no cloud coverage so paratroopers could be dropped on target without getting blown off course. Dr. Crane's expertise was critical to the success of Operation Overlord and saved thousands of allied lives.

After being assigned to Project Blue Book two years earlier, Conner consulted with Professor Crane on multiple UFO sightings, most of which he was able to explain scientifically. Due to the classified nature of the program, Conner had the professor flown to Wright-Patterson AFB to consult with after signing non-disclosure agreements. Conner thought it wise to meet with him in person since he would be in Madison.

Needing to refuel and wanting to give Dr. Crane a call, Conner stopped at a Texaco station just west of Indianapolis. At 29 cents per gallon, it would take well over four dollars to fill the sixteen-gallon tank on the Bel Air. Conner was sure to get a receipt for the purchase and marked it down on his expense sheet for reimbursement.

After paying for his gas, Conner took a moment to step into the phone booth located next to the filling station office. Putting a dime into the slot, he entered the number for the University of Wisconsin Science Hall. After waiting a few moments, a young woman picked up the line and said, "Science Hall, how may I direct your call?"

"Good morning. My name is Special Agent Conner Price and I would like to speak with Dr. Crane."

"Please hold the line and I will see if he is available."

Waiting on the line, Conner recalled his time as a student at the Science Hall. Dr. Crane was not only his professor but as a veteran himself, served as a mentor and a friend. Critical in helping Conner assimilate to college life, he also helped him face some of the demons left over from the war. The professor found the fact that Conner had been a fighter pilot very interesting and he often had questions related to aeronautics.

"Conner, old friend, are you still on the line?" asked the familiar voice.

"Yes, Doc, I'm still here."

"It's great to hear your voice. How can I be of service?"

"Doc, I am driving up to Truax AFB for a new case and was wondering if you would have some time to meet with me this evening for a consultation?"

"Of course, Conner. Would you like me to meet you at the base?"

"If it's not too far out of your way, that would be wonderful."

"Not at all, just tell me when and where."

"Well, I should arrive around five this evening and will need to meet with the local OSI agent and probably the base commander. Would seven pm at the base OSI detachment be too late?"

"That would be just fine. If you can give me an idea of what you are looking for, I can try and prepare a bit."

"Well, I guess I am looking for any atmospheric conditions or strange phenomena over Northern Wisconsin last night that would be of interest to the kind of thing I investigate."

"Sounds good Conner. I will see you tonight."

"See you tonight, Doc."

Continuing on his journey, Conner adjusted the radio dial to find another channel. Coming across Indianapolis WFBM radio, they were having a conversation about the new polio vaccine that had been approved just six weeks earlier. Developed by Dr. Jonas Salk, the vaccine proved successful against poliomyelitis, the virus that caused the crippling disease. In 1952 alone there were 50,000 new cases in the United States with 3,000 deaths.

The disease was commonly referred to as infant paralysis because it mainly affected children.

Conner couldn't help but think of his childhood friend Trevor. The two were inseparable and spent all their free time hunting and camping in the Montana wilderness. Conner was devastated when Trevor contracted the disease shortly after their seventeenth birthday. Crippled by the disease, he was unable to enlist in the military with Conner after the Japanese attack on Pearl Harbor. Trevor would live the war vicariously through Conner's letters and radio news broadcasts. It was hard to believe that the disease that left even President Franklin D. Roosevelt crippled, could be a thing of the past.

CHAPTER 6

As he pulled up to the front gate at Truax Air Force base in Madison, Conner glanced at his watch. Just after five o'clock, the Bel Air made good time. As the Airman came out of the gate shack, Conner held out his OSI credential and asked for directions to the base detachment. After providing the directions to the office, the air policeman rendered a salute. Returning the salute, Conner drove onto the installation.

Pulling into the parking spot in front of the local OSI detachment, Conner was not surprised at the subpar building occupied by the resident agent. Many of the base commanders were not very happy about being ordered to provide secure office space to the special agents whom they had no authority over. Because of this, some commanders provided some of the worst real estate the base had to offer.

Walking up to the small concrete building with metal doors and bars over the windows, the door opened before he had a chance to knock. A man in a black suit said, "Afternoon, are you the guy from Project Blue Book?"

"Yup, Conner Price," he replied while providing his credentials.

"After examining the identification and comparing it against his face, the man in the suit said, "Come on in. I'm Don Golden, welcome to our little castle."

Smiling, Conner replied, "Yeah, I heard the base commander was not a big fan."

"That's an understatement. Last month I charged his top contracting officer and golf buddy with fraud. He was taking financial kickbacks from a construction company for awarding them the new aircraft hangar project."

"The commander wasn't grateful?"

"Not so much. He felt I should have just let him handle the matter rather than conduct an official OSI investigation," replied Don.

"Speaking of Colonel Roberts, he's waiting over at his HQ for us. We should head over there as he is not the most patient man."

"Sounds good. I have a professor from the University of Wisconsin meeting with us here at seven o'clock. I hope that's ok?"

"Sure, whatever you need. I also took the liberty of getting you a room at the VOQ," said Don while holding up the key.

"Thanks," said Conner, taking the key and putting it in his pocket.

As the two agents were driving across the base to the headquarters building, Conner asked how many OSI agents were assigned to Truax.

Shaking his head, Don replied, "There are supposed to be four of us, but the most I ever had was two besides myself. Right now, I only have a rookie agent right out of the academy. I do have another agent assigned but he is deployed to French Indochina for the next six months."

"What's he doing there?" asked Conner.

"Cold War stuff in a little country called South Vietnam. The Japanese occupied it during the war. Now that the communists in the north are trying to move in, we are helping them build their own Air Force."

"Sounds like the makings of another Korean War," said Conner.

"No, we are just there as advisors this time. We are not doing any of the actual fighting. I don't think President Eisenhower will let us get too involved over there," said Don.

As the two agents arrived at the base commander's office, they were met at the door by Lieutenant Spalding.

Don introduced them, "Lieutenant Spalding, this is Special Agent Price from Wright Patterson."

Shaking hands, Lieutenant Spalding said, "Glad you are here sir, the colonel is getting a little impatient."

As the three men walked down the hall, Don asked if they had located the crash site yet.

"No sir, not yet. The area is heavily wooded with a very thick tree canopy. We have a huge area to search."

Coming to Colonel Robert's office, Lieutenant Spalding knocked once on the door.

"Enter," came a commanding response from within the office. Lieutenant Spalding opened the door and announced them.

"Sir, I have Special Agent Price from Wright-Patterson AFB and Agent Golden here to see you."

"Thank you, Lieutenant, that will be all. Gentlemen, please have a seat."

The two agents took a seat in front of the commander's desk while Lieutenant Spalding closed the door behind him as he left the room.

"So, you are from Project Blue Book, Agent Price?"

"Yes sir, I am."

"Good. I want some answers."

"I just arrived colonel, I haven't had the opportunity to investigate anything just yet."

"Well, I'm certain based on your position, you have some idea of what may have happened to my men."

"Unfortunately, I do not sir. I'm here to conduct a non-partial investigation and determine if there is any UFO-related aspect to your missing aircraft."

"Fine," he said with a tone of disbelief. It was clear the colonel was convinced that there was some sort of extraterrestrial explanation behind his missing plane and its two pilots. It was also clear he believed Agent Price had some knowledge about space aliens that he wasn't sharing.

"So, what are your plans, Agent Price?"

"This evening I will examine the known facts of the case with Agent Golden. Later tonight I have a meeting with an expert in meteorology and atmospheric phenomena from the University of Wisconsin. Tomorrow morning, I plan on driving up to Marinette County and speaking with local law enforcement. From there I will see where the investigation takes me."

"I expect to be kept informed of your investigation."

"Sir, I will keep Agent Golden in the loop. As the agent assigned to your base, he will serve as your liaison to my investigation."

It was clear the colonel was not pleased with that answer, however, he had no recourse.

"Agent Golden, I would like you to accompany Agent Price up to Marinette County tomorrow. And I expect regular updates."

"Yes sir," replied Don.

"Agent Price, I want to know what is special about that area up there. This is the second plane that has gone missing while investigating a UFO. Now there is even that damn UFO book written about my base."

"Sir, while I was not the agent who investigated the missing plane in 1953, it's my understanding that the situation was explained. The UFO was a Canadian Air Force C47 that was off course by thirty miles and entered controlled air space."

"Then what caused my plane to disappear?"

"That I couldn't say. It was the investigator's opinion that the pilot crashed into Lake Superior as a result of either mechanical failure or pilot error."

"And is that your official statement on the matter?"

"Sir, I don't have an official statement on the 1953 incident. All I did was read the report. I am here to investigate the current missing aircraft."

"Fine. That will be all gentlemen. I expect to be kept in the loop, Golden."

"Yes sir," replied Don as the two men left the office.

Once outside of the headquarters building, Don asked Conner how could so many people, including educated people like a base commander, believe in UFOs from outer space.

"Well, I guess a lot of it has to do with Hollywood. Movies like *The Day the Earth Stood Still, Invaders from Mars,* and dozens of similar science fiction films make people want to believe in existence outside of our world. Also, the Cold War makes people feel vulnerable. I like to think of the UFO hysteria as a social phenomenon. People want to think there is an extraterrestrial entity that will come to earth and save us from ourselves, prevent nuclear war and such."

"I can see that I guess. It just surprises me senior leaders like Colonel Roberts fall for it," said Don.

"A lot of folks much higher up than Colonel Roberts are believers," replied Conner. "A lot of pilots and senior officials have seen things they just can't explain any other way. That said, just because they can't explain it, doesn't mean there isn't a reasonable explanation."

"You don't believe in aliens do you, Conner?"

"I officially have to keep an open mind on the subject. I have investigated a lot of strange things while assigned to Blue Book. Most of which there was a scientific explanation for. Many more are intentional hoaxes. There have been a few things I simply can't explain. Doesn't mean they are extra-terrestrial though. Also doesn't mean there are not."

Back at the local OSI detachment, Don provided all the specific details of the disappearance of Scorpion 6 to Conner.

"So, there you have it. Any thoughts?"

"Have you pulled the medical and psychological profiles on the pilots?" asked Conner.

"Yes, Captain Glen Casper, callsign Ghost, is a West Point graduate with eight years of pilot experience. He served in the Korean War where he shot down two Mig 15s. He has an excellent flight record and is known to be calm and collected under pressure. He was about to pin on the rank of major and he is on the shortlist to be assigned his own fighter squadron. His last flight physical was in March. Other than slightly elevated cholesterol there were no issues noted. I did learn that his wife is expecting their first child. She informed him of the news just before takeoff."

"Was he upset by the news?" asked Conner.

"It didn't sound like it, but that information came from his wife. Who knows what was going through his mind during the flight?"

"What about the back seater, call sign Legend?" asked Conner.

Smiling, Don said "First Lieutenant Kelly Jensen, callsign Legend. He has been flying for just over two years and is a graduate of the University of Florida. He has a pretty big reputation as a skirt chaser. Kind of an overgrown frat boy who looks like Rock Hudson. He isn't the most mature pilot in the Air Force but he is a solid aviator. He's pretty cocky, even for a fighter jock. His last flight physical was in April."

"Anything pertinent on his physical?"

"He had a black eye and some cracked ribs that kept him out of the cockpit for a couple of weeks. Apparently, he was dancing with the wrong girl at a club in town. Her boyfriend took issue with it. But other than that, he had a clean bill of health."

"Do you know them personally?" asked Conner.

"Not really. I've seen them around the Officers' Club once in a while. I think everyone knew who Legend was around the base as he had a way of standing out in a crowd. When he was off duty, he was always sporting around on his Harley Davidson motorcycle wearing his leather flight jacket. You know the type."

"Yeah, I know the type," replied Conner.

CHAPTER 7

Hearing a knock on the OSI detachment door, Conner looked down at his watch. It was only half past six, the professor must be early he thought.

Don, peeking through the blinds, said, "It's not your professor, it's Mrs. Casper. The wife of the missing pilot. I wonder what she wants?"

Opening the door, Don greeted the woman and welcomed her inside the small building.

"Please come in Mrs. Casper. What can we do for you?"

"Thank you, Agent Golden. I was told that another OSI agent from Wright Patterson AFB was sent here to help find my husband. Is he here by chance?"

Seeing that Don was struggling to respond to the woman's question, Conner stepped up and introduced himself.

"Hello, Mrs. Casper. I'm Special Agent Conner Price. Please come in and have a seat."

The thirty-year-old military wife was well-dressed, articulate, and very confident. Although she was devastated by the situation, she maintained her composure and held herself together. Taking a seat at the small conference table across from Conner and Don, she thanked them for taking the time to speak with her.

"I'm sorry to meet you under these circumstances, Mrs. Casper. What can I do for you?"

"I was told that you are from a secret project that investigates UFOs, is that correct?"

Not sure where this conversation was headed, Conner trod carefully.

"Ma'am, I am here at the request of the base commander. I am assigned to a special project that investigates strange phenomena and unexplained aerial sightings. As there was some anomaly with the radar involving your husband's disappearance. I have been called in to take a look."

Cutting the small talk, the determined woman asked the question they were dancing around.

"Agent Price, do you believe my husband was abducted by space aliens?"

Evaluating the sincerity expressed in her eyes, he replied, "Ma'am, I have seen nothing that would draw me to such a conclusion."

Nodding in agreeance, she asked, "Are you a Christian agent Price?"

"Well, yes ma'am. I was raised that way, but admittedly, I'm probably not the best example these days."

"My husband and I are strong Christians. Glen is the son of our hometown preacher back in Alabama. I always thought he would follow in his father's footsteps someday. We have spent a lot of time praying that God would bless us with a child and I recently learned he has done so. Since Glen's disappearance this morning, I have continued to pray on the matter. I believe the lord has spoken to me and I know in my heart that Glen is alive and waiting to be rescued. I don't believe in space aliens and I fear precious time will be wasted on such endeavors."

Conner replied, "I understand Mrs. Casper. I can assure you that the Air Force will take every possible measure to bring your husband home safely. My function here will not divert any resources from the search for your husband or his crewmember. Their safety is everyone's number one priority."

"Thank you for that, Mr. Price. But like I was saying, I have prayed on the matter and I believe that the Holy Spirit has spoken to me. Are you familiar with the bible story of Daniel and the lion's den?"

"Yes ma'am, I recall the story. Daniel refused to stop his daily payers to the God of Israel so the king had him cast into a pit of hungry lions as punishment. The next day when the king came to check on him, he found Daniel unharmed. The King asked if his God had saved him and Daniel replied an angel was sent down from above to close the jaws of the lions. Is that the story you are referring to?"

"Yes, it is. This morning while I was praying for my husband's safety, I believe I had a vision. My husband was in the lion's den surrounded by danger, but God protected him for several days until an angel was sent to close the jaws of the lions and deliver him from evil. I believe you are to be the angel God has sent to bring my husband home."

Not sure how to respond to the woman who was experiencing grief, Conner replied, "Thank you for sharing your vision with me, Mrs. Casper. While I am not certain how to interpret what you told me, I promise you, we will do everything in our power to bring your husband home safe."

As the two shared an awkward pause while she continued to look him in the eyes, he replied in a more personal tone. "I will do everything in my power to bring your husband home to you."

"Thank you, Agent Price. I know in my heart that you will."

Once Mrs. Casper left the detachment, Don looked over to Conner and asked, "Well, what do you make of that?"

Scratching his head, he replied, "The woman has had a pretty traumatic couple of days with learning she is pregnant and now her husband going missing. The situation would make anyone emotional, even without pregnancy hormones."

"Have you ever had anyone tell you about a religious vision before?"

Laughing, he replied, "Well I have never been accused of being an angel before, that's for sure. But, yes, many of my Project Blue Book investigations have involved some highly emotional people. Some with mental health issues, some under the influence of drugs and alcohol, and other folks who got themselves worked up into a psychological frenzy. People that hold deep religious or personal beliefs often allow them to shape their perception of reality. I think Mrs. Casper is looking for reassurance right now and her spiritual belief system is providing it. I admire it. I've relied on faith before to help get me through extreme situations. While I'm not a textbook church-goer, I do believe in a higher power."

"So, what happens if we don't bring her husband back alive?"

"I imagine she will struggle with her beliefs, or at least reevaluate the vision she thinks she had. Either way, the woman seems to be grieving in her own way, even if she didn't physically present that way. I recommend you give the base chaplain a call and have him check in on her."

"That's a good idea, I'll do that. I'm not sure what the chaplain will think about her envisioning that her husband is surrounded by lions in Northern Wisconsin."

Looking at the younger investigator, Conner replied, "I think it's safe to say she used the parable as a metaphor. I don't think she was talking about actual lions surrounding her husband, or that I'm an actual angel sent from heaven."

Smiling, he asked, "You sure about that?"

Shrugging his shoulders and smiling, he replied "Yeah, I don't know."

Hearing another knock on the door, Conner again looked down at his watch. It was almost seven o'clock.

"Is that your Dr. Crane?" asked Don, while peering through the Vene-tian blinds.

Looking through the window to verify, he said, "Yeah, that's him."

Opening the door, Conner greeted his old friend and introduced him to Agent Golden. After inviting him inside, they all took seats around the small table. Without providing all of the details, Conner explained the general encounter that took place and asked if any atmospheric phenomena could explain.

Pondering all the potential explanations, Dr. Crane replied, "I suppose there are several plausible explanations, each one having different merits of course. We can rule out an elaborate hoax as this particular incident involved credible Air Force pilots and ground radar personnel. So, let's examine some of the potential atmospheric explanations."

"The most logical explanation would be some sort of classified military object. I know both the United States and the Soviets are testing new rockets, so I assume you have already ruled out anything of that nature."

"We are looking into that but I haven't heard conclusively just yet."

"I would assume an Atlas or Jupiter rocket could provide a bright light from a high altitude, either from a propulsion system or a reflection of moonlight off of its metal body. But I would assume the radar operator would have made mention of the high speeds a rocket would likely travel at as well as the rapidly changing altitude. The fact that the object turned around in flight would make the rocket theory highly questionable."

Writing down the potential hypothesis, Conner replied, "I would be very surprised if it were a rocket based on the radar data."

Dr. Crane hesitated to share his next theory as even he couldn't explain how it would have affected the pilots over Wisconsin. "There was an unusual anomaly that occurred last night. Although I can't explain how it would affect Northern Wisconsin, it's too unusual to discount completely. Today was a total solar eclipse but it was only visible from Asia. A solar eclipse occurs when the moon passes between the Earth and the Sun, totally or partially obscuring the image of the Sun for a viewer on the Earth. A total eclipse occurs when the Moon's apparent diameter is larger than the Sun's, blocking all direct sunlight, and turning day into night. The eclipse today lasted seven full minutes, which made it the longest solar eclipse since the 11th century. While I can't explain how that would provide a light in the sky over Northern Wisconsin or the radar reading, the coincidence is a bit too amazing to be dismissed altogether."

"That is quite a coincidence," said Conner.

Intrigued by the theories, Don asked if there were any other possible explanations.

"Oh, yes, there are several," replied Dr. Crane. "Other common atmospheric phenomena that have been mistaken for UFOs have been sprite flashes of lightning that occur well above the electric field during a thunderstorm, odd cloud formations, weather balloons, and even the planet Venus."

"Venus?" asked Don.

"Venus has been the explanation for several of my UFO sightings, especially by pilots," said Conner.

Dr. Crane explained, "Yes, the planet Venus is often mistaken for a UFO. The second planet from the sun appears as a bright light in the sunset sky occasionally. It can outshine all the other stars except for the sun. Because Venus orbits the sun inside our own orbit, from our perspective on Earth, it can dart in and out from the side of the sun, often being mistaken for a UFO. It should also be noted this can only be seen from looking to the west from North America."

"That was the same direction the P-89 was traveling when it reported the bright light in the sky. But they reported the light directly above them rather than to the west," said Don.

"What about the Northern Lights? They are visible from Northern Wisconsin at times?" asked Conner.

Dr. Crane explained, "Yes, the Northern Lights have been mistaken for extraterrestrial activity by people for thousands of years. The scientific name for them is Aurora Borealis. The bright dancing lights are actually collisions between electrically charged particles from the sun that enter the earth's atmosphere. But in Wisconsin, they are most visible during the long, dark nights of the winter months. It would be very unlikely they were visible last night."

"So, what would make the P-89 disappear or crash?" asked Don.

The professor looked at Conner and said, "Well that is outside of my area of expertise. I would assume you have some theories, Conner."

"I do, but I am trying not to let them skew my thought process. One theory would be when the pilot saw the light, whatever it was, he thought it was closer than it actually was and took evasive actions to avoid colliding with it. It's very difficult to judge the distance of light, especially when you are traveling at 600mph at an altitude of 45,000 feet. There could be several aeronautical or mechanical issues that could result in a crash. Perhaps he got disoriented, experienced a case of vertigo, or maybe his plane went into a flat spin or even had a bird strike. There are some very large storks up in that area that could easily take down a jet traveling at that speed, though not at that altitude. There is a list of potential things that could happen to a jet mechanically during high altitude evasive maneuvers."

"What about losing oxygen at that altitude?" asked Don.

Nodding in affirmation, Conner said, "Sure, hypoxia would kick in fast at that altitude. Atmospheric pressure reduces at high altitudes and with it, the amount of oxygen. With the lack of oxygen at even 12,000 feet, the pilot would experience dizziness and headaches. Above 30,000 feet the pressure would become far too low to push oxygen molecules into the lungs. If something happened to his oxygen supply at that altitude, he could lose consciousness and die pretty fast. I assume if and when we locate the crash site, we will learn a lot from the wreckage if there is anything left."

"Did you ever experience hypoxia?" asked Dr. Crane.

"Oh yeah, a couple of times. It was at a much lower altitude but pretty scary stuff," replied Conner.

"Are you a pilot?" asked Don.

"I was back during the war. World War 2 that is, not Korea. When I got shot down, I took a pretty good beating from some German prison guards. After that, I could no longer pass a flight physical so I switched career fields to investigations."

With a lull in the conversation as Conner slipped back into the dark memory of his time as a POW, Dr. Crane changed the subject in an attempt to bring his friend back to the present conversation.

"Conner, did the P-89 have one of those new ejection seats or would they have had to bail out?"

Conner knew the Doc was aware of the ejection seats on modern fighter aircraft so he assumed his friend was just trying to keep him from getting lost in his past.

"Yes, it had a Type C-3 ejection seat. But ejecting at such an altitude and such a fast speed provides a whole slew of complications. The pilots could have been killed or wounded during the ejection process, not to mention parachuting into a heavily wooded forest or over water at night. Of course, other theories could involve some advanced aircraft from the Soviet Union shooting it down and yes, maybe space aliens abducted them. But I prefer to follow the evidence rather than the theories."

Looking at Dr. Crane, Conner asked, "Doc, I remember you telling us about a huge fire in that part of the state in the eighteen hundreds where some people thought it was caused by aliens."

Smiling, Dr. Crane said, "Yes, the Peshtigo Fire of 1871. It was a huge forest fire in the northeast of Wisconsin and parts of upper Michigan. To this day it is the deadliest forest fire in recorded history. It killed between 1500 and 2500 people and burned 1.2 million acres."

"How have I not heard of that?" asked Don with a surprised tone.

"It occurred the same day as the much more famous Great Chicago Fire, October 8th. Even though it was five times deadlier, Chicago was a big city and got all of the publicity. There was speculation that it was not a coincidence the two fires occurred on the same day. Some people speculated that fragments of the Biela Comet had ignited both fires. Today we know this to be false as the comet fragments would have been cold to the touch by the time it hit Earth."

"Other theories focused on extraterrestrial causes. Some people claimed to have seen blue flames burning in the basements of houses. Modern fire theory explains this phenomenon as likely a product of burning carbon monoxide in poorly ventilated basements."

"Interesting," exclaimed Don. "I never considered there were so many scientific explanations for things."

"Not all of the conspiracy theories involving the fire were extraterrestrial. There was also a widespread theory that William Ogden, Chicago's first mayor, was responsible for both fires as part of insurance fraud. He owned thousands of acres of land and many businesses in both cities. While this theory was entirely conspiratorial, it was a popular one."

"So, Conner, what is the military definition of UFO? I assume there is one," asked the professor.

"Yeah, the Air Force has an official definition of just about everything. Last year we published Air Force Regulation 200-2. It defines a UFO as any airborne object which by performance, aerodynamic characteristics, or unusual features, does not conform to any presently known aircraft or missile type, or which cannot be positively identified as a familiar object."

"Yeah, that sounds like an Air Force definition," said Don with an eye roll.

"Thanks, Doc, you have provided a lot of information for us to consider. I appreciate you taking the time to come and educate us," said Conner.

After saying goodbye to his friend and mentor, Conner turned to Don and said, "I'm starving. Does the Officer's Club serve food this late?"

"Yeah, if you go to the bar side, they serve burgers and sandwiches until 10 o'clock."

Looking down at his watch, it was almost nine-thirty. "I'm going to run over and get a bite to eat before they close. What time do you want to head up to Marinette in the morning?"

"I suppose we better leave early if we want to get up there during business hours. If we leave at five o'clock, we should be up there by lunchtime. Do you want to ride together?"

"Sure, we can take my car, it's got air conditioning," said Conner.

"Sounds good, I will be over at the VOQ at five."

CHAPTER 8

Walking into the Officer Club bar, it was dimly lit and the mood was not as vibrant as it typically would have been. Monday nights were typically slow to start with, but the loss of two of their own had dampened the mood. There were only about ten customers in the club, scattered about with some sitting at tables and only a couple sitting at the bar.

Conner walked up to the counter and waited to place his order with the bartender. He noticed the attractive brunette sitting by herself at the bar drinking a martini and smoking a cigarette. She was probably in her late twenties and well put together. Fashionably dressed and with an overly sophisticated manner, she didn't appear like the traditional military wife. As the bartender walked up to the other side of the bar, he asked, "What can I get you?"

"Is the kitchen still open?"

"Sure, we take orders right up until 10 o'clock."

"Great. How about a BLT and a Coke?" asked Conner.

"It will be right up," replied the bartender.

"Thanks, I will be sitting over there," said Conner, pointing to the empty table in the corner of the room.

He preferred not to put himself in a position for small talk when he was on assignment, that was unless he was attempting to elicit information from someone. Sitting alone at the small table in the corner of the club, he maintained his back to the wall so he could view all of the activities and people who enter the room. He could see the attractive brunette sitting at the bar with her back to him. She was using the mirror behind the bar to watch him in the reflection. Knowing it was a tradecraft technique utilized by cops and spies, Conner was initially suspicious of her surreptitious actions. He quickly dismissed the notion as it was illogical to believe everyone was a spy fighting in the Cold War.

As the bartender delivered the meal to the table, Conner impatiently took the first bite as he was famished from the day's journey. As soon as his mouth was full with his oversized bite, the brunette appeared at his table and introduced herself.

"Hi, I'm Darlene, mind if I join you?"

Embarrassed, as he couldn't speak to the woman with his mouth full, he simply gestured with his hand for her to have a seat.

Wiping his mouth with his napkin, he introduced himself as Bill. Since William was his middle name, he often gave the name Bill to people he didn't wish to provide his actual first name.

"So, Bill, what brings you to base?" asked the woman.

"What makes you think I am not stationed here?" he asked.

Taken back by the redirection of the conversation, she replied, "Oh, I have just never seen you here before."

Smiling, he asked, "Do you know everyone on the base?"

"No, but you don't seem like a regular here at the Officer's Club."

Switching the line of questioning to her, Conner asked "So, what do you do here? You don't exactly seem like a WAF (Women's Air Force).

Smiling, she said, "No, I'm not in the service. My sister's husband is a pilot and I have been staying with them for a little while."

Wanting to keep the elicitation of information focused on her rather than himself, Conner wanted to see how truthful she was being. Knowing from experience that the devil lives in the details, he took her down the rabbit hole to see if her backstory stood up to the test.

"Interesting. What kind of plane does he fly?"

"I'm not sure. A big one, I think. But let's talk about you. There are not a lot of guys hanging out in the officer's club wearing black suits this time of night. Are you coming from a business meeting or something?"

"No, I just like to look nice when I go out for a BLT," he replied, not feeding her the information she was trying to obtain.

Putting the information press back on her, he asked, "Maybe I know him, what's his name?"

"Whose name?"

"Your Air Force pilot brother-in-law that you are staying with."

"Oh, him, his name is George."

"I know a couple of Georges, what's his last name?"

Taking a long sip of her martini to stall for time, she finally replied, "Patterson."

Finding humor in the fact she was getting frustrated by him turning the table, he just had to give it one more push.

"I think I know a George Patterson. What does he look like?"

"Oh, he is pretty average, five foot nine with a military haircut."

Wanting to get back on topic and knowing Conner was toying with her, she changed the subject to a more direct approach. "Did you hear a plane went missing last night?"

"No, what happened?" he asked.

Pausing, she said, "It was just something I heard. I don't know any details."

The cat and mouse game played on for another twenty minutes. While Conner was charming and flirtatious, he expertly avoided answering her questions. Seeing he was done with his meal and would likely be leaving the bar soon, she excused herself to go to the restroom. Before she left the table she said, "I will be right back, wait for me" in a seductive voice.

Once she was gone, Conner opened the purse she amateurishly left unattended on the table. Pulling out her driver's license, he read the information to himself: Sandra Jane Elliot, 3069 Pine Street, Chicago, Illinois. Placing the license back in the purse, Conner stood up and left some cash on the table to cover the bill as well as a tip. He wanted to be out of the bar when she returned from the bathroom. Reaching down he picked up a clean napkin and wrapped it around the stem of her martini glass, taking it with him.

Standing in a dark, concealed area outside the Officer's Club, Conner watched as the annoyed woman left the building and walked to her car. She got into a blue and white Ford Fairlane convertible. It was a good-looking car that Ford had just introduced that year. As Conner squinted to make out the license plate in the dim light, he could tell it was blue with yellow digits. As she backed out of her stall, he could make out the number as 257207. While the top of the plate was too dark to see the state, the bottom of the plate read "Land of Lincoln."

Getting into his own car, he followed her at a distance. Leaving the base, she drove about two miles into town and pulled into the Silver Spur motel. Conner parked on the road, shut off his headlights, and watched her from down the block. As she got out of her car, she walked to the pay phone on the corner. Once inside the phone booth, she inserted her dime and dialed a number. Her phone call lasted under five minutes. After hanging up the phone, she walked back to the motel and entered room number three. A few minutes later, the lights went out inside the room.

Giving her another twenty minutes to fall asleep, Conner walked across the dark motel parking lot with a flashlight tucked into his waistband. Using the light to illuminate the interior of her vehicle, he looked for any clues as to who this woman could be. In the back seat, he could see several changes of clothes and what looked to be a couple of wigs. It appeared the woman was savvy enough on disguises, but she clearly lacked the tradecraft skills of a professional counterintelligence officer. Conner assumed she was something along the lines of a private detective or investigative journalist.

Before leaving, Conner walked over to the pay phone and wrote down the identification number for the booth. As he drove back to base, he couldn't help but think about the woman. While it was obvious she had an agenda by flirting with him, he did enjoy the conversation. With the fast pace and secretive nature of his job, he rarely had the opportunity to converse with a beautiful woman.

Returning to Truax AFB, he drove to the OSI detachment in hopes that Don was still there. As he pulled up to the building, he could see a light on inside. After knocking on the door and waiting a moment, it was opened by a young man wearing agent attire. Conner identified himself and produced his credentials. The young man was the rookie agent Don had spoken of.

"Please come in sir. I'm Tim, I mean Special Agent Tim Patterson."

"Good to meet you, Tim, I'm Conner."

"What can I do for you sir, I mean Conner?"

Conner explained the encounter with the woman at the officer's club to the young agent.

"I was hoping you can find out who she is and what she was doing at the Officer's Club. She gave me the false name of Darlene but here is the identity from her driver's license and vehicle license plate," said Conner as he passed a piece of paper with the information written on it.

"Are you sure she wasn't a dependent wife just looking to step out for the evening? That happens, you know."

"Yes, I know that Tim," smiling to himself at the naivety of the young agent. "While that is a real possibility, I am more concerned about why she was pushing so hard for information. She seemed to have an agenda other than a wife's night out. I would also be interested to know who signed her onto the base and whom she called from the payphone. The pay phone identification number and time of the call are written on the paper."

"I'm on it, sir."

Handing him the martini glass, Conner asked, "Do they still teach lifting fingerprints at the academy?"

"Yes sir."

"Great, see if you can pull one from this glass. If you get one, run it through the FBI database."

"Will do," said the eager agent.

"Thanks, Tim. I'm going over to the VOQ to get some shut-eye before my road trip in the morning."

"Have a good night, sir."

"You too."

CHAPTER 9

5:00 am came early as Conner reached over to silence his travel alarm clock. It had become a common practice for him to wake up alone in strange hotel rooms across the country while conducting Blue Book investigations. He never wanted to be part of the special project and only did so at the request of his friend, General John Nix.

Eleven years earlier, Nix was a Lieutenant Colonel and the senior allied prisoner of war at the German camp where Conner was held. During a coordinated escape attempt where several prisoners tunneled out under the fence, Connor was assigned to create the diversion and draw the guard's attention. The next day, when the escape was discovered, Conner received a severe beating and spent six weeks in solitary confinement.

After the war, Conner was about to be medically discharged from the Air Corps as his injuries prevented him from returning to flight status. Knowing he would never fly again; Nix pulled some strings and got him assigned to the new investigative agency the Air Force was developing. A few years later when OSI needed an experienced agent with a working knowledge of aeronautics for Project Blue Book, General Nix asked Conner to take the position.

After showering and getting dressed, he folded his suit and placed it in the suitcase. While he was supposed to wear the agent attire in the field, Conner felt it was far more practical to wear casual clothes while interacting with locals in the Northwoods of Wisconsin. Carrying his suitcase out to his car, he found Don waiting for him, leaning against the Bel Air.

Smiling, he asked, "Did you get any sleep or did you spend the whole night chasing attractive women around the city of Madison?"

"I got a little sleep but it's never enough," said Conner.

"Not in this line of work," replied Don.

"Did Tim find anything out about that brunette?"

"Sure did. She is a journalist from Chicago. Looks like she was initially working on the corruption story involving the contracting officer I busted for taking the kickbacks. It was connected to an organized crime story she was writing down in Chicago. I'm guessing she got wind of the missing plane and the UFO theory and thought it was a juicier story."

"Who did she call from the payphone last night?"

"The number came back to 435 North Michigan Avenue, Chicago Illinois. That is the address for the Chicago Tribune newspaper."

"I assumed she was something along the lines of a reporter. Just to be safe, how long will it take to get the prints back?"

"That's up to the Bureau, probably a few days I imagine."

"Was the car's license plate registered to her?"

"No. It came back to a company called the Dewey Chemical Corporation, headquartered in London."

"Well, that's odd. Can you have Tim work with your FBI liaison to find out more about the company?"

"Sure," replied Don.

"Who signed her onto the base?"

"That's the interesting part. It was Lieutenant Spalding," smiled Don.

"Colonel Roberts's aide?" asked Conner.

"The one and only. I thought we could stop by and have a chat with him this morning before we head up to Marinette."

"Do you think the reporter is in cahoots with Colonel Roberts?"

"That would be very surprising, however, I wouldn't put anything past him."

"Did the search crew find the crash site yet?"

"No, but the sun is just coming up so they should start searching again soon. They have a huge area to search so it will probably be a lengthy process."

"OK, then I guess we have time to go have a chat with the young lieutenant before we head up there."

Thirty minutes later, they watched as Lieutenant Spalding kissed his wife goodbye in front of their house. His young bride was wearing a bathrobe and holding their baby in her arms. After closing the front door, he walked around to the front of the fourplex in the junior officer housing section of the base. He was surprised to find the two OSI agents leaning against his car.

"Good morning, lieutenant. I think we need to have a word with you," said Don.

Looking nervous, the lieutenant asked, "Is this about the missing plane and the UFO?"

"Maybe, but what we need to speak to you about is the lady that you signed on to base last night."

Nervous, the lieutenant looked back towards his house to ensure his wife wasn't looking out the window.

"Can we talk about this another time?" asked Spalding.

"Nope, we are going to talk now. Either here or at the OSI detachment," said Conner.

Looking deflated, Spalding spoke in a whisper, "She is just a friend."

"How long has she been your friend Spalding?" asked Conner with a strong emphasis on the word friend.

"It's not like that." Knowing he was caught in a lie, he explained "I play shortstop on the base softball team. Last month after a game we were drinking at a bar off base. I had lost a friendly wager I placed on the game. One thing led to another and I got involved with a guy who takes gambling bets."

"You mean a bookie?" asked Don.

Looking at the ground in shame, he replied, "Yeah, you could call him that. He is connected to some wise guys in Chicago. One thing led to another and I ended up owing him a lot of money. I just kept getting in deeper and deeper and they wouldn't let me out. I wasn't able to pay my debt so they made me a deal. All I had to do was provide them with information on future base construction projects. I didn't give them any military secrets or anything classified."

"No, but you did introduce organized crime and corruption onto the base and allowed them to get major construction contracts over legitimate bidders. Not exactly a shining example of a West Point graduate," said Don.

"I know. I have been regretting my decision since I did it. Especially since you arrested the base contracting officer last week, I knew this day was coming sooner or later."

"What was your part in the contracting officer taking bribes and kickbacks?"

"I had no part in that. All I did was tell them about the future construction plans. They must have contacted him separately."

"And how much money did you make on this deal?"

"Nothing. Well, they forgave my betting debt."

"Are you having any dealings with them currently?"

"No sir. Not since I provided them the information."

Conner interjected, "So this lady, Sandy Elliot, that you signed onto the base yesterday. How is she connected to this mess?"

"She isn't part of the group. She is a journalist who is doing a story on organized crime down in Chicago. The mob guy she is doing the story on was the one who bribed the base contracting officer for the construction projects. She was on base getting some photographs of the hangar construction for her story when she heard people talking about the plane that went missing. Then she heard about the UFO connection."

"And how did she know who I was and what I was doing on base?"

Still avoiding eye contact, he replied, "I told her."

"And what exactly did you tell her Spalding? And you will want to be very honest at this point."

Looking down at his feet he admitted, "I told her you were an OSI agent from a special UFO program and you came up to investigate from Ohio. I didn't know you would be at the Officer's Club; she must have figured that out on her own somehow."

"Does Colonel Roberts know about this?" asked Don.

"Of course not," replied Spalding.

"When are you supposed to meet with her again?" asked Conner.

"I'm not. It was a one-time thing. I gave her the information about you and signed her onto the base."

"And what did you get in return for that information?"

"She agreed to leave my name out of her article altogether."

"If you are withholding any information lieutenant, I will charge you with several crimes under the Uniform Code of Military Justice (UCMJ). Do you understand me?"

"Yes, sir."

"Is there anything else you would like to add?"

"No sir, I told you everything. Is Colonel Roberts going to find out about this?" he asked nervously.

Don made eye contact with the lieutenant and said, "I am going up to Marinette this morning. When I return to base and brief Colonel Roberts on my investigation, you had better have already informed him of your actions. Do I make myself clear?"

"Yes, sir. I will go tell him this morning." Looking back up at the two agents, he said, "I'm not a bad guy. I love my country and the Air Force. I just got caught up in everything."

Conner looked at the young lieutenant and said, "Son, you need to get your act together. You are an officer in the United States Air Force. Your indiscretions and lack of integrity may have placed your career in jeopardy. If you want to continue as an officer in the United States Air Force, you need to adjust your moral compass back to true north."

"Yes sir, I will," said Spalding, once again looking down, too embarrassed to make eye contact with the special agents.

"You are excused," said Conner.

"Yes, sir. I'm sorry about everything," he said as he got into his car and left for work.

CHAPTER 10

As they started their road trip to Marinette County, Conner asked "What do you think Colonel Roberts will do with Spalding?"

"I don't know, but he is not known to be the forgiving sort."

"I imagine that having his aide get caught by OSI won't make him very happy," laughed Conner.

"I expect not. So, what are your thoughts on this reporter, Sandy Elliot?"

"Well, I don't think she is a foreign espionage agent, so we have that going for us. But having a reporter poking around on an Air Force base, especially when there is a connection to Project Blue Book, isn't good for any of us. Some things are better left out of the headlines."

"Agreed. I'm sure Colonel Roberts won't care for a headline about major contract fraud and mafia connections on his Air Force base either," said Don.

"I can't blame her though. She is just trying to do her job and expose corruption. Unfortunately, her job gets in the way of us doing ours."

After an hour of traveling north, they were starting to lose the radio station. As Don turned the dial attempting to locate another station, he only found one without static which was playing the song "Rock Around the Clock" by Bill Haley and the Comets.

"I can't believe that a rock and roll song reached number one on the charts. What is the world coming to?" asked Don.

Laughing, Conner replied, "I don't know, but I kind of think it's catchy."

"You just like them because they are called The Comets," joked Don at the connection to the space phenomenon.

As they continued on their journey, they passed the sign for the small city of Ripon, Wisconsin. Below the city sign was the phrase "Birthplace of the Republican Party."

"Is that true?" asked Conner.

"Yeah, there is a little white schoolhouse there where it was started in 1854. It's a museum now," replied Don.

"Why Wisconsin?"

"At that time the Kansas-Nebraska Act was trying to permit the extension of slavery beyond the limits of the Missouri Compromise. People that opposed the expansion of slavery met there and started the Republican Party. In 1857 the Supreme Court handed down the infamous Dread Scott decision, declaring that black men had no rights that white men were bound to respect. That's when Lincoln joined the Republican Party and became the first Republican president."

"Interesting, I would have thought it was back east someplace."

"Another forty-five miles up the road we will get to Appleton. Senator Joe McCarthy is from the small town of Grand Chute next to it."

"Well, that's just great, he is the last person we need showing up at the crash site. That would turn everything into a huge media circus," said Conner.

"We are headed pretty far into the sticks. I would be surprised if he were to show up in Marinette County. Not a lot of news cameras up there."

"If the Senator can make any sort of a communist connection, I think he will gladly bring the news cameras with him. If it turns out a Soviet aircraft is involved, I expect our little brunette reporter friend will just be the first to make a showing."

What does Senator McCarthy think about UFOs?" asked Don.

"That's a whole other media circus we need to avoid."

"I don't follow?"

"I'm sure you have heard of the liberal journalist Drew Pearson?"

"Of course."

"Well, he's McCarthy's biggest critic and sworn enemy. A few years ago, Pearson attacked McCarthy on air and in his newspaper column, accusing him of lying about communist infiltration in the government. McCarthy responded by attacking Pearson on the floor of the US Senate and even called for a national boycott of his radio show. After a random dinner party, the two accidentally ran into each other in the cloakroom and their conflict turned physical. Sen McCarthy kneed Pearson in the groin and Senator Nixon had to pull him off of the reporter," explained Conner.

"That's crazy! But where is the UFO connection?" asked Don.

"Things escalated from that point. Pearson sued Senator McCarthy, claiming injury and McCarthy publicly accused Pearson of harboring communist sympathies. This is where the UFOs get involved. Pearson extended their feud into the realm of science-fiction."

"Really?"

"Oh yeah. In 1951, Pearson portrayed himself in the flying saucer movie *The Day the Earth Stood Still*. In the movie the government panics when the alien, with a left-leaning ideology, lands on Earth. Audiences watched Pearson play the anti-McCarthy voice of reason in the face of panic. McCarthy called him a communist tool for the film."

"I can see that."

"Yeah, that's why liberals prefer that movie while conservatives preferred the movie *The Thing from Another World*. In that movie, the space aliens had all the traits of a communist, such as a lack of emotion and a desire to conquer others. Only the mighty US Air Force in the film could stop the alien attack. It was a much more patriotic film and supportive of the

US military. Even Time magazine said the space aliens in the movie represented Russians."

Changing the subject, Don asked, "So, how do you like working on Project Blue Book?"

Careful not to say anything critical of the program, Conner replied, "It's a job, I guess. It keeps me on the road a lot but I don't have to testify in court like most agents."

"Well, that's one perk," replied Don. "How does an agent go about getting on a detail such as that?"

"You looking for a new job?"

Smiling, Don said, "No, just looking at what I can do to avoid getting such a job."

Laughing, Conner said "I was requested by an old friend to take the assignment. Someone I owed a favor to. Blue Book wanted an investigator with aeronautics experience and I was a former pilot. A lot of the recent sightings are by pilots and I can speak their language."

"So why are more pilots reporting UFOs all of the sudden?"

"The answer to that is classified Agent Golden."

"Of course, it is," he replied with a smile.

"So, tell me about Marinette County. What can we expect to find up there?" asked Conner.

"It's located on the bank of the Menomonee River, which feeds into Lake Michigan. The first European settlers were French fur traders in the 1700s. After the war of 1812, the US took over the region and stopped free trade with Canada. During the lumber boom of the late 19th century, logging was a big industry. Logs were floated down the Menominee River to Green Bay where they were shipped to communities around the Great Lakes. Today the county is known primarily for its paper mills. It's right on the border with the upper peninsula of Michigan."

"So, it's not very populated? Not a lot of folks to notice a plane crash?" asked Conner.

"The county spans 1500 square miles, most of which is forest and lakes. *Peshtigo* The plane disappeared from radar about ten miles east of Wausaukee and thirty miles north of Peshtigo. The search team will base out of Peshtigo as they have a motel and diner that can accommodate them. Peshtigo has about 2,000 people. There are a lot of places to hide a crash site up there," said Don.

"Peshtigo was the place of that huge fire in 1871 the Doc told us about."

"Yeah, I'm not sure if that's more strange or suspicious."

"Welcome to Project Blue Book. Most of the things I look into are both strange and suspicious."

"You ever seen any space aliens?" asked Don in a semi-joking tone yet with an ounce of sincerity.

"That too is classified," said Conner with a smile. "But, no, to answer your question, I have not."

Elaborating a bit, he continued "I have seen some strange things, and some incredible coincidences, but in the end, most have been explainable through good investigation and science."

"Most?"

"Yeah, there have been a few I haven't been able to explain, but that doesn't mean there isn't an explanation," replied Conner.

"Well, you can call me a skeptic, but I find the idea of space aliens to be a little too far-fetched. That said, I did get into a debate with Tim over the subject. He keeps bringing up the incident last year in Los Angeles that was witnessed by all those people and even the CBS news reporters. The one with the lights in the sky traveling in a V formation. I know it is explainable, yet I can't think of one. I suppose that is classified also?"

Laughing, Conner replied, "No, that one is not classified. It was easily explained but since it was witnessed by hundreds of people it got a ton of media attention."

"So, what were they?" asked Don.

"They were Air Force planes. A KC-97 aerial tanker aircraft was in-flight refueling some B-47 bombers. There are floodlights on the bottom of the tanker that illuminate the bomber so they can see to hook up the fuel nozzle in the dark. They were flying at a high altitude and a slow speed; therefore, no sound could be heard on the ground. Most people, including Air Force pilots, have never seen an in-flight refueling before, let alone one at night."

"That's it?" asked Don.

"Yep. That was all it was. It got a lot of people worked up, especially when CBS reported it as UFOs."

After driving another twenty minutes, Don asked, "Do you think we need to go all the way to the City of Marinette to the county Sheriff's department, or should we go directly to the town of Peshtigo?"

"Does Peshtigo have its own police department?"

"Yeah. They started their own police department four years ago. Just a small one with a chief and two officers. But I would guess with the Air Police up there searching for a crashed plane, there would be plenty of sheriff's deputies in town to assist."

"Let's just go directly to Peshtigo then. I want to connect with the local law enforcement before we check in with the search team. We will need to find a place to stay if that's possible."

"I already secured us a room at the local motel. I could only get one room with two beds as the others were all filled with the search party members. The Air Force rented the entire place," said Don.

"That's fine with me. We won't be spending much time in the room."

CHAPTER 11

As the Bel Air pulled up to the small Peshtigo Police Department, all of the parking spaces were occupied. It was apparent all hands were on deck as two Marinette Sheriff cars, two Wisconsin State Patrol cars, and two Air Force Police cars were parked in front of the small police department next to the single Peshtigo Police car. Not finding an empty space, Conner pulled his car into the diner parking lot located across the street.

"If everyone is at the police department in town, I wonder who is out searching for the crash site?" asked Don.

Walking across the street, they pulled open the glass door to the police department and instantly found themselves standing in the back of a press conference. There were four or five reporters with cameras and notepads standing in front of them facing the other direction. They were all looking at the group of lawmen at the front of the room who were smiling and posing for photographs. Conner assumed the big man front and center was the elected sheriff. He had the look of a politician playing lawman. Wearing a pressed suit, he had one side of his jacket pulled back to show off his gold star badge and a large revolver with ivory grips. He was flanked by uniformed officers from multiple agencies, including Major Gibson, the commander of the Air Police Squadron."

Conner looked over at Don and said, "So much for keeping this quiet. I have no desire to have my photo taken or answer any questions about Project Blue Book. I'll be over at the diner across the street. Let me know when the circus is over."

"Roger that," replied Don, watching as the group of local law enforcement executives put on a dog and pony show for the press.

As Conner walked back across the street to wait at the diner, he thought he may as well get a bite to eat. As he stepped up onto the sidewalk, he couldn't help but notice one of the cars parked at the diner was familiar. The Ford Fairlane convertible with an Illinois license plate with the phrase "Land of Lincoln" written across the bottom. The numbers written in yellow were 257207.

Impressed at the determination of the reporter, he scanned the front windows of the diner as he approached the front door. Using his peripheral vision, he saw a woman sitting in the corner booth with an unobstructed view of the police department. As he got to the door, the woman was already on her feet, walking to the lady's room in the back of the diner in an attempt to hide out. While her attire was very different, and her hair was now blond, she was unable to disguise the graceful way she walked.

After tracking Soviet spies in west Berlin, Conner was very astute in the small mannerisms that set people apart. A graceful gait was often a sign of inner confidence. When a person pronates their feet, like a dancer, they typically have high self-esteem. Also, a walk with a pronate foot is not the natural way of walking, but a learned one.

Smiling to himself, Conner entered the diner and took a seat at the bar. Taking his aviator glasses from his shirt pocket, he placed them on the bar, positioning them in a manner to use the mirrored lenses to view the bathroom door behind him.

As the waitress came to take his order, she asked, "What can I get for you, sweetie?"

"I don't know, what's good here?"

"If I serve it, you know it will be good," she said with a grin.

"I'm sure that's true," replied Conner. "How about a BLT and a Coke."

The waitress looked over her shoulder and yelled to the short-order cook working in the kitchen.

"Stanley, one BLT!"

"One BLT coming up," the man echoed from the kitchen.

Conner looked at the woman's name tag as she poured his Coke from the soda fountain.

"So, Lacie, you live here long?"

"Yup. My entire life."

"Are things always this exciting?" pointing his thumb over his shoulder towards the police station.

"No, this is new."

"What's all the excitement about?"

"An Air Force jet disappeared around here and all those folks are looking for it."

"Disappeared or crashed?" asked Conner.

"I suppose it crashed, but some of the young military police guys had dinner here last night and were talking about a possible UFO abducting it. One thing led to another and now the entire town is all excited. Folks are keeping guns in their trucks and even the county sheriff came to town."

"Is there an election coming up?" asked Conner with a smile on his face.

"The primary is in five weeks," she said with a chuckle.

"So, besides the MP's talking, does anyone else around here know anything about a missing airplane and UFOs?"

"Well, now that folks are talking, a few people are claiming to have seen UFOs around here. But those same folks are the ones who claim to see Big Foot when people start talking about that as well."

"Big Foot?" asked Conner.

"Yeah, people like to have a story to talk about and not too much goes on around here."

"Order is up!" yelled the cook from the kitchen.

As the waitress turned to get the plate of food, Conner glanced down at his sunglasses. He could see the lady's room door crack open momentarily to see if he was still there, then close again. Conner couldn't help but laugh to himself at the thought of the attractive reporter hiding out in the bathroom.

"What's so funny, sugar?" asked the waitress.

"Oh, I was just thinking about Big Foot."

Smiling, she replied, "Most of the folks around these parts are pretty normal. Boring really. Unless the conversation is focused on the Green Bay Packers or deer hunting, there's not much to talk about."

"I think your little town is rather charming," Conner said, not wanting to sound judgmental.

With a sense of community pride, she said, "We like to think so. A lot of our boys served in the wars and we have a pretty strong VFW here in town. We have a lot to be proud of."

"I'm sure you do," replied Conner, while glancing at his sunglasses.

"Other than that crazy religious cult in the north woods, there isn't all that much to gossip about."

His attention now peaked, Conner asked, "Crazy religious cult?"

"Yeah, sort of a cult. That's what I call them. It's just some sort of inbred, backwoods hillbillies that keep to themselves."

"What do they call themselves?" asked Conner.

"I don't think they have a name. At least not one I know of. There was a town south of here back in the day called Egersund, but it was wiped out in the big fire in 1871. People say some of the survivors moved up into those woods and keep to themselves. Every so often a hunter or trapper will come into contact with them but it's not very often."

"Other than being a separatist group, what do they do that's crazy?" asked Conner.

"They spook a lot of the town's folk. They think because they are Scandinavian, they are descendants of Vikings. Hell, plenty of us here are Scandinavian and we are just Lutherans," she joked.

Paying for his lunch and leaving a tip, he thanked Lacie for the conversation.

As the door opened for him to exit, the bell tied to the handle jingled.

Once he was gone, the blond waited a minute before exiting the restroom. Paying her bill with cash, she looked out the window to ensure Conner's car had gone. Confident he had left, she hurried out to where her car was parked on the side of the building in an attempt to catch up and follow him.

Walking at a fast pace, she instantly slowed when she turned the corner to where her car was parked and Conner was casually leaning against her driver's side front fender.

"Hello, Darlene, doing something different with your hair these days?"

"I don't know what you are talking about sir, have we met?" she asked with a thick Boston accent.

Grinning, Conner said, "Sorry, I guess I mistook you for an old friend," he said as he stepped away from her car.

"I get that a lot," she said, as she opened the door and got behind the wheel.

Pulling down his sunglasses to look over the top, he said, "You have yourself a nice day Ms. Elliot," before turning and casually walking back to his car which was now parked in the alley behind the diner.

Sitting in the car, Sandra just looked forward and smiled to herself, knowing that Special Agent Conner Price was onto her. Maybe he would not be as easy to crack as she had anticipated.

CHAPTER 12

Watching as the Sheriff and reporters slowly departed after the press conference, Conner made his way across the street, back to the Peshtigo Police Department. As he entered, Don was sitting at a table with Major Gibson, examining maps of the search area.

"Agent Price, this is Major Bob Gibson, the Air Police Commander from Truax AFB."

Shaking his hand, he said, "Please call me Conner."

Taking a seat at the small table with the two men, Conner asked, "So how was the press conference?"

Don and Maj. Gibson looked at each other uncomfortably before answering, making it obvious that words had been shared over the indiscretion.

"Oh, it was about what you would expect," related Don. "A not-so-popular sheriff facing election time with an opportunity to grab some headlines."

With a disapproving look on his face, Conner said, "I do this sort of thing often and I typically find it advisable to stay out of local politics….and the media spotlight."

"Roger that," said Major Gibson, looking down at the map on the table to avoid eye contact.

Changing the subject, Don pointed down to the map to show Conner the areas that have been searched by air, as well as where the ground search teams are starting to look.

"Without spotting a crash site from the air, it's very unlikely we will find anything just searching on the ground. The woods are just too thick and there are few roads. There are several lakes and wetlands which could easily swallow up an airplane. We have plenty of challenges ahead of us, that's for sure."

"Any status on getting a helicopter up here?"

"They are working on it but it will take at least two or three days for it to make its way up here. They fly a lot slower and have a far shorter range than fixed-wing aircraft."

"I think the helicopter will be the game changer. Those things are amazing," said Don.

"I agree. I still can't see how they stay in the air," replied Conner.

As the men looked over the map, two more cars pulled up in front of the police department.

"This could get interesting," said Don, as he watched the Air Force staff car and a second unmarked vehicle parking through the department window. Colonel Roberts exited the back seat of the staff car, accompanied by a Captain wearing a service dress uniform.

"Looks like Lieutenant Spalding has already been replaced," said Conner.

"Yeah, looks like it," replied Don.

A younger man wearing a business suit exited the second vehicle carrying a briefcase.

"Do you know that guy?" asked Don.

Taking a closer look, Conner said, "Yeah, he is from Wright-Patterson AFB. He is one of the classified couriers. I was expecting him to show up at some point."

The door opened and Colonel Roberts walked in, not waiting for his new aide who was struggling to keep up.

Once inside the police station, he observed the three men, now standing at the small table looking at maps.

"Welcome to the party Colonel, we weren't expecting you," said Conner.

Looking annoyed, the colonel replied, "Agent Price, a classified courier arrived at Truax this morning looking for you. He arrived shortly after you departed. I assumed it was time sensitive so I thought it best to bring him up directly."

"I appreciate that sir, but the classified couriers are trained to deliver messages without the need of an escort, especially a wing commander escort," replied Conner.

"I know that! But I don't have the time to wait until you return to Truax to brief me on what the message is," replied the colonel in a stern tone.

Looking a bit annoyed himself, Conner replied "Colonel, I don't yet know what the message is either, but I will not be sharing it with you unless you have both the need and the proper security clearance to know what it is."

"I am a colonel in the United State Air Force with a Top-Secret security clearance!"

"Yes, sir, I understand and respect that fact. But I am afraid you are confusing your rank with my authority," replied Conner.

"Don't you get insubordinate with me; I will have your badge!" shouted Roberts.

"Yes. sir. Now if you will excuse me, I have some urgent business with the courier."

"Follow me," Conner said to the young man as he exited the building.

Once outside and across the street at Conner's car, he turned to speak with the courier.

"That was rather intense," said the young man in the suit.

"Sorry about that. Sometimes wing commanders get excited when they can't call the shots."

"Yes, sir. He demanded that I leave the classified message with him as you had already left the base. He was pretty excited when I told him I couldn't do that. I told him I would bring the message up here directly but he insisted that he follow me in a staff car."

"You did just fine and sorry about the extra trouble." Conner pulled his credentials out of his pocket so the courier could verify his status, even though he knew him by sight. Once his identity was verified, the young man placed his briefcase on the hood of his car. His left hand remained on the briefcase handle as it was attached by a special handcuff.

Conner entered the combination to unlock the briefcase, a combination that was unknown to the courier. Once the briefcase was opened, the courier looked away as per his training.

Conner removed the sealed brown envelope and opened it up. After reading the short message, he returned it to the envelope and resealed it. After securing it back inside the briefcase, he signed the chain of custody card and indicated on the document it was to be returned to Wright-Patterson. Conner then relocked the briefcase.

"Thank you, son. You can return the message to Special Agent Johnson back at Wright-Patterson."

"Yes, sir," replied the courier as he returned to his vehicle to start the journey back home.

Pondering his options after reading the note, Conner decided it best to give his boss a call. Opening the trunk of his car, he grabbed an envelope containing documents and non-disclosure agreements before returning to the police station. As he entered the building, the colonel was anxious to learn what was in the message, however, he knew the special agent was correct and his superior rank was irrelevant in this situation.

Walking to the front desk, Conner asked the police receptionist if there was a phone he could use in private.

"You can use the chief's phone in his office, he won't mind," the older woman said.

"Thank you," replied Conner, as he took her up on the offer.

Once in the office with the door closed, Conner dialed the number for the Blue Book Office back at Wright Patterson AFB. After a few rings, a male voice answered the phone.

"Air Force OSI, this is Agent Tucker, may I help you?"

"Hey Tuck, it's Conner. Is the boss in?"

"Where is my car, Conner?"

Laughing, he replied, "It's in Marinette, Wisconsin."

"That's some dirty pool, Conner. I am headed to Kentucky in the morning and I'm stuck with the old Ford and no air conditioning."

"Sorry about that, it's the car Jan assigned to me. Maybe take it up with her."

"Yeah, have fun on your double date!"

Laughing, he replied, "Have fun in Kentucky. What are you doing down there?"

"I'm not too sure yet. Apparently, a family was attacked by little space men which led to some sort of gunfight."

"What?"

"That's the initial report. Who knows what kind of shenanigans I will find when I get there?"

"I can't wait to hear that story!"

"Yeah, well the story would be better if I had air conditioning. Stand by and I will transfer you to the boss."

The phone rang three times before it was picked up. "Special Agent Johnson."

"Hi boss, it's Conner. I just got your message."

"Have you found the crash site yet?"

"No, and we may not for a long time with the geography up here. It's not very conducive to a search."

"What is your recommended course of action, Conner?"

"Under the circumstances, I think it may be best to provide a classified brief to Agent Golden and the Wing Commander, Colonel Roberts."

"You sure that's the best way to play this?"

"I think it's the best option at this point in time. The courier arrived at Truax after I left and the colonel tried to get him to hand off the message. When the kid refused, the colonel followed him all the way up to Marinette County to see what was in it…and it was a six-hour drive. The colonel seems to have very strong feelings that his men were abducted by aliens and that we know something about it. He believes the 1953 plane that went missing was also abducted. I feel it's in the best interest to provide a level 2 briefing. I want him focused on finding the downed aircrew rather than watching the skies for answers."

"Do you have blank non-disclosure agreements with you?"

"Yeah, I have all the necessary documents if you give me the go-ahead."

"OK, just those two individuals and only a level 2 brief. Give them both the Blue Book and the Dragon Lady briefings. File all the paperwork when you get back and I will document it on this end."

"Will do. On another topic, an investigative reporter is poking around and trying to get a scoop on a UFO story."

"That's not so unusual."

"I know. The local sheriff already held a press conference in front of a bunch of reporters."

"Of course, he did," said Agent Johnson, with a tone of sarcasm.

"But this reporter is different. It's a female journalist who was look-ing into a mafia connection with contract fraud on the base. She got wind of the missing plane and UFO angle and she's digging into it pretty hard. She already approached me at Truax wearing a wig and using an alias to try to elicit information. Now she is up here at the search location with a different wig. She's pretty determined."

"I see. Is she a determined journalist or an attractive one?"

Laughing, Conner replied, "Both actually."

"Ok, do you want me to look into her?"

"No, I already have the local detachment at Truax doing that. I just wanted to inform you about her."

"OK, anything else?"

"No, that's about it for now."

"OK, let me know if that colonel has any issues after you brief him."

"Roger that sir," replied Conner before he hung up the phone.

As Conner returned to the others, he advised them he had received permission to provide a classified briefing to the two officers, but they would need to do so at a secure location. He suggested they all drive to the Army National Guard Armory in the city of Marinette.

CHAPTER 13

Leaving the colonel's driver and aid behind at the police department with Major Gibson, Conner drove the staff car with Don and the colonel to the city of Marinette. Arriving at the National Guard Armory, they parked near a memorial to Company A, 127th Infantry Regiment.

The Wisconsin National Guard Unit that served with the 32nd Division, nicknamed "Red Arrow" had a proud and distinguished history in both world wars. The symbol, consisting of a red arrow with a line through it, was earned on the front lines of WW1 for piercing the Hindenburg line trench system. From May until the armistice on November 11th, the Red Arrow was in the thick of every campaign and suffered 13,000 casualties.

In WW2, the Red Arrow fought in the South Pacific, logging 654 days of continuous combat, more than any other division in the war. They would battle the Japanese in New Guinea and in the Philippines, recapturing the largest island of Luzon. The battle ended with the surrender of General Yamashita.

As the three men entered the armory, they were greeted by Master Sergeant Pompa who was waiting for them.

"I appreciate the use of the facility," said Conner.

"It's our pleasure to host you, sir," said the Master Sergeant as he led them to the secure briefing room.

"This will work out just fine, thank you."

"Can I get you all anything?"

"Would it be possible to have a guard posted outside the door at the far end of the hall?"

"Yes sir, most of our guys are out helping with the search party. There are only a couple of us in the building. I will stand guard personally."

"Thank you, Sergeant," replied Conner as he closed the door to the briefing room where Colonel Roberts and Special Agent Golden were waiting.

Securing the door behind him, he said, "We just have some formalities before I can provide the briefing gentlemen. I will need to personally verify both of your military identification cards while you complete these non-disclosure agreements."

Both men were familiar with the classified briefing protocols as both possessed Top Secret Security clearances due to their positions. The briefings they were about to receive were part of special access programs code-named Project Dragon Lady in addition to Project Blue Book. Once all the required security documentation was complete, Conner began the briefing.

"Dragon Lady is the code name for a Top-Secret, high-altitude, reconnaissance aircraft operated by the USAF and the CIA in a joint venture. Its numerical designation is the U-2."

Looking confused as he expected the briefing to be about space aliens and UFOs, Colonel Roberts asked "You mean to tell me it's a reconnaissance plane?"

"Yes sir, a spy plane actually. It flies at 70,000 feet, placing it above Soviet radar and out of range of even the most advanced Mig 17s. It's even too high for Soviet surface-to-air missiles. It's designed to operate over enemy territory and take special high-altitude photographs."

"It can fly over the Soviet Union? What happens to the pilot if it goes down?" asked Don, knowing the extreme risk the pilot would face and the United States not being able to save them.

"Each pilot is issued a liquid cyanide L-pill that causes death in fifteen seconds. They understand the threat of going down over Soviet territory."

"How high is 70,000 feet in miles?" asked Don, the only non-aviator in the room.

"It's thirteen and one-quarter miles in the air."

"But a human can't survive at that altitude," replied the colonel.

"We found a way to do it. The pilots wear a pressurized flight suit. Before take-off, they sit in a booth and breath 100% oxygen for a full hour to get the nitrogen out of their systems."

"Did we get this technology from extraterrestrial intelligence?" asked the colonel.

"Not at all," replied Conner. "It was developed by Clarence "Kelly" Johnson, the same man that developed the P-38. He works for the Lockheed aircraft company, but in a smaller, classified division known as Skunkworks. But the U-2 does account for a lot of UFO sightings, especially those by pilots."

"Was there one of these spy planes in the area when my patrol plane disappeared?"

"Yes, sir. That was the message I just received from the courier. We verified that the CIA had one in that very area at the time and place the P-89 disappeared. It was supposed to be flying at an altitude of 70,000 feet, above our radar. But the pilot had mechanical issues and the plane dropped down to 60,000 feet for a period of time. That's when the ground radar system picked it up over Lake Superior. That's when your patrol fighter was dispatched."

"Did they collide?" asked Don.

Shaking his head, Conner said "No, the U-2 was far above the P-89. There is no possible way they could collide. We don't know what happened to the P-89 or what made it crash. But we are relatively certain the U-2 was the blip on the radar screen that they were sent to investigate."

"What was the light the P-89 pilot saw above him? Surely it wasn't a landing light?" asked Colonel Roberts.

"No sir. It was very likely the silver, metal wings of the U-2 reflecting the sun. It has been said it can appear like a bright fiery light in the sky to other aircraft at altitudes of around 40,000 feet."

"How could it reflect the sun at night?" asked Don.

"At thirteen miles high, the curvature of the Earth comes into play. The sun shining over the horizon is much more apparent at that altitude than to planes at typical altitudes of under seven miles. Basically, the spy plane flies so high in the atmosphere, it sees the horizon long before the planes at lower altitudes," explained Conner.

"So that is the explanation for the recent increase in UFO sightings by military pilots?" asked Colonel. Roberts.

"Yes, sir, the majority of them anyway."

"How could the Air Force hide such a program?" asked the colonel.

"It was funded through the Central Intelligence Agency (CIA) budget, not the Air Force budget. Although it's primarily Air Force pilots who fly them, they must resign their military commission and join the CIA."

"So, is it a CIA operation or an Air Force program?" asked Colonel Roberts.

Smiling, Conner replied, "Well both, but I would say its 49% Air Force and 51% CIA. Air Force General LeMay wanted to have total control of the program but President Eisenhower opposed military personnel flying it. That's why the pilots resign their commission and join the CIA.

"Where are these things based? There has to be hundreds of Airmen who know about these aircraft on the bases they operate out of," said Don.

"Yeah, that was one of the initial problems we had to overcome. We built a secret test base out at a place called Groom Lake in the remote Nevada Desert. That way only key personnel would be exposed to the aircraft. That's why the majority of the new UFO sightings have been in that part of the country."

"We have a secret Air Force Base?" asked the colonel in disbelief. "What is it called?"

"Yes, we do. It doesn't have a name as we don't acknowledge its existence. While people in the program use unofficial nicknames like "Dreamland" and "Paradise Ranch", most folks simply refer to it as Area 51."

"What does Area 51 stand for?" asked Don.

"It was the number associated with the Atomic Energy Commission who used the region for nuclear weapons testing. The Yucca Flats test facility is out that way."

Both men got quiet as they absorbed this unbelievable information.

Colonel Roberts asked, "So, this U-2 spy plane is the primary cause of this recent UFO hysteria?"

"Yes sir, one of the major ones recently, especially among credible witnesses like pilots."

"So, what explanation do you give while protecting the spy plane?"

"We usually claim it to be a natural phenomenon, such as ice crystals or temperature inversion. While that does explain some of the UFO reports, it's a hard-to-refute explanation that covers the spy plane's existence."

"So that's why there was an increase in UFO reports over the last few years," asked Don.

Smiling, Conner replied, "Well, yes and no. The U-2 and other classified programs explain some of it, but there is also a disinformation program that spreads the UFO theory."

Shocked, both men asked, "What was that?"

"A disinformation program. The powers that be felt the best way of hiding the secret program is to give the people something shiny to distract them. If they are looking for UFOs, then they are not thinking about our secret spy plane program."

Don understood exactly. It was just a very large-scale program of the counterintelligence techniques OSI employed in Europe. If you wanted to hide what was in the right hand, they would use something in the left hand for a diversion.

As they all sat in silence for a moment, Conner asked, "Can I answer any other questions?"

Any idea what happened to my P-89 and its crew?" asked Colonel Roberts.

"Nothing concrete Colonel, but my theory based on the evidence is this: The P-89 pilot approached the area of the blip that was reported by the ground radar screen. The backseat officer could not locate the U-2 on the short-range plane radar because of the huge altitude difference. When the ground control informed them the object was at an altitude of 60,000 feet, the pilot probably looked up just in time to see a solar reflection from the U-2's silver wing tip. As it is very difficult to judge distance when looking at a light in the dark, the pilot may have thought a collision was imminent. His evasive actions at 600mph may have resulted in the mechanical failure of his aircraft. Perhaps something along the lines of a flat spin, engine flame out, hydraulics failure, loss of oxygen, etcetera."

"Interesting theory Agent Price," said Colonel Roberts.

"Well, it's just a working theory based on the facts we have so far. I think we will learn more about what happened to the P-89 when we find the crash site."

"So, just for my education, do we have any information on extraterrestrial existence?" asked the colonel.

"Not to my knowledge sir. I have investigated plenty of strange sightings under Project Blue Book. Most of them have been explainable by classified projects like the U-2 or scientific investigations. A lot have simply been hoaxes intended to trick drinking buddies that got out of hand. There are a few things that I have not been able to explain, but that doesn't mean there isn't an explanation. But I cannot speak definitively as I only know of my own investigations."

"Was the alleged UFO that crashed near Roswell in 1947 related to the U-2?" asked Colonel Roberts.

"No sir, that was a different program altogether. That program was code-named Project Mogul."

"So, was it just a weather balloon that crashed as the official report stated?"

"No, sir. It was a high-altitude spy balloon with secret microphones and long-range sensors. We flew them over the Soviet Union to detect their testing of nuclear weapons. When the one crashed near Roswell, the cover story was that it was simply a high-altitude weather balloon."

"Interesting," replied the colonel.

"Now that you both have been briefed on the situation, there is something else I want to mention," said Conner.

"Go ahead," said Colonel Roberts.

"The female reporter that approached me at the officers club last night."

"Yes, I know. I apologize for that. Lieutenant Spalding came to me just before the courier showed up from Wright-Patterson. I haven't had time to formally look into the matter yet but I relieved him from duty until I have the opportunity. I don't want any unnecessary attention on this investigation, especially now after getting this briefing. And I will not tolerate a lack of integrity by an officer under my command."

"Thank you sir and I appreciate that. But my concern is not about Lieutenant Spalding, it is about the female reporter. She is here in Peshtigo," replied Conner.

"Did you see her?" asked Don

"Yes, across the street from the police station at the diner. She changed her hair from brunette to blond and took on a Bostonian accent, but it's her. She attempted to hide from me but I was able to follow her to her car. It was the same Ford Fairlane with Illinois plates. "

"Did she admit it was her?" asked Don.

Smiling, he said, "Nope, she stuck to her story. But it was definitely her…and now she knows that I know."

"Again, I apologize about my Lieutenant."

"No need for an apology colonel. But if we could try and keep a lower profile while we conduct the search it would certainly be appreciated," replied Conner.

"Of course. Was there an incident?" asked the colonel.

"Well, last night some of your Air Policemen were over at the diner eating supper and speaking of the UFO theory. The locals overheard them and it created a type of UFO hysteria. Many of the locals are arming themselves and now some of them are coming up with their own UFO sighting claims. It's not only unhelpful, but it brings a lot of attention to the matter."

The colonel's jaw clenched in frustration as he could picture his young troops shooting their mouths off at the local diner. He knew that just the fact an Air Force official, even a low-ranking Airmen in uniform, speaking about UFOs would add credibility to the theory.

"OK, I will put a stop to that. Anything else?"

"Yes sir, if we could avoid being part of the media circus and local political campaigns, it would be helpful."

Colonel Roberts looked over across the table to Don who explained. "Yes sir, the Marinette County Sheriff is up for reelection in a few weeks. He is not very popular in this part of the county, which is why the town of Peshtigo started its own police department two years earlier. Having all this excitement in town has provided him with a new platform to campaign on. Seeking free media attention, he has capitalized on the Air Force search party and already called a press conference where he took center stage. The media left just before you arrived in town."

"That's just wonderful," said the colonel with a sarcastic tone. "I will be sure that my men stay far away from the press…and the local political squabbles."

Don, looking a little uneasy as Major Gibson was a friend, said, "Well, sir, that ship may have already sailed."

"What do you mean?" asked the colonel.

"During the press conference, Bob…I mean Major Gibson of the Air Police, was standing behind the sheriff along with a State Patrol Sgt and the Peshtigo Police Chief. On a side note, the Police Chief is running against the sheriff in the upcoming election."

Looking angry, the colonel said, "I see."

In an attempt to provide a lifeline to his friend, Don told the colonel "Sir, Bob didn't say anything to the reporters and I advised him of the problem with the optics."

"You know damn well he didn't need to say anything to the reporters. His Air Force uniform said all they needed to know. He added credibility to whatever that politician, I mean sheriff, wanted to say."

"Yes, sir," replied Don.

With the briefing now concluded, Conner secured the non-disclosure agreements and opened the door to the conference room. The National Guard Master Sergeant was sitting in a chair at the far end of the hallway as requested. When he saw Agent Price, he stood and approached him.

"Agent Price," called Master Sergeant Pompa.

"Yes."

"I didn't want to disturb you during your meeting, but we just received a call from the search team. A Wisconsin Department of Natural Resources (DNR) Conservation Warden thinks he found the crash site. It's about thirty miles north of Peshtigo near Lake Noquebay. I guess it's in a difficult location to get to. Major Gibson is bringing in the crash investigation team from Truax AFB tonight now that they have a location. The Game Warden will lead the team in at first light."

"I take it there was no possibility of survivors?" asked Don.

"From what I could gather over the radio, the crash site consisted of multiple burned pieces of debris spread over a large area.," said the sergeant.

"The key will be if the ejection seats are present at the site. If not, the pilots could have ejected long before the plane hit the ground. If they punched out at 40,000 feet of altitude they could have come down in Upper Michigan," said Conner.

CHAPTER 14

Sunrise came shortly after five o'clock. Conner and Don were already dressed and waiting in the crowded parking lot of the motel. They were accompanied by over forty Air Force and other personnel assigned to find the crash site. The group included policemen, rescue personnel, aircraft mechanics, civil engineers, and crash investigators. Many of them drove up overnight after the crash site was located.

"Gentlemen, can I have your attention over here by the colonel's staff car?" shouted Major Gibson.

As the various personnel gathered around him to listen to the mission brief, he continued.

"Last night, shortly before sunset, a Wisconsin State Conservation Warden received word of a suspected crash site. The site is about twenty-nine miles north of here near a large lake. It will be a challenge to get to the site due to geography and rough terrain. The command post will be established near the boat launch. We will have three teams working from boats and a separate team walking to the crash site over land. Conservation Warden Roeske will provide the details," said Major Gibson as he handed the briefing over to the warden.

"Good morning, men. Lake Noquebay is the largest lake in the county, spanning more than 2400 acres. It's a freshwater lake with a thick marsh and wetland on the eastern portion. The lake is at least fifty feet deep in places. The suspected crash site is in the wetland off to the east. A local fisherman saw smoke rising from the area and when he eventually got over there, he saw a large section of burnt grass and scattered debris that appeared to be an aircraft wreckage. There are few telephones in that part of the county and it took him all day to be able to report what he found. I have secured the use of three civilian boats to get to the crash site. Mr. Otto Bargenquast here is a local hunting guide and he will lead the ground team," said Warden Roeske.

The hunting guide looked like a mountain man from the movies. In his late fifties wearing an eye patch, he had a long grey beard and wild unkempt hair. Wearing a buckskin fringed coat, he looked as if he had just led a Lewis and Clark expedition. He carried a homemade tomahawk tucked into his leather belt.

"Good morning, fellas. You can call me Otto. I was in the army too but it was back during the first World War. I have been out for thirty-seven years now so my marching aint too good. But where we are going, there won't be a lot of marching going on. The terrain is very inhospitable and you can expect to fall and get stuck in the mud the entire trip. I suggest you bring minimal gear with you, just what you need. There are plenty of deep spots in the wetlands and you can easily find yourself underwater. So, if you aint a good swimmer, you should stay behind. Are there any questions?" asked the hunting guide.

As nobody had any questions, they were divided up into teams and mounted their vehicles to travel to the lake.

As Conner and Don followed along in the motorcade, they discussed what actions they would take when they arrived.

"Do you think we should go in one of the boats or walk in?" asked Don.

"I'm not about to walk through that swampy mess. I spent nine days hiding in a swamp during the war. After getting eaten near to death by mosquitos, ticks, and everything else, I was just about ready to surrender to the Germans voluntarily," replied Conner.

"Do you think I should go on the ground team?"

Looking over to his companion, Conner laughed and said, "In that suit?"

"It's what I brought. OSI dictates we wear agent attire in the field. We don't all have a Project Blue Book clothing waiver," he joked.

Smiling, he replied, "Blue Book doesn't have a clothing waiver. But most agents have enough sense to wear a suit at the office and change into appropriate clothes when out in the field. Where were you assigned prior to Truax?" asked Conner.

"I was assigned to OSI headquarters in Washington D.C."

Smiling, Conner said, "OSI duty in the field is a little different from a headquarters assignment."

"So, I'm told."

"Do you think we both need to go out in a boat then?"

"I'm here as part of a Project Blue Book investigation. Now that we know the U-2 was the culprit for the unidentified object, my job is pretty much complete. I just need to learn from the crash investigation team what their assessment is. If the aircraft crew members are alive, I need to interview them as well. I'll be hanging back at the Command Post."

"Do you think they could still be alive?" asked Don.

"Probably not but it's always possible. If they were able to eject is the main question I'm looking to answer. I know firsthand a pilot can survive in those conditions, even if injured. But then again, I bailed out from a propeller plane going far slower and flying much lower. And these guys were strapped to one of those new rocket-powered ejection seats. That alone could have done them in."

"I think I'll ride out in one of the boats and assist with the search," said Don.

"That's a very good idea, Don. Although you don't fall under the base leadership, you need to maintain a solid working relationship with them. Do your part to assist, but remember, we don't investigate airplane crashes.

They will all look to you for guidance because you are OSI but that is well out of our area of expertise.

"Roger that," replied Don.

As the caravan of cars arrived at the boat launch area of Lake Noquebay, the various groups of men assembled into respective teams. While the Air Police Commander, Major Gibson was in charge of the search team, Lt. Colonel Lebsack was in charge of the crash investigative team. A command pilot with specialized training in crash reconstruction, it would be his job to determine what actually brought down the aircraft.

Lt. Colonel Lebsack and his technical team would accompany Warden Roeske in the boats while Major Gibson would take the ground team in with the hunting guide. Agent Golden would ride in one of the boats while Agent Price remained with Colonel Roberts and a few others at the command post.

"Be sure and provide updates over the radio," instructed Colonel Roberts.

"Yes, sir," replied the leaders of both teams as they departed on their respective missions.

Looking over at Conner, he said, "Well, now we wait." I have some coffee in my staff car. You care for a cup?"

"I never turn down free coffee," replied Conner.

As the two men walked over to the staff car, Colonel Roberts advised the young airman driver and the captain that had become his fill-in aide, that they could stand down and take a walk. This let Conner know the colonel wanted to chat in private. As the two men took a seat in the back of the 1952 Nash Rambler painted Air Force blue, the colonel closed the door.

"I thought those mosquitos would be the death of us," replied the colonel while opening a thermos of coffee.

Smiling, Conner replied, "I don't envy those guys walking through the wetlands."

Making small talk, the colonel asked, "So Conner, how long have you been with the OSI?"

Taking a disposable paper cup filled with hot coffee, Conner replied "Going on seven years now."

"I bet you have seen some interesting things?" said the colonel.

Assuming the senior man was buttering him up in an amateur attempt to elicit some Blue Book information, Conner had to laugh to himself. It would not be hard to turn the tables on the old man. One thing a fighter pilot liked to talk about, was himself.

"Yes sir, I have seen some interesting things in the past few years but it wasn't my first career choice."

"Oh," replied the colonel.

"No sir, I had a career change after I was no longer qualified for flight duty." Seeing the interest peak in the aviators' eyes, Conner knew the trajectory of their private conversation had now changed.

"You were a flyer?" asked the colonel.

"Yes sir, during the war." Conner kept his answers intentionally vague so the older man would waste questions on that topic rather than OSI or Project Blue Book.

"What kind of aircraft were you on?"

Conner knew the colonel was attempting to determine his actual Air Force rank based on the question. Enlisted personnel typically served in-flight roles such as aerial gunners, engineers, and radio operators while officers typically serve as pilots, navigators, and bombardiers. While a handful of sergeants served as pilots, they were elevated to the rank of flight officer, a rank between enlisted and commissioned officers.

"I flew a P-38 lightning," replied Conner. Taking a sip of his coffee, he continued, "I served with the 95th Fighter Squadron. Early in the war we started off in North Africa, based out of Algeria and later Tunisia. We did a lot of anti-submarine patrols and shot up some enemy ground targets. In 1943 we moved north and supported the invasion of Sicily. In 1944 we moved the unit up to Italy and conducted a lot of bomber escort duty over Europe."

Now that the conversation had been redirected away from sensitive topics, Conner was able to have a conversation with a fellow war veteran and aviator.

"I see you spent some time in that part of the world as well," said Conner, pointing to the brown and green ribbon on the officer's service coat (the European-African-Middle Eastern Campaign Medal).

Nodding, the colonel replied. "I commanded a P-51 Mustang squadron based out of England. We flew a lot of bomber escort duty over Europe as well. I'm sure we flew a lot of the same air."

Conner could see the old aviators' memories returned to the war.

The colonel continued, "I lost some good men over there. On my twenty-second mission, I got shot down over Bordeaux, France."

"Were you captured?" asked Conner.

"Thankfully no. I evaded for a few days until the French resistance found me. It took a few weeks but they were eventually able to smuggle me to Spain. I spent the next few months recuperating from my injuries then sent back to the states to lead a training unit."

The colonel was lost in thought and the conversation took a pause. Conner knew exactly where the older man's thoughts were. While he rarely shared his POW experience with anyone, it felt right to share it with the colonel.

"We certainly did share some of the same air," replied Conner, in a tone of understanding. "I was shot down over Romania in 1944. I spent the rest of the war in a German Prisoner of War camp with a bunch of Russian Army prisoners.... Stalag VII-A."

"Much respect," said the colonel, now viewing the special agent in an entirely new light.

"You also. It's hard enough getting yourself shot down over enemy territory, but it's a whole different hell being a squadron command and having your men get shot down."

Nodding as he remembered his fallen brothers, he said, "I can still picture each of their faces after all these years.

"Here's to the ones that didn't come home," said Conner, while holding his coffee cup up as if to toast.

"Here's to them," said Colonel Roberts.

CHAPTER 15

Standing in the small lobby of the Peshtigo Police department, Sandy waited for the uniformed officer to walk out of the building before approaching the elderly civilian woman who worked the reception desk. She hoped she could engage the woman in conversation and gain some information for her story. Holding a clipboard and trying to look official, she approached the desk.

"Good morning, ma'am, how are you doing today?"

"Oh, I'm doing fine, thank you. All this activity is very exciting."

"Yes ma'am, I know it is. While the search team is out looking for the crash site, I was asked to see if there were any local reports of UFOs or other strange sightings. Can you help me with that?"

"I thought the Game Warden found the crash site last night?" said the police receptionist.

Learning the news and not wanting to blow her cover, she replied, "Yes ma'am, they sure did. I wasn't sure if that information was releasable just yet. Do you have officers helping at the scene?"

"No, that area is way out of our jurisdiction. But I'm sure the County Sheriff and the State Patrol are giving them a hand."

Trying to find a not so obvious way of asking the location of the crash site, Sandy asked how large their jurisdiction was.

"Oh, we just police the Peshtigo area, the sheriff does the rest of the county."

"I see. How long would you say it would take to get to the crash site from here?"

Looking a little confused, the receptionist asked, "What agency did you say you worked for again?"

Thinking fast on her feet, she said, "I work for the Wisconsin Office of Military Assistance. It's the link between the Air Force and the Governor's office."

"The what office?" asked the elderly receptionist.

Smiling, Sandy said, "You probably know of it by its three-letter acronym, OMA."

"Oh, yes. I think I have heard of it," said the woman in an attempt to appear knowledgeable of the many agencies the government has.

"Oh, look at the time," said Sandy while looking down at her watch. "I'm running late for another meeting. Thank you so much for your time and have a nice day."

"You too," said the confused woman as Sandy exited the department.

Walking across the street to the diner, Sandy was hoping the waitress had heard some gossip about the location of the crash site. Having a seat at the counter, she waited for her moment to strike up a conversation with the only waitress on duty. The waitress seemed annoyed and not very friendly. Moments later, another woman ran into the diner apologizing.

"Oh, Mable, I am so sorry. I got here as soon as I could."

"You are thirty minutes late! I told you I would cover your breakfast shift but I had to be out of here by ten o'clock at the latest."

"I know, and I am so sorry. I will make it up to you I promise."

As the two waitresses continued to argue, Sandy saw an Air Force Jeep pull up outside the diner with a young airman driving. Looking back towards the arguing waitresses, she watched Mable take off her apron and place it on the counter before storming out of the diner. When the oncoming waitress walked into the kitchen to speak to the cook, Sandy snatched the apron off the counter and walked outside.

Wearing the apron, she walked around the corner of the diner to the parking area and greeted the young airman.

"Hi sweetie, you down from the crash site for some food?"

"Yes ma'am, I am."

"You don't have to call me ma'am, please call me Mable," she said in a flirtatious manner while adopting the persona of her new character.

"I was sent down to try and get some food to take back up there."

"I can help you with that. We just finished waxing the floor so I can take your order right here."

"Ok. I need eighty hamburgers and eighty bottles of Coke."

"Wait right here and I will go place the order."

Walking back to the front of the diner, she removed the apron and left it outside on the bench before re-entering. Going back to the counter she placed the order to go and watched the airman through the window to ensure he didn't try to come inside. Luckily, he took the opportunity to catch some shut eye and napped uncomfortably in the canvas seat of the jeep.

When the order was ready, she paid the bill and said thanks.

"It's a lot of food, let me help you carry it out to the car," said the waitress.

"That's ok, I can make a few trips," said Sandy as she didn't want the real waitress to foil her ruse.

"It's not a problem at all."

"No thank you I said. I got it."

"Suit yourself," said the waitress, with an insulted tone.

Sandy made four trips carrying the food and drinks from the dinner out to the parking lot. Once all the food was outside, she put the apron back on and carried the order the rest of the way to the jeep.

Once it was all loaded in the back of the jeep, she woke the sleeping airman up by patting him on the shoulder.

"Your order is ready, Airman," she said in an overly sweet tone.

Startled, the young man jumped as he woke up.

"Sorry ma'am, I guess I dozed off."

"That's ok, you seem exhausted. Did you have a long night?"

"Yes ma'am, I drove all night from Madison. I arrived just in time to go up to the crash site and now they sent me back down for food."

Sandy had originally planned on following the jeep up to the crash site, but she thought better as she knew Conner would be there and could easily identify her convertible.

"How much do I owe you for the food ma'am?"

"It's not ma'am, it's Mable," she said in a flirtatious voice.

The young airman couldn't be more than eighteen years old and presented as very naive. Sandy determined that flirting was not the best way to manipulate the service member so she switched to the motherly and insistent character.

"What is your name sweetie?"

"Airman Basic Swanson, ma'am."

"What's your first name?"

"It's Albert ma'am."

"Well Albert, the owner of the dinner is a World War 2 veteran and he insisted that I give you the food at no charge. But he also insisted that I ride up there with you to deliver it personally."

"I don't know about that ma'am. I wasn't told I could bring anyone back with me."

"Albert, it will be just fine. They didn't specifically tell you not to bring anyone back, did they?"

"Well, no ma'am, they didn't, but…"

Before he could finish his sentence, she was already climbing into the passenger seat of the jeep.

"It will be fine Albert, now let's get going before these burgers get any colder."

CHAPTER 16

There were four men on the boat with the Game Warden as he shut the outboard motor off and lifted it out of the water to avoid getting it tangled in the tall grass. The 18-foot long, 1949 model Chris Craft boat floated forward with momentum into the wetlands as the water grew shallow. Mosquitoes swarmed the boat as it floated in the stagnant water. Warden Roeske, wearing a set of hip waders and suspenders, handed a second set to Lt. Colonel Lebsack. As the boat slowed to a stop near a large piece of burnt metal debris protruding from the water, the game warden sat on the edge of the boat and swung his legs over the side. Using a long pole, he checked the depth of the water.

"It's about three feet right here. This is about as close as we will get without getting the boat stuck," said the Warden. The warden and Lt. Colonel Lebsack slipped out of the boat and into the waist-deep water. Two men from each of the other two boats also slipped into the water to assist. Don stood in the boat and took photographs with his OSI crime scene camera to document the scene as much as possible.

"This was definitely a P-89 Scorpion," said Lt. Colonel Lebsack.

While the aircraft was in pieces and badly burned, the soft marsh with a watery bottom prevented it from total destruction upon impact. Struggling as he waded through the mud and water, Lt. Colonel Lebsack shouted "I can see the fuselage about thirty yards to the east in the tall grass. As the men slowly made their way to the burned-out wreckage, they all fell several times due to the muddy uneven bottom of the marsh. Lt. Colonel Lebsack tried to climb the side of the aircraft hull but the slick, mud-covered boots of the waders made it impossible to get any traction. The game warden assisted by taking a knee and allowing the Lt. Colonel to use him to boost himself up high enough to get a look inside the mangled cockpit.

All the men present were silent, waiting to learn the fate of the two aircrew members. Would this be a tomb for two American airmen or would the search for survivors continue?

Climbing down from the wreckage, Lt. Colonel Lebsack turned to the rest of the men and shouted, "Nobody on board. Both ejection seats are missing from the wreckage." With a sigh of relief, there was still a possibility that the missing aircrew members could be alive.

Back at the Command Post, the radio came to life with a broadcast, "Waterborne Search Team to Command Post."

Colonel Roberts, using the radio mounted in his staff car replied, "Go ahead for Command Post."

"Colonel Roberts, we have located the crash site and confirmed that it is a P-89 Scorpion. Both ejection seats are missing. I repeat both ejection seats are missing. No aircrew members located."

"Roger that search team, crash site located, both ejection seats unaccounted for," repeated the colonel.

"Thank God! There is still a chance," said Conner.

The colonel switched frequencies on the radio to communicate with the Airborne Search Team.

"Command Post to Airborne Search and Rescue."

"Go for Airborne Search and Rescue," came the reply from the pilot up above.

"The crash site has been located. Both ejection seats are missing. Continue the airborne search for any sign of parachutes or pilots."

"Roger that Command Post! The search continues. Airborne Search and Rescue out."

CHAPTER 17

"**M**ajor Gibson!" shouted Airman Second Class Barber in a thick southern accent. As the ground search team communications Airman, the weight and bulk of the AN/PRC-10 backpack radio made it difficult to walk in the muck. With a range of almost five miles, the twenty-six-pound radio allowed them to remain in communication with the Command Post.

"What is it, Barber?" replied the Major, trying to hide the fact that he was winded from the strenuous journey.

"Sir, I just overheard a communication between the boat guys and the Command Post. They found the crash site and verified both aircrew members ejected before it crashed. They are still unaccounted for."

Trying to reevaluate his situation, Major Gibson told his search team to take a five-minute break while he contacted Command Post. The men, covered in mud and standing in the swamp glanced at one other with an incredulous look. None of them had a clue what to do while on break except to continue standing in the swamp.

Airman Barber turned around while the major operated the radio pack that was strapped onto his back.

"Ground Search Team to Command Post."

"Ground Search Team to Command Post, come in Command Post."

"Airman Barber, I think we are about out of range for the short antenna, set up the long one."

"Yes sir," replied the young airman.

Barber removed the standard three-foot antenna from the radio pack and started to assemble the longer range ten-foot antenna. The longer antenna was a collapsible seven section whip style joined by a stainless-steel cable. With the antenna extended and secured to a tree branch, he informed the major that it was ready to go.

Speaking into the telephone handset, Major Gibson repeated his earlier message.

"Ground Search Team to Command Post."

"Go for Command Post," came the reply.

Luckily the longer antenna extended the range of the radio enough to reach them.

"Command Post, we overheard a transmission that the crash site was located and both crew members had ejected. Can you confirm?"

"Roger that Ground Search Team. That is confirmed."

"Permission to adjust destination? Rather than continuing on to the crash site, recommend we turn towards the last known airborne location and proceed to look for surviving air crewmembers."

"Roger that Ground Search Team. Proceed to a general heading of 105 degrees due east of your current position."

"Roger that Command Post. Proceeding to a heading of 105 degrees due east. Ground Search Team out."

Hanging up the handset, Major Gibson gave new instructions to his team.

"OK, guys, new plan. We are headed east now, away from the lake and this godforsaken swamp. Rather than walking one in front of the other, we are now going into search mode. I want you to walk in a line, side by side, spaced out about ten yards between each man. Be sure and look up every few steps and scan the tree canopy for parachutes that may have gotten caught up there. If you see something, call out. Any questions?"

There was no reply.

"Good. As soon as Barber changes antennas back on the radio, we will move out."

Walking over to their civilian hunting guide Otto, Major Gibson said, "I hope the terrain gets easier going to the east."

The rugged old hunting guide was an odd sort of man. It was obvious he spent a lot of time alone in the backwoods. It was apparent he was tough as nails but he was also socially awkward. Casual conversation was difficult at best.

"Yes, the farther we get from the lake the less water we will be walking in," he replied in a gruff, monotone voice.

"Well, that will be a nice change of pace. I wouldn't mind getting away from these mosquitos."

"Yes, the mosquitoes are worse closer to the stagnant water."

Looking towards the thick forest, the major asked, "Does anybody live in those woods?"

"Some," replied Otto with a dead look in his eyes.

Not wanting to continue the awkward conversation with the creepy hunting guide, the major gave the order to move out. The men lined up as instructed while Airman Barber struggled to stow the long-range antenna into its pouch.

It took about twenty minutes of walking east for the team to move from the wetland onto dry ground. With every step Major Gibson took he could feel the water squish in his combat boots.

"Flight Halt! I want everyone to take five and put on dry socks," commanded Major Gibson.

Trench foot, or immersion foot syndrome, is a serious condition that results from feet being wet for too long. The condition became well known during WW1 when soldiers got it from fighting in the cold and wet conditions in the trenches. Trench foot would lead to the death of 75,000 British soldiers during WW1.

Thankful that he finally had a dry place to sit for the first time all day, Major Gibson sat on an old fallen log as he unlaced his boots. Pulling each one off, he poured the remaining water out. Pulling his socks off, he twisted them, wringing out the water. Laying them on the log next to him, he pulled a dry set from a waterproof sack inside his field pack.

Waiting a few minutes for his feet to dry before putting his new socks on, he took a drink from his canteen. Placing it to his lips, he tilted his head back and poured the water into his mouth. As he opened his eyes, he noticed something strange hanging from the tree above his position.

Putting the cap back on the canteen, he stood to examine the strange symbol. Hanging from a tree branch about fifteen feet in the air were three deer antlers, intertwined with one another and tied into position with twine.

"Hey Otto, what is that?" he asked the guide while pointing to the ornament.

"Triple Horn of Odin" the man said as if it was common knowledge.

Everyone in the group looked up at the symbol then slowly back to Otto.

"What is a Triple Horn of Odin?" asked Airman Barber.

"It is a tribute to the Gods of War" he replied.

The group of airmen silently made eye contact with one another, then to the major. The major, looking back at his troops, shrugged his shoulders as if to say he had no idea what the hunting guide was talking about.

"Is that some sort of witchcraft symbol? Are these woods supposed to be haunted or something?" asked Airman Barber.

Otto didn't smile or make eye contact with anyone when he spoke. He said in a monotone voice, "The woods are not special, but the ones who dwell among them are the chosen. The Gods have placed them here to look after the forest and wait for a new leader to emerge."

Airman Barber's eyes grew wide as he turned his head towards Major Gibson and sarcastically mouthed the words, "Well that's just wonderful."

The airmen started chatting amongst themselves, discussing that the woods were creepy enough without the spooky symbols hanging from the trees or the ramblings of a crazy backwoods' mountain man.

Not knowing what else to do, Major Gibson said "OK, then…Let's get our boots back on fellas and continue with our mission." Once the airmen were formed back up in the search pattern, the line seemed considerably shorter than before. Looking to his left and his right, Major Gibson observed his men were now only five yards apart from each other in the thick woods.

Laughing to himself, he commanded his men, "Spread out—ten yards apart! The woods are not haunted!" Once the line was properly adjusted, he commanded them to move out. As the men walked through the thick forest, they came across addition symbols, some hanging from branches and others carved into the trees themselves. Although there was no visible threat to react to, Major Gibson would have felt a little more at ease if his men had been armed. Being that it was a search and rescue mission; rifles were not essential and deemed too cumbersome to carry. The only two Air Policemen who were armed were MSgt Tratnyek and himself, and they were only Smith and Wesson, K-38 revolvers.

As the group walked through the dense forest, one of the airmen joked, "Maybe we should call this mission Operation Hansel and Gretel," causing laughter among the men.

"Ok, let's stay focused gentlemen, we have two missing airmen to find. They could be injured, stuck in a tree, and likely dangerously dehydrated. Time is not on their side," said Master Sergeant Tratnyek.

That hit home to all of the young air policemen walking in the forest. They could each picture themselves alone and injured, waiting for help. They additionally imagined how their mothers or wives would feel under the circumstances.

"Major, thirty yards ahead and a little to your right!" shouted one of the airmen.

"What do you see?" he shouted back, as the thick forest provided each man a different visibility vantage point.

"Not sure yet, but a possible helmet over by the fallen log."

"Hold the line!" shouted the major as he moved in the direction to investigate.

As Major Gibson got closer to the area pointed out by the member of his search team, he could see the white helmet on the ground next to the old log. Picking it up to examine it, he heard Master Sergeant Tratnyek ask from behind him, "Can you confirm its from Truax?"

Looking the helmet over, he replied, "It's the new P-3 fighter pilot helmet. Our guys just got them a few weeks back."

"How can you tell?" asked the Sergeant.

"The wind blast visor. With the new ejection seats and the much faster aircraft, the jet pilots now face new extremes. In 1953 the Air Force started to standardize the helmets by attaching this visor onto the older P-1 helmets to protect the pilots during ejection. Truax just got ours."

Turning the helmet over to look inside, he saw the call sign "Legend" written in ink. He also noticed blood on the helmet strap and buckle.

CHAPTER 18

The sun was moving across the sky as the boat search team made its way back to the command post. Looking down at his watch, Conner noticed it was half past three as the boats pulled up to the shore and the men climbed out. They looked rough as they walked up to the command post. Eight hours of searching the wetlands left them exhausted, sunburnt, and covered in mosquito bites.

The team walked over to the Air Force Jeep containing food and drinks. Colonel Roberts had sent one of the men from the Command Post back to the diner in Peshtigo to buy as many hamburgers and Coca-Colas as he could get. As the search team devoured the late lunch, Lt. Colonel Lebsack and Don brought theirs over to Colonel Roberts and Conner to eat while providing a briefing.

The four men gathered around the hood of the colonel's staff car, using it as a makeshift table while they ate and briefed.

Lt. Colonel Lebsack reported, "While the geography makes it near impossible to conduct a by the book crash investigation, here is what I can determine. We found the fuselage and one of the wings. We still have yet to locate the tail section and right wing. There is a very good chance they are submerged in water. The most important thing is that both ejection seats and the canopy were not present. It appears the aircrew punched out at some point prior to the crash."

"Was there any indication that the P-89C was shot down or collided in air with another aircraft?" asked the colonel.

"Well sir, I can't conclusively rule that out without a complete inspection of all of the parts, however, I didn't see any indication of that from what we found today. The damage and charring I found were consistent with the aircraft impacting the ground."

"Do you have any theories on what mechanically brought the plane down?" asked Conner.

Scratching his head, the Lt. Colonel said "Well, it's not enough to make a conclusive determination just yet, but I do have a theory that seems to fit the evidence, at least so far. There are a few contributing factors that support my hypothesis. I will explain."

1. The aircraft in question is the P-89 Scorpion "C" model. The C variant had some issues and the aircraft design was upgraded multiple times over the past few years to resolve some of them. This year we are already up to the "J" variant.

2. The C model introduced the more powerful Allison J35-A-33 engines. The airframe wasn't strong enough to accommodate the increased power at higher speeds and higher altitudes. They only made 164 "C" models before they noticed the issues and upgraded to the next model.

3. There was a similar incident in El Segundo, California a few years ago. A P-89-C was making a high-speed pass and the right horizontal stabilizer peeled off resulting in the plane coming apart in the air. The pilot was able to eject and survived but the back seat officer perished. After the crash investigation, the cause was determined to be high-frequency, low-amplitude aeroelastic flutter in both the horizontal and vertical stabilizers.

4. A similar incident occurred in 1951 at an air show in Detroit, Michigan killing both the aircrew and a spectator on the ground. That P-89-C

experienced severe torsional aeroelastic problems. That incident led to the temporary grounding of all "C" models.

5. Two years ago in 53, we lost another one of the "C" models from Truax AFB that was forward deployed to Kinross AFB in upper Michigan. It went down in Lake Superior killing both crew members.

Lt. Colonel Lebsack concluded, "So based on my limited examination of the crash site, historical aircraft mishaps of similar nature, the age of the particular aircraft, and the conditions it was operating in (speed and altitude), I would say it is highly likely the aircraft came apart while taking evasive maneuvers."

This information was enough for Conner, at least in regard to Project Blue Book. Knowing the classified U-2 spy plane was what the fighter pilot was trying to avoid when his plane could not withstand the evasive maneuvers, he could now close his portion of the investigation.

As the briefing was concluding, a broadcast came in over the radio.

"Ground Search Team to Command Post."

Colonel Roberts picked up the radio handset to respond.

"Go for Command Post."

"Command Post, we have located a pilot's helmet with the callsign "Legend" written inside. It appears there is blood on the strap and buckle. Nothing else located at this time. Our position is about six miles southeast of the crash site. There is a thick tree canopy above us. Requesting permission to pop smoke so the Airborne Search and Rescue Team can get a vector on our location."

"Command Post to Airborne Search and Rescue Team."

"Go for Airborne Search and Rescue Team."

"Did you copy the last transmission?"

"Affirmative Command Post. We are in position to acknowledge smoke and mark the location."

"Roger that. Command Post to Ground Team, you are cleared to pop smoke."

Major Gibson looked over to Master Sergeant Tratnyek and gave him a thumbs up. The sergeant, understanding the nonverbal command, removed a green canister from his belt. Putting his finger in the ring, he pulled the pin from the M18 smoke grenade before tossing it onto the ground a few yards away. Three seconds later the canister started to emit a huge cloud of yellow smoke. Waiting about thirty seconds for the smoke to rise above the tree canopy, Major Gibson spoke into the radio handset attached to Airman Barber's pack. "Ground Search Team to Airborne Team, look for yellow smoke now."

"I see your yellow smoke Ground Team. I'm marking your position and starting a new search grid based on your location."

CHAPTER 19

C olonel Roberts looked down at his wristwatch to estimate how much time was left in the day to conduct a search. It was half past four and the sun would be down around eight. Knowing it would get dark far earlier in the thick forest, he asked Lt. Colonel Lebsack how long it would take for the ground team to walk back to a location where vehicles could pick them up.

After reviewing the map in relation to where they found the helmet, he replied, "Probably a couple hours if they don't run into any trouble."

"Please communicate with the ground team and have them start heading toward the pickup location. It will be around nine by the time we can get back to Peshtigo. The guys will all need a good meal and a night's sleep before we start again in the morning. "

"Will do colonel."

"Oh, and Lebsack, make sure we have a search plane up all night long in case the downed pilots set a signal fire."

"Yes sir, but just for informational purposes, Warden Roeske did inform us about some people who live out in those woods. There will be no way to determine if a fire is a signal by the pilots or just a cooking fire by the locals."

"What kind of people live out there?" asked Colonel Roberts.

"Not too sure, but the warden acted like they were different."

"Different how?"

"He didn't really elaborate but I assumed they were hillbilly types who didn't assimilate well with modern society. Maybe moonshiners?"

"Ok, but I still want the planes up at night. If my men are alive, the sound of aircraft over head will give them hope" emphasized the colonel.

"Yes, sir."

Looking back down to his watch, Colonel Roberts hated pulling the search team out of the woods for the night, however, it was the smartest decision. They would need to be rested to conduct a thorough search again tomorrow.

Looking back down at his watch reminded him of when he had been shot down in the war. It was the same Omega CK2129 watch he wore on that fateful day. It was a gift from a friend in the Royal Air Force while he was serving in England. The watch was developed for British pilots in 1940 when it was decided they required a rotating bezel to help pilots time certain events while on a mission. This simple tool resolved a lot of issues in the cockpit and helped fighter pilots coordinate with their bomber pilot counterparts in the air.

Concerned that the local diner may not stay open late enough to feed his troops, Colonel Roberts walked over to the Command Post airman who had brought the burgers up for lunch.

"Airman Swanson, what time does that diner close back in Peshtigo?"

"Eight o'clock sir."

"That probably won't be late enough. I want you to drive back to Peshtigo and ask if they will stay open late for us. If they won't, then order another eighty burgers and drinks before they close. We will be back in town around nine or ten I suspect."

"Yes sir, I'm sure they will accommodate us. That lady over there works at the diner," he said pointing to an attractive woman with red hair.

"What is she doing out here?"

"She insisted she bring the food personally. Her boss is a World War 2 veteran and donated the meal to the Air Force, free of charge."

"Well, that is appreciated, but I think the Air Force can afford to pay our own way and that is a big order for a small diner."

"I thought so too, colonel, but when I pulled up, she asked me how the search was going. When I told her I was fetching lunch for the boys, she insisted I wait in the Jeep while she went in and brought out the food. They were waxing the floors and didn't want me to walk on it. She insisted that she drive out here with me to serve the troops."

"Why would they choose today to wax the floors when they are probably having the busiest day they have had in a long time?"

"I couldn't say, sir."

Thinking that scenario sounded a bit strange, Colonel Roberts told the airman to stand by.

Walking back over to the staff car where Conner was standing, he related the airman's story to the investigator. This piqued Conner's curiosity so he walked around the many military trucks and police vehicles to get a look at the woman from the diner. Smiling to himself, he knew another change of hair color could not disguise the way the woman carried herself when she walked.

Returning to the colonel, Conner smiled and said, "Yeah, that's her. She knew I made her car and she obviously needed a new ride and an excuse to get out here."

"What do you think we should do about it?" asked the colonel.

Handing his OSI car keys to the colonel, he asked "Can you please give these to Agent Golden? I'll drive the jeep back to town with the young lady. Have the airman load her up in the Jeep and stop by the staff car on his way out? Don't tell him why."

Smiling, Colonel Roberts replied, "That sounds like a wonderful idea."

CHAPTER 20

As the dark blue Air Force jeep drove around the parked military vehicles, it came to a rest near the colonel's staff car. The female passenger was looking down as if she was searching for something in her purse in an attempt to hide her face.

The airman said, "I'll be right back, just need to check out."

"OK sweety, I'll be right here," she said while keeping her head down and not looking in the direction of the staff car. Moments later, the jeep started up again and headed towards Peshtigo. With a sense of relief, the woman looked up, but to her surprise, Special Agent Conner Price was behind the wheel.

After several minutes of driving in silence, Conner finally looked over at his attractive red-haired passenger with a smirk and said, "You doing something different with your hair?"

Trying to conceal her facial expression, the woman looked off to her right as she failed to contain her laughter.

Still not getting an answer, Conner asked, "So, how long have you been working at the diner?"

Smirking back, the woman turned towards the special agent and replied, "I never specifically told him I worked at the diner. I just offered to buy lunch for the search party. I can't help it if he assumed I worked there."

"Sounds like an innocent mistake. I'm sure the apron with the Mable name tag played no part."

Smiling, she looked over at him and said, "Well, you are one to talk, "Bill.""

Looking forward while driving, he replied, my middle name is actually William and I never tried to mislead you. The fact of the matter is you already knew who I was before you ever approached me."

"What makes you think that?"

Looking in her direction, he said, "Lieutenant Spalding has been relieved of duty for his part in your shenanigans."

After a long pause, she tried to explain, "Well I certainly didn't mean for that to happen. I even agreed to keep his name out of my story."

"You're writing a story?" asked Conner inquisitively.

Now knowing that Special Agent Price had more knowledge than she originally thought, she replied "I think you know who I am and what I do for a living."

"Who exactly are you?" he asked with a smirk.

"I think you know who I am, Mr. Price."

Conner smiled to himself as he knew she was expecting him to correct her by calling him mister rather than Special Agent. Denying her the opportunity to transition the conversation to his relationship with Project Blue Book or OSI, he let it slide. It was apparent the woman had some skills at eliciting information through conversation, however, compared to Conner, she was a rank amateur.

"Why don't you tell me who you are?" he asked, both toying with the woman but also curious to see what story she would come up with this time.

Sensing she had hit a wall with her ruse, she decided to come clean and hope that honesty would work out for her.

"Sandy Elliot. I'm an investigative journalist."

"What paper do you work for?"

"I'm technically an independent reporter, but lately I have been writing for the Chicago Tribune."

"Do they have a lot of woman investigative reporters at the Tribune?

Raising an eyebrow in annoyance at the question, she replied, "I often use a male pen name for my articles; however, something tells me you already knew that."

"Well, times are changing fast. They say as of this year, half of American homes have a television set. Maybe you can get a TV job next."

"Yeah, that's not a very sexist industry at all," she replied with a sarcastic tone. "Mabey I could be the next naive housewife who is bad with money on a situational comedy. Like America needs another Lucille Ball."

Looking over at the woman, Conner smiled as he said, "Well, you already have the red wig."

No longer interested in hiding her emotions, the woman laughed at the comment as this was her third hair color in as many days. As she continued on her rant about the male patriarch dominating her industry, she eventually realized the crafty special agent had manipulated the conversation to a topic she was passionate about in an attempt to lower her guard. What was worse was that it had worked.

Working to switch the conversation back onto Conner, she asked "So how long have you been a special agent with the Air Force OSI?"

Smiling, he replied, "Well that's a pretty abrupt and clumsy transition for a seasoned journalist such as yourself."

Trying to project a serious tone, she said, "I no longer care for the flirtatious dance with words you like to play Mr. Price. You think you are so crafty with your conversational psychology mixed with a failed attempt at charm."

Smiling, Conner replied "Only a failed attempt at charm?"

She smiled at his reply but wasn't sure how to proceed. While she didn't want to feed his ego, she did enjoy their verbal dance with words...and his attempt at charm was certainly no failure.

"It would be a lot easier if you would just allow me to interview you, Conner."

"Truax Air Force Base has a public affairs officer assigned and it's his job to deal with all media inquiries. I find it best to stay in my lane."

"And what exactly is your lane Mr. Price?"

"What do you think it is?"

"I think you are Conner Price, a special agent with the Air Force Office of Special Investigations and assigned to Project Blue Book. You are based out of Wright Patterson AFB in Ohio and you travel around the country investigating UFO encounters." Smiling to herself, she concluded with "I do my homework also special agent."

"I'm not sure I would call blackmailing a young lieutenant for confidential information the same thing as doing homework."

Embarrassed at the accusation, even though it was correct, she replied "Sometimes you need to break a few eggs to make an omelet…or get a story."

"I think you are confused about that?"

"Confused about what, Conner?"

"I'm not the story."

"What is the story then?"

"The story is Captain Glen Casper and Lieutenant Kelly Jensen," replied Conner matter-of-factly.

"And just who are they?" she asked.

"They, are the two United States airmen we are searching for. The two brave aviators might be injured, suffering, and possibly even dead. They risked their lives for their country and their loved ones are very concerned about them right now."

Embarrassed that she missed it, and at how calloused her remarks must have sounded, she wasn't sure how to respond. It was easy for a journalist to get target fixated on the juiciest story and somehow look past the personal interest piece. Conner was correct, there were real men missing. Maybe she had been too focused on the "what" and "why" and not enough on the "who."

Softening her tone, Sandy said "Of course I am concerned about the pilots. But personal interest stories don't sell like UFOs right now."

"Maybe that's what's wrong with our country today. Folks are more interested in shiny objects in the sky and conspiracy theories than they are in each other and what's going on around them. Much of that rests with Hollywood and the media as they are the ones telling the masses what they should believe and how they should feel," replied Conner.

"Insightful words from a man who spends his days investigating UFOs."

Smiling, he replied, "I'm not investigating anything right at this moment. I'm just giving a pretty lady a ride into town."

Smiling, she replied, "Well that's a pretty abrupt and clumsy transition for a seasoned investigator such as yourself."

Laughing, he said, "Sometimes I stumble during my flirtatious dance with words."

As the jeep came to a stop at an intersection in town, Sandy looked over to the small movie theater on the corner. The movie being advertised was a science fiction film called "*This Island Earth*." The movie poster depicted flying saucers and green space aliens grabbing humans.

Smiling, she pointed to the movie poster and asked, "Care to comment on that film Agent Price?"

Looking over to the side of the theater where the movie posters were hanging, he saw the movie was a double feature, running along with "*Abbot and Costello meet the Mummy*".

"I always enjoy a good mummy flick," said Conner, grinning at the redirect.

Both smiling, their eyes made contact for the first time during their conversation. Her brown eyes were softer now, no longer trying to hide behind false personas and trickery.

"Are you asking me to a movie, Mr. Price?"

"No time for a movie tonight, but I can buy you dinner if you are hungry. I know of a good diner in town."

The conversation was interrupted by the sound of a car horn honking behind them. Realizing they were holding up traffic, Conner gave a friendly wave and proceeded through the intersection toward the diner.

CHAPTER 21

Captain Glen Casper was floating in and out of consciousness as he listened to the rhythmic sounds of the pitch-black forest. Sounding similar to crickets, the yellow rail is a small and elusive bird that is seldom seen. A master of camouflage, the male of the species emits a loud "tik-tik-tik-tik" sound to attract a female mate during the warm summer months of northern Wisconsin. The continuous sound was hypnotic.

As he adjusted his position, he could once again feel the pain radiating through his body from his many injuries. As horrible as that was, he was thankful he once again had feeling in his lower body. While the rocket-powered ejection seat had surely saved his life, the tremendous violence of its action was highly traumatic to the human body. His back ached so bad he assumed he sustained thoracic vertebral fractures, a common injury with ejection seat use. The intermittent loss of feeling in his lower body was both a blessing and a curse.

The more immediate situation was the large elm tree he was stuck in. After ejecting into the dark abyss, his ejection seat eventually separated from his body as designed, allowing him to fall to earth with the aid of a parachute. Disoriented from the ejection and having no visibility in the dark night, his body was limp when it crashed through the heavy tree canopy where each branch impacted his body like a baseball bat. His left ankle painfully wedged into the crook of a tree branch, leaving the rest of his body dangling upside down with the blood rushing to his head.

Unable to free himself from the tangled, inverted position, he used his upper body strength to pull against the parachute, which was stuck higher up in the tree. Once he was able to pull himself into the horizontal position, he used his rescue knife to cut a hole in the silk parachute. Pulling his head and shoulders through the hole, he was able to use the silk parachute as a makeshift hammock, preventing him from dangling upside down and taking some of the pressure off of his obviously broken leg.

Injured and suspended in the tree, he floated in and out of consciousness as he waited for a rescue team to locate him. He knew he had been there at least several hours but more likely a number of days. The passage of time was a blur. He was dehydrated and famished, but all he could think about was his pregnant wife, Becca.

Opening his eyes once again, it was now dark in the forest. Off in the distance, he could hear the howls of a wild pack of animals. Wondering if they were coyotes or wolves, he was actually thankful he was not lying wounded on the ground. He wondered if his partner, Legend, had made it out of the aircraft and if he was still alive. After seeing the bright light and taking evasive actions, he wasn't sure what happened next, but his aircraft violently came apart in the air. He was barely able to eject and wasn't sure if his back seat partner was able to do so.

Looking off into the dark he could see a series of dim lights approaching him from his left. Unable to focus his eyes, or his thoughts, he couldn't determine what he was actually seeing. Was it more UFOs returning? Was it several search planes flying in a row? Nothing was making sense to him.

As the lights continued to get closer, he started to orient himself. The lights were actually on the ground as they were approaching. Was it the glowing eyes of nocturnal predators such as a pack of wolves? Looking through his blurry eyes, he could eventually tell the lights were flickering. They were candles! Each was a single candle carried inside a glass jar.

He was having a difficult time making out the people carrying them as they were all dressed the same, in what appeared to be dark hooded robes. While he struggled to understand why the Air Force search and rescue team was wearing robes and using candles, he slipped out of consciousness once again.

Waking momentarily by an intense pain shooting through his back, Casper could tell his position had changed. He was no longer hanging suspended from the tree. Now he was lying flat on his back with his hands resting in front of him yet he was unable to move them. Were they tied? Was he paralyzed from the back injury? He wasn't sure.

Feeling motion underneath him, it appeared as if he was being transported on some sort of wagon or cart being pulled through the forest. Every bump in the ground sent radiating pain through his body. Looking up towards the tree canopy after dark, he was unable to see anything. The black abyss was all-encompassing.

"Legend?" Casper attempted to ask the people who were transporting him if his crew member had also been rescued. But there was no answer. Only silence and the sound of the cart being pulled through the rough terrain. It was hard to speak as his mouth was dry from lack of water.

Waking again sometime later, he was now laying on a mat on the ground. There was a strong smell of burning incense in the air. His helmet had finally been removed, making it easier to rest. Someone was holding his head up and helping him to drink water from a wooden bowl. The cool fluid was refreshing. It was dark and the only light was a flicker from a candle across the room. Where was he? Was Legend safe? With his throat now moistened, he attempted to speak once again.

"Legend?" he asked, looking for information about his partner.

The elderly female voice in the dark replied, "Not a legend...a prophecy."

Confused, he attempted to ask again, "Is Legend safe?"

The elderly female voice replied, "The prophecy is safe."

"I don't understand."

"It has been foretold that Odin would send a great warrior to our people from the heavens of Asgard. This wounded God would fall to Earth and would fertilize the egg of the chosen."

"What? I don't understand," said the confused pilot.

"Odin pursues knowledge throughout the world. It is written that the God of War, Odin, in an act of self-sacrifice, hung upside down in a tree for nine days and nights to gain knowledge of the runic alphabet. He then passed the knowledge onto the people giving them wisdom."

More confused than ever, Casper asked, "Where am I?"

"Odin placed you upside down in a tree to gain the knowledge of my people. We have been repenting for eighty-four years. Finally, Odin has recognized our sacrifices and sent you to us."

"Look lady, my name is Captain Glen Casper, United States Air Force. I need you to contact the police department. They will be looking for me."

The elderly woman's boney fingers stroked the pilot's hair as she said, "The Queen of Forest Egersund will hear from the Gods and only they can decide your fate."

"What does that mean?"

"You must rest now," she said as she stood to leave the room, closing a heavy wooden door behind her.

Casper looked around the room in an attempt to evaluate his situation. The room was dark and damp. There were no windows. The only light was from a single candle burning on a wooden table across the room. Once his eyes adjusted, he could tell the walls were made of limestone bricks and the small room was only about eight feet wide and ten feet long. He assumed the room was below ground, in a basement of sorts. Decorating the walls were several animal skulls and odd symbols made out of sticks and antlers. Taking a closer look at the skull that sat on the table next to the candle...it was human.

Starting to panic, he worked to control his breathing. Slowly inhaling through his nose and exhaling out his mouth. He knew his situation was dire. Where was he? Who were his captors? Had he dropped into a coven of witches or a strange religious cult? Looking around the room for anything he could use as a weapon or to signal for help, he found nothing.

He tried to sit up but was unable. He had to take an assessment of his injuries in order to devise a plan of action. His lower back was in extreme pain when he attempted to prop himself up onto his elbows. He was certain he had damaged his vertebrae during ejection which was causing paralysis of his lower extremities. Trying to move his hands, he could now determine they were bound together in front of him, resting on his stomach. His flight suit had been removed and he was laying there in just his underwear. His only hope was for the Air Force search team to rescue him before it was too late.

Closing his eyes, he said a prayer from a Psalm of David.

The Lord is my shepherd; I shall not want. He makes me lie down in green pastures. He leads me beside still waters. He restores my soul. He leads me in paths of righteousness for his name›s sake. Even though I walk through the valley of the shadow of death, I will fear no evil, for you are with me; your rod and your staff, they comfort me. You prepare a table before me in the presence of my enemies; you anoint my head with oil; my cup overflows.

While comforted by his faith, he was still worried about his partner.

CHAPTER 22

Walking up to the counter, Conner was greeted by a waitress with the name tag Norma.

"Evening, how's business?" he asked.

"Oh, it's about normal. I was expecting all those military boys for dinner but haven't seen them yet."

"Well, they are coming and will be hungry. But it might not be until nine or ten o'clock before they get back to town. Any chance you can stay open a bit later tonight for them?"

"Of course, we can honey. Anything for our service men. Now what can I get you?"

Pointing to the booth Sandy was sitting at, he said, "We will both have the special and two slices of cherry pie."

"Coming right up," she said.

"Thank you."

Returning to the table, he took a seat across from the beautiful reporter.

"So, when are you headed back to Ohio, Agent Price?

"Please, call me Conner."

"OK, Conner. Why is it you never answer any questions?"

"Don't I?"

"No, you don't. You always deflect, change the subject or answer with a question of your own."

Smiling, he said, "I guess I'm just not much of a conversationalist."

Grinning, she looked him in the eyes and said, "No, you sure aren't."

Smiling back at her, the two shared another intimate gaze, only to be interrupted by Norma delivering their meal.

"Thanks, Norma," said Conner.

"Anything else I can get you?"

"No, I think we are all set. Just keep the grill warm for when the rest of the guys show up."

"Will do," she replied and walked back to the counter.

Breaking the awkward silence, Conner asked "So, Sandra Jane Elliot from Chicago, is that where you were raised or did you move there to be a journalist."

"You seem to know so much about me, why don't you tell me where I grew up?"

Rubbing his chin with his hand, he looked at the woman as if he was trying to figure her out.

"Well, based on the way you mangled that Boston accent, I think I can rule out Massachusetts."

Laughing, she said, "No, I'm not from Massachusetts, but I do believe that accent was spot on."

Continuing the eye contact, Conner said, "You come from means and probably attended a fancy preparatory academy or a finishing school for girls.

Laughing, she asked, "And what pray tell would make you think that?"

"Just your mannerisms. I get the sense that while you did well in that environment, you despised it because they focused more on teaching social grace and upper-class culture, rather than actual academics and things with a real-world application."

"Really?" she asked while looking into his eyes.

"Well maybe…or maybe not. It's just a guess"

"So, what else can you tell about me Mr. Price?"

Scratching his chin once again to insinuate he was thinking hard, he replied, "You have had training in dance, probably ballet or classical."

Impressed, she asked, "And why would you say that?"

"It's the way you move your body."

"The way I move my body?" she asked, trying to sound insulted, but flattered by the observation.

"Yeah. Look at Norma over there behind the counter", he said without looking back at her. She is slouched, her hand on her hip and she leans forward when she walks. Her head bounces up and down a bit as she moves because she walks flat-footed."

Watching the hard-working waitress as she delivered food to another customer, Sandy was impressed with Conner's observation skills.

"And how exactly do I walk?"

Taking a sip of his Coke and setting the bottle back on the table, he replied. "You walk with your chin up, eyes forward, body straight, and relaxed shoulders. You lead with your thighs and allow your legs to swing from your hips. You keep your feet pointed straight so your heel hits the floor first. You then roll your feet from heel to toe, to prevent head bob."

Smiling and flattered that he had noticed all of those things about her, she said, "Ballet class at Miss Porter's Prep School, Farmington, Connecticut, class of 1947."

Their eyes meeting once more, he said, "Let me guess, you and your friends would walk back and forth in the dorm balancing books on your head?"

Laughing, she said, "I think you may have seen too many movies."

"I'm sure I have…but am I wrong?"

"No…you are not wrong," she said, while holding eye contact longer than necessary.

"And let me guess, there was a girl with a Boston accent in your class?"

Laughing, she said, "No. But there was a girl named Jacqueline in my class who also became a journalist. We were good friends. A couple years ago she married a congressman named Jack from Massachusetts who had a Boston accent. I suppose my accent may have been influenced by him to some degree."

Smirking, Conner said, "I think your normal manner of speaking suits you better."

Trying to hide her growing infatuation, she rolled her eyes and asked, "Any other observations that set me apart?"

Taking another sip from his Coke, he replied, "Someone close to you had some specialized training that you try to emulate. Maybe a police officer or a private eye. You clearly possess some rudimentary knowledge of trade-craft like surveillance, disguises and elicitation. While you employ those skills with some success, it's apparent you haven't been formally trained."

Knowing that she would get emotional thinking about her father, she changed the subject.

"You seem to know a lot about me, now tell me something about you."

"Not much to tell really, I'm just your average government employee who goes where he's told and does what's expected of him. Not very exciting at all."

"Something tells me that's not the case Mr. Price."

Smiling, he redirected the conversation yet again, "So what does tomorrow hold for you? Are you going to attempt to sneak out to the Command Post in another disguise?"

"Would you try and stop me if I did?" she asked in a playful tone.

"No. I am actually quite entertained by your Lucy Ricardo style antics. I can only imagine what you would try to pull if you had your sidekick Ethel with you."

Grinning, she replied, "They are hardly Lucy Ricardo style antics."

"OK, tell me this then. Yesterday when you were trying to hide from me in that bathroom over there, how many times did you attempt to crawl out the window before you realized it was too small?"

Embarrassed, she replied, "I don't know why places like this have such small bathroom windows."

Laughing, Conner said, "I don't know but I would have loved to see you trying."

Sandy was growing more infatuated with the man by the minute. Not only was he confident and charming, but he had a rugged quality about him. He was unlike the society men she was used to interacting with who put on airs and tried to impress. This secretive lawman was intuitive and could see her like no one else. Not only could he see through the many disguises she wore, he could also see through the hard journalist exterior she worked hard to portray.

In an attempt to penetrate his hard exterior, she tried a new approach. She would avoid asking specific questions but would make personal observations and allow him to open up while explaining. A tactic that he had used successfully on her.

"I bet it's lonely," she said while looking once again into his eyes.

"What's that?"

"Your job. Your life. As an OSI special agent, you operate in the shadows. You don't have the same opportunity for comradery and to let your hair down as a typical Air Force officer. And as a part of Project Blue Book, you operate in the shadows even from the other OSI agents. You are always on the road and I'm sure it's difficult to maintain any sort of a relationship. With your guarded persona, I'm sure it's difficult to get close to anyone." She reached across the table and placed her hand on top of his. It was an intentional move that could either be interpreted as a consoling gesture of understanding or a flirtatious sign, both of which were accurate.

Conner wasn't sure which way to take the hand grasp or the comment, but he did enjoy her touch. She was correct, his job and his life were lonely. He had no close relationships or substantive friendships due to the secretive nature of his work. He also had a lot of demons from his past which occupied much of his alone thoughts.

Smiling, he replied, "I guess it's not unlike being an investigative journalist. I am on the road a lot, I work alone, and I always have my guard up."

She was both impressed and annoyed at the way he answered her question, shining the light back on her vulnerability. Trying a different approach, she tried asking him innocent questions to see into his psyche.

"So, who is your favorite author?"

"What?"

"What is your favorite book?"

"I don't read much," he replied.

"I don't believe that for a second. You are too well read to not… well, read."

"So, what do I look like I would read?"

Rubbing her chin with her hand in an attempt to mimic him, she said, "You look like an Ernest Hemmingway kind of guy. Probably *the Old Man and the Sea.*"

Impressed, Conner replied with a quote from the book, "*But man is not made for defeat. A man can be destroyed but not defeated.*"

Sandy was impressed with herself that she was finally able to penetrate his hard exterior. She knew a man like Conner was well-read and likely deep on multiple levels. Hemmingway was the first author that came to her mind when looking at him. She wanted to know more about this man of mystery and intrigue.

Looking her in the eyes once more, he said, "You look like you're proud of yourself."

Laughing, she said, "You are not an easy man to get to know, Conner."

"Are you trying to get to know me for your story?"

"I just get the feeling you are a man worth knowing," she said while squeezing his hand.

Turning the tables back on her, he asked "So what's your favorite book?"

Playfully, she asked, "What do I look like I would read?"

Conner looked up as if he was thinking hard about the question.

Looking back at Sandy, he said, "You don't actually know who your favorite author is or your favorite book...but I do."

"Really? Do tell."

"*Ideal,* by Ayn Rand."

"Why would you say that?" she asked, both interested and afraid of the answer.

"You see yourself in the story."

"Why is that?"

"It's the story of a beautiful but tormented actress. Accused of murder, she turns for help from six different fans for support, but each has a completely different personality. Like a chameleon, she conforms to each fan individually; a respectable family man, a far-left activist, a cynical artist, an evangelical, a playboy, and a lost soul. Each reacts to her plight in their own way and their reactions are a glimpse into their secret selves and true values."

Understanding his analysis, she was embarrassed to admit the similarities to her own life.

"So, you think I'm a chameleon?"

"I think you are far more than that, but I'm not sure you see it."

"You don't think I know my inner self?"

"Few people do," he said while taking a bite of pie.

Sandy wasn't sure how to respond. She had never looked at herself in that light before, but he was spot on. She had made a career out of assessing a target and conforming her personality to further the story. Even when not undercover, she would conform her personality to succeed in her environment. Whether it was the old boys club of journalism or to appease her father, she was no longer sure who the real Sandra Jane Elliot actually was.

"And you think you are an open book?" she asked.

Taking another bite of pie, he replied "No, I am guarded, a necessity of my job…but I'm honest with myself about who I am and my values. I know my faults, my personal demons, and where I'm vulnerable."

"You do hide your vulnerabilities well, Conner. But I can sense you are lonely."

Taking the last bite of the pie, he replied "Unfortunately, that's another necessity of my job."

"It doesn't need to be," she said while giving his hand a gentle squeeze.

Smiling, Conner replied "I wish that was the case…I really do. But I'm not the answer to your struggle. I would only complicate your life more."

"Often times the best things in life are complicated."

Squeezing her hand, he replied "I better call it a night. I have a big day tomorrow. Can I drop you somewhere?"

Disappointed, she replied "No, my car is out back. But thanks for the dinner."

"It was my pleasure…and I do mean that," he said with a tone of sincerity.

Walking outside to the jeep in the parking lot, Conner climbed into the canvas driver seat and started the engine. While he knew he had to drive away, he also knew he desperately wanted to go back into that diner. He could talk to her the rest of the night if she would let him, but he also knew it would eventually lead to heartache due to both of their professions.

CHAPTER 23

The clock on the wall of the diner indicated the time was half past nine. Norma and the short order cook were preparing for the arrival of the search members by staging paper bags, napkins and hamburger buns so the two could try and keep up with the anticipated rush.

Sitting in a booth in the rear of the diner, Sandy was jotting down article ideas while waiting for the search team to arrive. With hopes she would overhear something important or possibly elicit information from a naive young airman, she waited patiently. It was hard to keep focused on her journalism as her mind kept returning to Conner. Not only were his astute observations making her second guess herself, she was growing more infatuated with the man.

She felt alive when she was near him, vulnerable yet excited at the same time. She had been so focused on being successful in her career, she forgot about who she really was. She was starting to second guess what exactly she wanted out of life. She did know one thing for certain…she wanted to see Special Agent Conner Price again.

Gazing through the window of the diner while daydreaming of what a future with Conner could look like, she was brought back to the present by several Air Force vehicles pulling into the parking lot. As the men filed into the restaurant, it was apparent they had a very long day. Many of the men were filthy, sunburned and looked completely exhausted.

Sandy was conflicted. Now was the time the men would be vulnerable to her verbal elicitation techniques, yet she felt haunted by Conner's words about the missing aircrew being the real story. Was she being a good journalist or had she been reduced to a tabloid hack by chasing the UFO angle?

Once the weary men had been served, they all sat in the diner conversing with one another. It was difficult for Sandy to select which conversation to eavesdrop on as each group's chatter was competing for her attention. She quickly learned that the two pilots had ejected and the team would continue the search for them in the morning. Her UFO story was falling apart; however, a new angle was starting to develop. Had the pilots survived the ejection? Were they wounded? Had they been living off the land for the past few days? Conner was right. These brave men had been the real story all along. How could she have missed it?

While the missing airmen were her new focus, one new aspect of the story intrigued her. Listening to many of the young air policemen, it was apparent the woods they had been searching were creepy at best and haunted at worst. Apparently strange symbols and tree markings had been enough to spook the young service members, many of whom had seen too many horror movies. While Sandy didn't believe in ghosts or paranormal activities, she knew the story may intrigue readers and sell newspapers.

She saw her opening when three of the airmen at a booth left, leaving a single young air policeman dining alone.

"Mind if I join you?" she asked in a friendly voice.

"No ma'am, please sit down," said the airman who was still in his teens.

"Thank you. We don't see a lot of military men up here in Peshtigo. My name is Kelly, Kelly Munes. What's your name?"

Nervous, the young man replied, "Airman Second Class Henry Ness, but people call me Hank."

"Nice to meet you, Hank," she replied while extending her hand.

Hank wiped the hamburger grease from his hands onto his fatigue shirt before grasping hers.

'It's nice to meet you also," he replied nervously as his voice cracked.

"So where are you from Hank?"

"Hutchison Kansas, Ma'am."

"I bet it's nice there. Do you miss it?"

"I've only been gone a few months, but I guess everyone misses home sometimes."

"I bet. I would be excited to get out of Peshtigo but I think I would miss it if I ever did."

"You have never been out of Peshtigo?"

"My parents took me to Green Bay when I was a kid, but that's about as far as I have been."

"So, you have never been to Madison?"

"Madison? Is that where the Air Force base is?"

"Yeah," replied the young man as his confidence with women was starting to build.

"No, I have never been to a big city like Madison. I would love to visit but I would have no idea where to start or what to do. It sounds kind of intimidating."

"I would be happy to show you around sometime. I live in the barracks but I could borrow a car from someone, I'm sure."

"Airman Ness, it's time to go!"

The conversation was interrupted by a Master Sergeant who had noticed Sandy targeting the naïve young airman, much like a cheetah hunting the slowest gazelle in the herd.

"Yes Master Sergeant," replied the nervous young man, not long out of boot camp.

Looking up at the confident sergeant with six stripes on his sleeve standing by the table, Sandy read the name tag on the man's uniform.

"Master Sergeant Tratnyek? Is that Russian?"

The confident sergeant pointed to his other name tape that read U.S. Air Force.

"No ma'am, I'm an American."

Laughing in a flirtatious manner, she replied, "Yes, I am aware of that sergeant. I was referring to your family's heritage."

"Yes ma'am, I am aware of what you were asking. Let me save you some time. If you have any questions for me or any of my airmen, I will refer you to Captain Merritt, the public affairs officer at Truax Air Force Base."

"I didn't mean to get the young airman in trouble, sergeant, it was just small talk. It's not often a small-town hairdresser gets to see so many handsome servicemen all in one place. Especially one with so many stripes on his sleeve."

Not swayed by the batting eyelashes and flirtatious comments, Master Sergeant Tratnyek replied, "As I said, you can direct your questions to Captain Merritt, the public affairs officer at Truax AFB,"

Looking annoyed, Sandy replied, "Yes Sergeant, you already said that."

"Good. Then we are clear. Have a good evening, ma'am," he replied while he ensured all of his men had exited the diner.

Sandy wondered if the sergeant saw through her façade by himself or if he had been tipped off by Conner beforehand. It didn't matter as she already overheard what she needed to. She knew the pilots were still missing and the search crew would continue in the morning. She could look into the creepy haunted forest angle by talking to the locals.

Once all the airmen had departed, Sandy took a seat at the bar while Norma cleaned up from the late-night dinner rush.

"Norma, some of the airmen were saying the woods up there are haunted."

The waitress, putting down her cleaning rag, came closer to her to share some of the local gossip.

"There are a lot of rumors about those woods but I don't like to gossip," replied Norma.

Knowing the ladies who say they don't like to gossip are the best source of unconfirmed information, Sandy pressed on.

"They aren't really haunted, are they?" asked Sandy in an attempt to get the woman talking.

"Well, I don't think they are haunted, but a lot of weird things do happen up there. Most of the locals stay far away from them."

"What sort of things?" prompted Sandy to keep the waitress talking.

"A lot of folks have gone missing up there over the years. They say a coven of witches lives in those woods."

"Witches?"

"Yeah, I don't believe it either, but those woods are creepy. The folks who live up there are pretty strange and don't come out of the woods. They are all tall, pale and look sort of inbred. They live like it's the olden days."

"Are they some sort of an Amish community?" asked Sandy.

"No, they aren't Amish as they believe in violence, but they don't have electricity or cars. People say they are sort of like a combination of Vikings, witches and hillbillies. Either way, they scare the locals. They were the big gossip in these parts until that UFO abducted the Air Force plane, but I don't like to gossip."

"No, neither do I," replied Sandy. Who would have more information on these Viking witches?"

"I suppose the person who would be the best to speak with would be Sabrina Duchateau if she is still alive. She is an old woman who survived the Great Peshtigo Fire back in 1871. She has to be in her nineties by now. Her aunt was a Catholic nun who had apparitions from the Virgin Mary. They say the Virgin Mary protected them from the fire. That group in the woods is somehow connected to them I hear."

"Where can I find this Sabrina Duchateau?"

"I would start at the Chapel of Our Lady of Good Help down in Champion, Wisconsin."

"Where is Champion?"

"Champion is a small community south of here in Brown County. The Chapel of Our Lady of Good Help is a Catholic Shrine because the Virgin Mary made her apparition and performed her miracle there. That's where the chapel was that they took shelter in when the great fire passed them over. Back in the day a lot of Catholics would make a pilgrimage to that place. If anyone knows the real story about the people in those woods, you would likely find it there."

CHAPTER 24

The morning shower was refreshing as Conner allowed the water to cascade over his body. His mind drifted back to the conversation from the previous night with Sandy. Thinking about what she said to him, she was correct in her assessment. He was lonely. His lifestyle made it difficult to have a relationship with a woman and his personality was so closely guarded that few knew the real Conner. It was an existence that made it easy for the demons from the war to live on in his memory. He needed something enjoyable in his life and he wanted someone to share it with.

Smitten with Sandy, he could not get her out of his mind. Her blue eyes, her infectious laugh and even her feminine hand on his were burnt into his memory. She was articulate and witty yet still had a vulnerable human quality about her. He was charmed and longed for his next encounter with her. One that he hoped would come soon.

Once dressed, he exited the bathroom into the motel room with the double beds.

"You ready for breakfast?" he asked Don.

"Starving," replied his fellow agent while looking in the mirror and adjusting his tie.

"Good." Looking at his watch it was half past six. "The search team should be out of the diner and entering the woods right about now. Maybe we can get a seat."

As they drove from the motel to the diner, Don filled Conner in on the story of the haunted forest.

"The air police guys were pretty spooked when they got back to the command post. It was pretty funny actually."

"What made them think the woods were haunted?" asked Conner

Laughing, Don said, "For starters, that spooky old hunting guide set the tone."

"Yeah, that guy gave me the creeps too."

"I wonder what made him the way he is?" asked Don.

"Well, he said he was a World War 1 veteran and he has that eye patch. I wouldn't be surprised if he had some shell shock or psychological problems from his experiences. He probably spent the rest of his time sheltered away from society in those woods because he felt like he didn't fit in." Once Conner said that out loud, he couldn't help but notice the similarities between himself and the crazy mountain man. Was he sheltering himself away from people in his own way as a Project Blue Book investigator?

Don continued with his story about the spooked airmen. "Then, when they got into the woods, they came across a few strange symbols hanging from branches and carvings on some of the trees."

"What kind of symbols?" asked Conner.

"Not sure exactly, but I guess they were made out of animal antlers, bones, sticks, and sage. The guys said they looked like some sort of witchcraft or voodoo symbols. It got pretty dark before they got out of the woods and they started hearing an animal howling. I guess Master Sergeant Tratnyek started telling them a bigfoot story to wind them up further."

Laughing, Conner said, "That's hilarious. Did you ever find out what the symbols were?"

"No. After breakfast, I want to stop over at the local police department and see what they have to say. I guess there is a group of people that live back in those woods and keep to themselves. I want to find out how we can locate them to see if they have seen any trace of the missing pilots."

"Good thinking. I bet the game warden or that spooky hunting guide may have an idea as well.

As the men ate breakfast at the diner, Conner filled Don in about the reporter situation.

"I can't believe she bluffed her way out to the command post," said Don.

"Yeah, she knows how to get what she wants. If she is anything, she's crafty," replied Conner.

"And determined," said Don.

Just as their breakfast was being served, the Peshtigo Police Chief walked into the diner for his breakfast.

Waiving him over to the booth, Don asked him to join them.

The chief looked over at the waitress and said "Mable, I'll have my usual breakfast over at that booth."

"Coming right up Chief," she replied.

"Chief Squier, this is Special Agent Price," said Don, introducing the two men.

"Please, call me David," said the chief as he sat down with them.

"I'm Conner."

Don started the conversation, "Chief, we were just headed over to your office after we ate."

"Oh yeah? Well, what can I do for you?"

"The military police team that was searching the woods for the missing aircrew last night came across some spooky symbols in the woods."

Smiling, the chief said, "Let me guess, they are searching in the woods a few miles east of Lake Noquebay?"

"Yeah, that's the area" replied Conner.

"Yeah, that section of woods is pretty creepy. It's well outside of my jurisdiction as the chief of Peshtigo, but when I was with the sheriff's department, we would have to go out there once in a while."

"What kind of calls would you get out there?" asked Don.

"Typically, missing persons. About once a year someone would go out there on a dare or to poach deer out of season. It is rough terrain and easy to get turned around. As you get closer to the lake the wetlands can be dangerous with plenty of drop-offs and thick mud."

"What kind of dangerous predators are in those woods?" asked Don.

"Well, the mosquitos will carry you away during the right time of the year and the ticks are just terrible. But there are some black bears in those woods as well as wolf packs. What scares me are the cougars. They will just sit up in a tree and let you walk right under them."

"How about the people that live back in there? Are they a threat of some sort?"

Smiling, the chief replied "Well, it just depends on who you ask. There are plenty of rumors about a religious cult, a coven of witches, ritual sacrifices and such out in those woods. We usually don't find a person who goes missing out that way, which feeds into the conspiracy theory. I've seen no proof, but the stories have been around for years. My grandpa used to tell me stories about those woods being haunted."

"Some of the military police said there were strange symbols hanging from trees. They said it looked like witchcraft or voodoo symbols."

"Yeah, you will find some strange things in those woods. I suspect it is that clan of people that live back in there just trying to scare the locals to keep them away. It's just my theory but there were a lot of moonshine operations up here during prohibition. I could see those symbols being used to mark territory or scare away outsiders."

"Why would moonshiners come way up here?"

"A lot of Chicago gangsters used to come up to Wisconsin to hide out from the law. I imagine they were the inspiration for much of it."

"Chicago gangsters?" asked Don.

"Yeah, plenty of them. Northern Wisconsin is remote and isolated. We played host to several infamous figures including Al Capone and John Dillinger. Even Baby Face Nelson had a big shootout with the FBI over at the Little Bohemia Lodge in Lac Du Flambeau. Still to this day, Capone's brother Ralph operates the *Rex Bar* over in Mercer."

"Interesting," said Conner. "How would we go about finding the folks who live in the woods?"

"Beats me," said the chief. "The deputies usually don't go into those woods unless they absolutely have to. I guess I would check with the DNR Game Warden. We just got a new one for the county. His name is Chris Roeske and he just transferred over from Waupaca."

"We met him briefly. He's out with the search team at the lake. We'll check with him later on," replied Don.

"So, does the theory still involve space aliens and UFOs?" asked Chief Squier.

Smiling, Conner replied, "No, that was never a theory, just a lot of folks buying into UFO hysteria."

"Good to hear it. Maybe you all could leak that around town. Folks are far more spooked about the UFO stuff than they ever were about those spooky woods."

"Why? Did something happen?" asked Conner.

Taking a sip of his coffee, the chief replied, "You haven't heard about the helicopter yet?

"No, we haven't checked in with the command post yet this morning. What happened?"

"I guess the Air Force helicopter coming from Illinois was in a hurry to get here so they flew up in the dark early this morning. They were using a spotlight to try and locate the landing area Major Gibson designated for them. A couple drunk locals saw the strange light hovering in the sky, moving too slow to be an airplane. Thinking it was the UFO that abducted the jet, they started shooting at it with their hunting rifles."

"Did they hit it?" asked Conner.

"Oh yeah. If these guys can do anything besides drink beer, it's shoot guns. Major Gibson said they hit the helicopter a couple times but I haven't heard the extent of the damage they did. I'm just now coming from their farm; they're still pretty freaked out. It never occurred to them it was a helicopter. Folks around here have never seen one of them before, especially at night. Although drunk and not too bright, they honestly thought they were defending themselves from space aliens."

"So, I guess you didn't charge them with anything?" asked Don.

"No, I just took the report. That way the Air Force can try and get restitution for the damage they caused. But those two don't have anything of value so good luck with that."

CHAPTER 25

Captain Casper awoke to the sound of noises coming from the other side of the heavy wood door. The candle that illuminated the room had gone out at some point during the night. Casper assumed it was night, but with no windows, it was only a guess. He felt like he had been there for several hours, but as he had slipped in and out of consciousness it may have been longer.

The noise outside the door sounded like someone hammering nails into wood. Casper wondered if it was best to call for assistance or just to wait in silence. With no good option in front of him, he decided to call out.

"Hello! Is someone out there?" he shouted.

The hammering stopped, but nobody answered his call.

"Hello! Who is out there?"

He could hear heavy footsteps as they walked away.

As he lay there in the dark, he wondered if he was actually alone in the room. Unable to see anything in the pitch-black environment, he had no idea if someone or something was in the abyss with him. Trying to move his legs caused severe pain to shoot through his back. Moving his head and neck from side to side, it was apparent they were sore but uninjured. His hands were still tied together in front of him.

Casper worked to move his hands back and forth in an attempt to stretch or loosen the bindings. As he was just starting to notice a little bit of progress, he heard footsteps approaching. The heavy door creaked open and the dim light from a candle poured into the room. Two large figures entered the room wearing brown robes with oversized hoods.

One of the figures sat the candle down on the table next to the human skull, then walked to the head of the mat he was lying on. The other man walked to the foot of the mat. Both figures stood well over six feet tall and had very large frames.

"Where am I?" asked Casper.

The men didn't say a word as they reached down and took hold of him. The man at his head placed his hands under Casper's shoulders while the other man wrapped a large arm around his knees. As they lifted him off the mat, pain shot through his body for a moment before it went numb. Casper feared the rugged movement would cause irreparable damage to his spinal cord as the possibly fractured vertebra moved back and forth.

As the large men carried him out of the room and into the corridor, he tried to look around for clues that would tell him where he was or something about his captors. The dark corridor opened into a larger room that was probably fifteen feet wide by twenty feet long. It was apparent they were underground as the far end of the room contained a stairway leading up. There were no windows and the larger room was illuminated only by candle-light. The floors and walls were made of limestone bricks and there were few furnishings. More strange symbols decorated the walls and in the center of the floor was a large tub of water, also made of limestone.

The two large men placed Casper into the water as the man at his head adjusted him so he was in a sitting position. The water was cold, which sent a shock to his system.

"Where am I? Who are you guys? Am I a prisoner?"

His questions continued to go unanswered.

Once he was positioned so he would not slip under the water and drown, the two large men walked up the stairs without a word. As his eyes adjusted, Casper looked around the room for anything that may aid his escape. On one side of the room was a very rugged wooden table. There were multiple items on it, however, from his low angle he could not make out what they were.

Moments later, two smaller figures walked down the stairs wearing brown hooded robes. When they got to the bottom of the stairs and entered the large room, they removed their robes. Once out of the heavy garments, Casper could tell they were women. Both were tall, standing close to six feet. The younger one was probably in her late teens while the older woman was in her forties. Both had long, dirty blond hair but the older one had hints of gray. They were fixed in an elaborate style, with a large braid on the crown of their heads, which worked into smaller braids that hung down to their shoulders.

Under their robes, they wore sleeveless tunics made out of animal skin. Their bare arms were very toned and Casper could see the definition between the muscle groups. Both women had several designs on the skin of their hands, arms, and necks. It was difficult for him to tell if they were tattoos, brands or skin etchings in the poor light. Both women had depictions of an elm tree on their right arm and what appeared to be a compass-type symbol on their left arm. Other unfamiliar symbols decorated the rest of their exposed skin.

"Where am I?" asked Casper.

"You are in the Forest Egersund," replied the middle-aged woman.

Thankful that someone was finally speaking to him, he asked "Am I a prisoner?"

"You are the prophecy," the woman replied.

"What does that mean?" he asked, trying to appear calm and collected.

"The Gods foretold of your coming many seasons ago. We have been waiting patiently for many generations. Odin has finally heard our prayers and sacrifices. He sent you here to give us wisdom and to provide a new leader."

"By Odin, do you mean the Mythical Norse God of War? The Viking God?" asked Casper, trying to understand his predicament.

"Odin is one of the Gods of War, but he is the one who sent you here."

"Did Odin send just me or was there another man dressed like me? With the same clothes and helmet?"

"Odin sent two, but one is a false prophet."

"What happens to the false prophet?" Casper asked, trying to understand the thought process of the strange community.

"Odin will enlighten us, but we will be provided knowledge from both of you."

"Who is the Queen of the Forest? The older lady last night spoke of a queen."

The middle-aged woman stood behind Casper and started to wash his hair while the younger woman retrieved a knife from the table. Casper watched nervously while the younger woman used the sharp blade to remove his soiled t-shirt and boxer shorts.

The middle-aged woman spoke. "The Queen of Forest Egersund is Thordis, my grandmother. The woman who cared for you last night is Gyda, my mother. I am Nanja and this is my daughter Randalin."

"So, you are royalty?" asked Casper.

"What is this royalty you speak of?"

"Will you will become queen of the forest someday?" asked Casper in a calm voice as he was trying to understand his captors. A technique he was taught at Air Force survival school.

"If it is the will of the Gods, then yes. But if the prophecy comes true, my daughter, Randalin will be the next queen."

"When will my fate be decided?"

"That is up to the Gods of course," replied Nanja.

"Can I see the other man dressed like me?"

"You will see him soon."

"Can you untie my hands?" asked Casper.

"I cannot. The queen has instructed you to remain bound for now."

"I am injured. I need to see a doctor."

"I am a healer," said Nanja.

Trying to keep calm, Casper said "I need to see an Air Force doctor."

"I do not know this Air Force doctor. I am the healer."

"I think my back is broken; I can't feel my legs."

"I healed your leg but it will take time."

"What does that mean?"

"I put the bone back together but it will take time to mend."

Casper heard the sound of someone coming down the stairs into the basement. As he looked up, he saw the two large men wearing robes returning. They were carrying a large animal skin and spread it out on the ground next to the tub. The two men then took their places at the head and foot of the tub. Reaching into the water, they lifted him out of the bath and placed him on the large animal skin on the floor. Grasping the skin, they lifted him up, using it as a makeshift litter. Once they were up the stairs, Casper tried to look around to orient himself and make note of anything potentially useful. The men carried him through what appeared to be a large gathering hall with benches on both sides of the center aisle. As they continued to move, he didn't have a chance to observe much inside the building.

When they exited the building, the bright sunlight caused him to squint as his pupils constricted involuntarily. Trying to look at his surroundings while he had the chance, he forced his eyes open enough to see he was in some sort of old-world village. There were several small structures made out of natural materials. Most were wood with sod-covered roofs while some had walls formed out of limestone, a common resource in Northeast Wisconsin.

Between the structures were small fenced-in areas containing farm animals and gardens. He could see about five or six people wearing brown hooded robes milling about the compound doing various tasks. Confused by the situation, Casper started to wonder if he had died and if this was some sort of afterlife. Perhaps he had gone back in time or was transported to an alternate universe by the UFO. Was he just hallucinating? Nothing was making sense.

At the far end of the compound, the men carried him into a new structure made of wood with a roof of sod and moss. It looked almost as if a grass lawn covered the structure. Casper noted it would be near impossible for a passing aircraft to differentiate the structures from its surroundings because of it, especially through the thick tree canopy.

Inside the building, the single large room was divided by several half-wall partitions, similar to a horse corral but not nearly as elaborate. The men carried him into one of the small partitioned stalls and laid the animal skin onto the soft grassy floor. This room was brighter as it was above ground and there were a few window openings, without glass, to let in the light. Casper was finally able to prop himself up onto his elbows to look around. The small partitioned section he was in was empty with the exception of a thick wood stake hammered into the ground. Looking down at his wet, naked body, his eyes were drawn to his left leg. There were two branches affixed to either side of his leg secured by strips of cloth. He assumed he had a leg fracture and Nanja splinted it while he was unconscious. As he looked closer, he could see a long incision extending from his ankle to halfway up to his knee. The sutures consisted of a thick string that was crudely applied. He wondered just how badly damaged his body was and what kind of "healing" that strange witch doctor performed on him.

As the two men left the structure, they closed the heavy wood door behind them. Casper heard what he believed was a board being placed across the outside of the door as a means to prevent him from opening it. Now that he was alone, he had to craft some sort of an escape plan, however, his incapacitated body would make it very difficult.

"Who are you?" came a whispered voice from the other side of the partition...

CHAPTER 26

As the Ford Fairlane drove south through the green rolling hills and majestic forests, it came to the small unincorporated community of Champion, Wisconsin. While it was only about twenty miles north of Green Bay, you would never know it by the untouched scenery.

The chapel of *"Our Lady of Good Help"* was the prominent location in Champion. The new building, built in 1942 was a Tudor Gothic style that accommodated three hundred parishioners. The outdoor area contained a Rosary walk and a Station of the Cross walk, where people could pray and meditate. The largest annual gathering at the chapel was on August 15th, the feast of the "Assumption of the Blessed Virgin Mary". It was observed with a mass and a procession around the grounds. The chapel was certainly a unique feature in rural Wisconsin.

After parking the car, Sandy walked to the chapel, dressed in very modest attire. Entering the glass front door, she was greeted by a young lady.

"Good morning, how may I help you?"

"Good morning, I was hoping to speak with Mrs. Duchateau."

"She doesn't normally meet with visitors, is she expecting you?"

"Not exactly, I traveled all the way up from Chicago to speak with her. It is about her aunt, Adele Brise. Is there any way she will see me?"

"I can ask, but she is very old and needs her rest. Whom may I say is calling?"

"My name is Sandra Brise."

"Oh, are you related to her?" asked the young lady.

"Well, I'm not certain but I think I may be. I wanted to speak with her about it."

"Let me see if she is up for a visit."

The young lady walked away and returned a few minutes later. "Mrs. Duchateau will meet with you in the garden by her aunt's grave. There is a nice bench there you can sit on while you chat. But please remember, she is a very old woman and tires easily. She needs her rest."

"Of course, I will be brief," said Sandy.

Walking out of the chapel into the garden and nearby cemetery, the grounds were immaculate and the grass well-manicured. Sandy could see an elderly woman in a wheelchair sitting next to a white bench. As they approached, the young lady introduced her as Sandy Brise.

"Please have a seat, Ms. Brise," said the elderly woman.

"Thank you, ma'am, please call me Sandy."

"So, what brings you all the way to Wisconsin, Sandy?"

"I'm not certain ma'am. I just felt a strong need to travel here all of the sudden. I'm not sure if it was some form of divine guidance or just a curiosity about my heritage."

"I don't understand dear," replied the older woman.

"Back in Chicago, my uncle was looking into our genealogy and trying to piece together our family tree. While he is not done yet, he said I may be related to Sister Marie Adele Bise, your aunt. I just felt a strong impulse to travel up here. I prayed on it and feel I am supposed to do this. I know that sounds strange," said the crafty journalist, using the ruse to gain the woman's trust.

"I don't find that strange at all young lady. The Lord works in mysterious ways."

"Thank you, ma'am. What can you tell me about your aunt?"

"That's a very interesting story. Our family settled here in Wisconsin in 1855. My aunt lived on the family farm with her parents and siblings. One of her older sisters was my mother, Catherine Brise Duchateau. In the year 1859, while carrying grain to the mill, Adel had an apparition from the Virgin Mary. She kept that vision to herself, but the following Sunday while walking to mass, the Blessed Mother again appeared to her, in the very same location. This time she reported the vision to the local priest who told her that if it appeared again to ask who she was and what she wanted of her. When the apparition happened a third time, Adel asked who she was. The lady identified herself as the "Queen of Heaven" and told her to gather the children in this area and teach them what they should know for salvation. The apparition also told her to teach the children their catechism, how to sign themselves with the sign of the cross, and how to approach the sacraments..."

"That's amazing Mrs. Duchateau," said Sandy, while placing her hand on the old woman's knee.

"Child, our story gets even more amazing. In the year 1861, a chapel was erected on the site of the apparition and a school was built five years later. In 1871, a great fire consumed the entire countryside around here and killed two thousand people. Sister Adel along with a few others took refuge in the chapel and prayed to Mary for their safety and protection. The fire burned everything around them but spared the chapel and school, along with those inside. I was ten years old and survived in that chapel with the others."

"I don't even have any words for such a thing," said Sandy, playing up her dramatic role.

"My uncle also said something about a coven of witches that may be related to the family up near Lake Noquebay?" prodded Sandy, to see what the old woman knew about them.

"Oh, dear, there is no relation between those awful people to our family. Where did you hear something as outlandish as that?" asked the woman with real concern.

"I'm not sure, my uncle was just talking about historical things but I was too focused on the story of Sister Adel. Surely there are no witches up there."

"No, not witches, but there is a religious cult up there. I haven't heard of them in many years."

"So, there is no relation to us at all?"

"No, of course not. The same year our family immigrated from Belgium, that group immigrated from Norway. While most Norwegian immigrants in this area were Lutherans, this group was led by a deranged man named Guenther Hansen. He believed they were descendants of Vikings and he instructed his clan to worship Norse Gods that allegedly spoke to him through visions. He was a deranged man and led his flock astray. Guenther had joined the Union Army during the Civil War and served with the 7th Wisconsin Volunteer Infantry Regiment and in the famous Iron Brigade. In 1863, he was shot in the head during the Battle of Chancellorsville. He somehow survived his wound, but his brain was certainly afflicted by the musket ball lodged in his skull. When he returned from the war, he claimed to have witnessed all sorts of visions from the Norse Gods. His clan, mostly uneducated and inbred, believed him."

"So, they also survived the fire of 1871?" asked Sandy.

"Just a few of them did. There were rumors that the clan was sacrificing people up near Peshtigo but it was never proven. There were also rumors of inbreeding and that Guenther had fathered all of the children in the clan since returning from the war. People said they were about to sacrifice a young girl when the Peshtigo fire wiped out the village. The girl who was being sacrificed had a little sister named Thordis, who had been sent outside during the ceremony. She and a few others took refuge in a well and the fire luckily passed over them."

"That's incredible. The little girl's name was Thordis?" asked Sandy.

"The little girl was just a year or two older than me. The name, Thordis, was Scandinavian and meant Thor's Goddess. She and her little brother were orphaned in the fire and were brought to live at the school here with us. They were both very odd and people assumed it was due to inbreeding. She had mental issues and continued to believe in her father's deranged religion. When she learned of the story of Sister Adel seeing the Virgin Mary, she adopted the story as her own and claimed to have visions of the Norse Gods Thor and Odin. After three years she had become such a disruption the school was in the process of placing her in an asylum. Before they could lock her up, she ran away, taking her little brother and the other orphans from the clan with her. The rumor is that they are the "witches" that have been haunting the woods up there for the past eighty years."

"That is so sad. You said they live in the woods east of the lake?"

"Well, it's actually more east of the town of Wausaukee."

"Now dear, who is your uncle and exactly how does he think we are related?"

"Well, I'm not exactly sure I have all the details right in my head. Let me run to my car and get the documents he gave me. I'll be right back," said Sandy as she hurried away towards the parking lot.

After several minutes had passed, the young assistant who brought Sandy to her asked "Everything ok Mrs. Duchateau?"

"Just fine dear. The young lady just went to her automobile for some papers. She will be right back."

"Mrs. Duchateau, that young lady just drove away..."

Back in the car, on her return trip to Peshtigo, Sandy tried to figure out what angle her story would take. There were just so many different perspectives she could focus on. Deciding she needed to go find this clan of people herself, she would need to get some clothes suitable for a trek in the forest. She recalled a farm store on the outskirts of Peshtigo. Hopefully, they would have some clothes that were more appropriate for her new mission.

Walking into the Peshtigo Farm Supply Company, she could see the store had a little of everything a farmer could want. As she was looking around, an older salesman approached her and asked if there was anything he could help her with.

"Yes sir. I am taking a hike in the woods and need some clothing that is a bit more appropriate. Do you have farm clothes for ladies?"

"Yes ma'am, we have some but the selection is pretty limited. Basically, just dungarees and overalls."

"That's perfect. Do you also sell hiking shoes?"

"Well, we have a small selection of work boots. They probably are not the best for hiking but will do you far better than those fancy shoes you have on now. The clothes and footwear are towards the back. There is a dressing room also."

"Thank you for the help, I will be fine from here."

"Yes ma'am. Holler if you need anything."

Walking to the back of the store, the selection of women's clothing her size was pretty limited. She selected a pair of dungaree overalls but couldn't find any women's boots close to her size. Seeing a section for Boy Scout uniforms, she observed a large advertisement for the new official Boy Scout hiking boots made by Weinbrenner. Settling for a men's size six, she also picked up a Boy Scout neckerchief and a pair of thick wool socks she hoped would take up the extra room in the oversized boots.

Changing in the dressing room, she was content that the new outfit would better serve her while hiking in the woods. Bringing her old clothes up to the front of the store, she paid for the new clothes and put her old ones in the bag. Returning to her car, she looked over at her large, unfolded map in an attempt to try and find the best way to locate this strange clan of people. Not sure where to start, she focused on the closest municipality, the town of Wausaukee.

CHAPTER 27

"**A**re you going to wear that business suit and dress shoes into the woods to search for the crazy religious cult?" asked Conner sarcastically.

Looking down at his agent attire, Don replied, "Yeah, I guess I better change."

Laughing, Conner said, "They'll think you are trying to sell them insurance."

"OK, there is a farm supply store up the road. I'm sure I can get some clothes and boots there."

"Great, drop me off at that barber shop while you go shopping. If there is any good gossip in a small town, you can find it at the local barber shop," replied Conner.

As the Bel Air pulled up in front of the Peshtigo barber shop, Conner stepped out and removed his light Jacket, exposing his revolver and OSI badge. In a small town such as this, that visual would start the gossip chatter all by itself. As he stepped up onto the sidewalk, he greeted the two old men sitting on the bench reading the newspaper. It looked as if it was the daily perch for these old-timers. He could see their eyes glance down to his badge as they said good morning.

Stepping into the small, two-chair shop, one barber was giving a man a shave and the other barber was sitting in a chair reading a magazine.

"Good morning, you all got time for a haircut?"

"Sure do, have a seat in chair number two," said the barber who was reading the magazine while waiting for a customer.

Before Conner sat down, he walked past the men to look at the examples of haircuts they offered from the poster on the wall. His real reason was to allow the men an opportunity to see his badge which would jump-start the conversation organically.

"Well, I'll take a number three but don't go too short, just a little trim," said Conner as he picked up the June 6th issue of Life magazine and took a seat in the chair.

As the barber placed the gown over Conner, he made eye contact with the other barber and the customer in the next chair. Conner, pretending to read the magazine, watched the men in the mirror with his peripheral vision. Looking at the cover of the magazine, it was a photo of Henry Fonda wearing a Navy uniform from his new movie "*Mr. Roberts.*"

The barber started the conversation, just as Conner had planned. "So, you up here with those Air Force boys looking for that missing jet?"

"As a matter of fact, I am. I'm headed up to the search area as soon as my partner gets back to pick me up."

"You military police?"

"Sort of. I'm a Special Agent with the Air Force Office of Special Investigations."

"What's that?" asked the barber.

"It's sort of like the military version of the FBI, I suppose."

The barber glanced at each other while Conner pretended to read. "So, are you here because folks are talking about UFOs?"

Laughing, Conner said, "No, I'm not here for UFOs. I'm here to help search for the missing aircrew. Apparently, they ejected over some woods up north of Lake Noquebay."

The customer getting a shave in the next chair spoke up, while trying to hold his face motionless to avoid getting nicked by the straight razor. "Well, I hope they have side arms if they bailed out in those woods."

Keeping his head straight, Conner asked, "Why would they need pistols?"

"There is a crazy coven of witches in those woods that perform human sacrifices."

Conner could see the barber doing the shave roll his eyes, indicating he didn't believe the myth his customer was talking about.

"Sacrifices?" asked Conner.

"Those are just rumors, and nothing true about them," said the barber giving the shave.

"A lot of folks do go missing up there though," said the barber giving Conner the haircut.

"Missing?" asked Conner, prompting the man to explain.

"Seems like once or twice a year someone goes missing up there."

"It's not that often Merl," said the other barber.

"Well, it's often enough to keep me out of those woods. People say the folks that live there can turn into wolves at night. Not like the werewolves in the movies, that would be silly. These ones are shapeshifters, like from the old Indian tribes. I don't believe it, but folks say it."

The barber giving the shave said "Don't pay them no mind, mister. These knuckleheads do more jaw-jacking than they do thinking. But if you are going up to them woods, do be careful."

"Most rumors have a grain of truth in them. How did this clan of people come to live in those woods?" asked Conner.

The barber giving the shave said, "There are all kinds of theories about that. Most are just crazy notions like they are descendants of Bigfoot, or space aliens whose flying saucer crashed out there. Other theories are that they are half-Indian and half-white men from the early days when the French fur traders were here. Probably the most realistic theory is they were survivors of the Great Peshtigo fire of 1871 and never assimilated back into society."

"Interesting theories. I'll be sure to keep an eye out. Did you boys hear that a couple of local fellas took some shots at the Air Force helicopter early this morning? I guess they thought it was a UFO?"

"Sure," said the man giving the shave. "Not much happens around here that doesn't get talked about in the barbershop. You know the old joke, there is the telegraph, the telephone, and tell a barber."

"Funny," replied Conner.

After his haircut, Conner paid his bill and walked outside to wait for Don. He had obtained twenty minutes of gossip about the group in the woods by only exposing his badge and uttering a few words. He was amazed at how much one could learn by simply shutting up and listening.

A few moments later, the Bel Air Pulled up and Conner got in. Looking over at Don, now dressed in appropriate woods attire, he gave him a nod.

"OK, let's head up to the search area and see if the game warden can tell us how to find the scary witches," said Conner.

While Don drove, he asked, "What does that reporter gal look like?"

"She changes her look all the time, why?"

"A girl was leaving the farm store as I was walking in. As I was checking out, the clerk asked me if I was with her. When I told him I wasn't, he said she was also buying a set of clothes and boots she could wear into the woods."

"Well, that sounds like her. What did she look like today?"

"About 5'4", slim, attractive. When she walked out, she was wearing a pair of women's dungaree overalls with a short sleeve shirt and a Boy Scout scarf in her hair."

"What color was her hair today?" asked Conner.

"Light brown, I think. I only saw her for a second as she passed me on her way out. Think we will run into her in those woods?"

"Those are some pretty big woods, but knowing her, it wouldn't surprise me if she found our coven of witches before we do," joked Conner.

"I hope she isn't biting off more than she can chew."

"If even half of the rumors and myths are true, she may find herself in over her head."

About forty minutes later they arrived at the command post at Lake Noquebay. They could see the helicopter parked in an empty field near the boat landing. Parking next to Colonel Roberts' staff car, they got out to look for the game warden. About thirty yards away, they saw Colonel Roberts and Lt. Colonel Lebsack standing by a large yellow tarp on the ground. Resting on the tarp were several charred aircraft parts recovered from the crash site.

As the two agents approached the men, Conner asked if there was any new evidence that would indicate something other than a mechanical issue.

Lt. Colonel Lebsack, scratching his head, said, "So far everything seems to point to the plane coming apart during high-speed maneuvers."

"Any news from the ground search team?" asked Don.

"No, not yet," replied Colonel Roberts.

"Has anybody seen that game warden today?"

Lt. Colonel Lebsack replied, "Yeah, Warden Roeske. He should be back here soon. He is out on the lake bringing back pieces from the crash site."

"What about that hunting guide?" asked Conner.

Colonel Roberts replied, "Yes, he was here this morning to guide one of the ground search teams but ran off when the state trooper pulled up to assist. Must be some sort of local matter he is involved with."

"Good, that guy gave me the creeps," said Lt. Colonel. Lebsack while kneeling over an aircraft part to inspect it.

"Yeah, he is a different sort, that's for sure," said Don. "I was hoping that he or the game warden could tell us how to contact that group of people who live back in the woods. Maybe they have seen some sign of our missing pilots."

Smiling at the woman, Sandy said, "I was hoping you could point me in the direction of someone who could tell me about that clan of people who lives out in the woods east of here."

Scratching his head, Emanuel said, "Well, they pretty much keep to themselves and don't ever come near town. Once in a while, a hunter will run across one of them in the woods but they typically avoid town folk. You will hear plenty of rumors and stories about them people but I would take it with a grain of salt."

"What kind of stories?" asked Sandy in an attempt to elicit more information.

"You know people like to gossip in a small town. You will hear all kinds of stories from witches to werewolves and even that the woods are haunted. But I just think they are folks who want to live their lives secluded. They are a strange lot and live like they are back in the old days," said Emanuel.

"Is it some sort of religious cult?" asked Sandy.

"While I don't like to speak badly of another's religion, I don't think they are Christians. From what rumors I hear, the folks out in those woods follow some sort of pagan belief system from the old country. It's hard to separate what's true from the stories embellished by drunk hunters."

"Tell her about Oddball Otto," said Betty.

"Now Betty, this young lady doesn't need to get herself mixed up with the likes of him," scolded her husband.

"Oddball Otto?" asked Sandy.

Emanuel explained, "That's just an unfortunate nickname some of the town folk gave the poor man after the war. The first World War that is."

"What is so odd about the man?" asked Sandy.

"Well, Otto was a bit of an odd duck even before the war. He was a couple of years behind me in school, but the war changed him. He is of German descent and his father forbade him to go fight against the homeland. We were all pretty patriotic and when we all enlisted, he did so without his father's permission. He was only seventeen and lied about his age. We were assigned to the 32nd Division and we were the first US troops to reach German soil. We remained at the front until the end of the war and took an incredibly high casualty rate. While I served as the unit quartermaster, Otto was right up on the front line. During an infantry charge, he was badly wounded by an enemy bayonet to the face, causing him to lose an eye. While that was bad, his more significant injury was psychological. He suffered a bad case of shellshock and spent close to a year in the Veterans Administration hospital in Milwaukee after the war."

"That's terrible," replied Sandy.

"When he finally returned home, his family had disowned him for fighting against Germany. The townsfolk were not very sympathetic as some viewed shell shock as just a form of cowardice. While his face was disfigured, it's his broken mind that makes him act strange…or odd. He eventually moved into the forest and somehow got affiliated with that strange clan. He lived among them for twenty or thirty years."

"Where does he live now?"

"About five or six years ago, something must have happened out there and he tried to return to civilization. But after living in the woods all those years he was even more "off" than before. He seems to be a man without a country nowadays. He works odd jobs here and there. He looks like some kind of a bizarre mountain man but I have only known him to be friendly. It's a sad story really."

"That is a sad story. Where could I find him?"

"Well, he wanders around a bit but he sometimes stays in a shack down by the old railroad tracks. It's the only one out there and looks like it's about to fall over."

"OK. Thank you so much, Emanuel."

"But even so, I recommend you stay away from him if you are all by yourself. Even though folks are mean to him and make up stories, he is still a very unpredictable sort.

"I understand and will keep my distance," said Sandy as she left the store.

Back in the Fairlane, she pulled back onto the road and pressed on towards the old train tracks. The now deserted train stop once served as a loading point during the logging heyday many years before. As she came around the corner, she saw the old shack positioned in the far back corner of the empty railyard. Consisting of scrap wood nailed together, it was small, only about eight feet wide by eight feet long with no windows. The gaps where the wood didn't fit together was filled in with sod. The door consisted of a heavy canvased tarp hanging over a makeshift doorway. This had to be where Oddball Otto lived.

Parking the car in the empty lot of the abandoned train stop, she sat and observed the shack for a moment. The area was secluded and she wondered if her idea may be more dangerous than it was worth. What if the man was violent? Would anyone hear her scream for help? Wausaukee was an unincorporated community and didn't have a police department. It was unlikely a state trooper or county sheriff's deputy was anywhere near this small town.

Knowing she was on her own but dedicated to her story, she stepped out of the car and walked to the rear, opening the trunk. Looking in her suitcase, she reached into the side compartment and removed a Colt 1908 vest pocket pistol chambered in .25 auto. The tiny pistol was nickel plated and wore ivory grips. As many of her stories involved unsavory characters, she kept the pistol handy in case she needed to defend herself. She selected the easily concealable weapon after seeing it in the movie *Maltese Falcon* with Humphrey Bogart.

Holding the small gun in her hand, she had to smile as she could hear her father quoting General George S. Patton when asked about the grips on his famous revolvers during the war by a reporter: "*They're ivory. Only a pimp from a cheap New Orleans whorehouse would carry a pearl handled pistol.*"

After ensuring the pistol was loaded with six rounds of ammunition, she concealed it in the small chest pocket on the front of her denim overalls. Feeling a little more confident, she approached the shack to see if the odd man could tell her how to find the clan of people in the woods. Knocking on the wood frame of the shack, she said, "Hello. Is anybody home?"

Hearing stirring on the other side of the hanging tarp, she took a step back, wondering if she had made the right decision. As the tarp was pulled back, Sandy instantly recognized the man as the bizarre hunting guide the Wisconsin game warden used to help the Air Force search party. This helped set her mind at ease. If the game warden trusted him, then he couldn't be too dangerous.

"Good morning, my name is Sandy Elliot. Are you Otto?"

"I'm Otto," he replied in a gruff, monotone voice.

"I work with the Air Force. I am here to help with the search for those missing pilots. I was told that you may have some information about that group of people who live in the woods?"

Looking her up and down, he replied "You don't look like a woman soldier."

Smiling, she said, "No sir. I am just the commander's secretary. He heard that you may know about the group of people who live in the woods. He asked me to come up here, buy you lunch, and see what you had to say."

"Lunch?"

"Yes sir. Is there a diner or restaurant around here?"

Nodding his head, he said, "There is a diner up the road on Main Street."

"Great, shall we go? We can take my car."

"Ok," said the mountain man, while tying an animal skin sash around his waist to serve as a belt. Once tied, he placed his tomahawk inside the belt.

As they walked to her car, Sandy wondered what was the bigger story, the missing pilots, the clan of witches in the woods or this bizarre mountain man veteran of the first World War. If she played her cards right, this story had the potential for several articles, maybe even a couple novels.

CHAPTER 29

"Legend, is that you?" asked Casper, speaking to the voice coming from the other side of the wooden partition.

"Ghost?"

"Yeah, it's me. Where the hell are we?" asked Casper.

"Not sure exactly. It's like we are lost in time. Some sort of religious cult I think."

As the senior officer, Casper had to take command of the situation. Like all military aviators, he attended the USAF Survival, Evasion, Resistance & Escape course, commonly referred to as SERE. While this situation was different from a traditional POW matter, he would need to modify his actions accordingly. It was unlikely this strange cult would follow the Geneva Convention or the international rules of the humane treatment of prisoners. While his actions were limited based on his physical condition, he first had to keep faith with his fellow airman and determine what resources they had to utilize.

"Are you injured?" asked Casper, trying to identify the immediate concern.

With labored breathing, Legend replied, "I'm pretty sure my left shoulder is broken or dislocated. When I was ejected from the plane, I hit something in the process. Must have been a part of the aircraft, or maybe the canopy. I was dazed after that and hit the ground hard as I couldn't see to anticipate the landing. When I woke up, I found I had been impaled by a sharp branch sticking up from a felled log. The branch was about three feet long and entered my right butt cheek and exited above my right love handle. When I came too, the sun was just starting to come up so I estimated I had been there a couple of hours at least. Dangling from that branch, there was nothing I could do to free myself and I was losing blood. I lost consciousness again and when I woke up, I was here."

In an analytical manner typical of a command pilot, Casper asked, "So what is your current condition?"

"My left shoulder is very painful and I can't use my left arm at all. My entire right flank hurts with every breath I take. Once they got me off that branch, they must have sewn me up because I can see crude stitches when I look down to my side. I'm very weak as I lost a lot of blood. Although I haven't tried, I'm not sure if I can walk. I'm naked, laying on a straw mat with my right hand secured to a heavy wood stake in the ground."

Assessing the information, Casper replied. "I'm currently paralyzed below the waist so I can't walk. I hurt my back during the ejection. When I came down, I crashed through a thick tree canopy. I have a broken lower left leg and I think I have some broken ribs, but the major thing is my back. My left leg got wedged in a nook of a tree branch and I hung upside down for a very long time, days maybe, before these folks got me down. I just noticed a huge stitched-up incision on my left ankle. They must have set the bone and stitched me up. I'm naked with my hands tied in front of me. My left leg is in a splint."

"Well, you win as usual Ghost," said the junior pilot with a laugh that turned into a painful coughing fit.

"Try not to laugh, Legend. You will only make it worse," said the senior officer, trying to take as much control as the situation would allow.

Speaking in a low voice to avoid being detected, Legend said, "This seems to be some sort of old-world forest community. There are about ten or twelve wooden structures with sod and grass roofs. No electricity or running water. They have been feeding me fish and some kind of animal meat. The people all seem to be very large and mostly blond or redheads. They usually wear those robes but when they take them off, they are dressed in buckskins and leather. They all have several tattoos and what looks like brandings. The tattoos are strange symbols that I don't recognize. They also seem to have what looks like letters tattooed on them but they are not English."

"Yeah, I observed the same thing. Have you met the Queen yet?" asked Casper.

"No, but they have talked about her some. Apparently, she gets visions from God and will decide our fate."

"Her name is Thordis and she must be pretty old. I spoke with her daughter Gyda last night and she must have been close to seventy years old. Today her granddaughter Nanja and great-granddaughter Randalin bathed me."

"A bath you say? So, what does this great-granddaughter look like?" joked Legend which caused him to start coughing again. Military men often use black humor in dire situations to lessen stress.

Laughing, Casper replied, "Slow your roll there, jet jockey. That girl may be more than even you can handle."

"Nonsense, I love a challenge!" replied Legend, sparking another painful coughing fit.

"Well, neither of us are in a position to make a run for it, so we need to stay alive until the search team finds us. We'll need to play along with their psycho game until we can find a way to get a message out for help. Try not to anger them as we can't defend ourselves in our present state. I think they believe in the Norse Gods. They refer to Odin a lot. I think the strange letters they have tattooed on their faces and arms are from the Runic alphabet."

"I have never heard of the Runic alphabet."

"They were used a long time ago to write some of the Germanic languages before they adopted the Latin alphabet. Each one sort of represents a letter as we know them but also has a specific meaning. That's about all I can recall.

"How do you know that?" asked Legend, always impressed with Casper's knowledge.

Laughing, he replied, "My first assignment was in England and I saw some of it there on Viking stuff in the museum. While that sounds more academic, I saw it a lot more in the new book series I have been reading."

"What book series?"

"That new series by J.R.R Tolkien called *The Lord of the Rings*. He uses a lot of the Runic alphabet on the maps in the books."

"Never heard of it."

Laughing, he replied, "Well that doesn't surprise me, Legend, as it doesn't have a centerfold."

"So do those books have a happy ending at least?"

"Not sure, the last book in the series doesn't come out until October."

"Well, let's just hope we are still around for you to see how that book ends."

CHAPTER 30

Waiting at the boat launch, Conner and Don watched as the game warden's boat slowly approached. They could see two men in the boat along with the warden. One was in a State Trooper uniform and the other in Air Force fatigues. As the boat killed its outboard engine and floated the rest of the way in, Warden Roeske tossed the rope to shore where Don pulled the boat in the rest of the way and secured it to the small dock.

Looking into the boat, it was filled with various debris from the crash site. As the men worked together to unload the charred aircraft parts and place them on a tarp for Lt. Colonel Lebsack to examine, Conner asked the warden if they could chat.

"Sure, what's up?"

"Couple of things. Can you tell us about the group of people that live in the woods that got the search team all freaked out?"

Smiling, Warden Roeske said, "Yeah, I heard about that. Unfortunately, I can't tell you much as I just transferred into this county from Waupaca last week. This area is new for me also."

Don asked, "What happened to the last game warden for this area?"

"He was killed in a boating accident last month, right here on this lake actually. I was sent in to serve as his replacement until a new one can be assigned."

"Sorry to hear about the loss of your warden," said Conner.

"Yeah, we still haven't recovered his body."

"What about that mountain man, hunting guide you had helping us with the search team? Would he know anything about the people in the woods?" asked Conner.

Smiling nervously, Warden Roeske said, "Yeah, he may not be the best person to chat with. It turns out I shouldn't have accepted his offer to assist us with the search. He introduced himself as a local hunting guide who knew the area well. He was pretty insistent that he help out. Being new here, when he volunteered his services, I gladly accepted. But after hearing how he acted during the first day of the search I was a little concerned he wasn't all there. Then this morning, when the state trooper arrived to help, Otto recognized him and ran off into the woods. I guess they have a history."

Looking over at the trooper standing by the boat, Conner asked, "Is that the same trooper that Otto ran from?"

"Yeah, that's Trooper Bruce. He's been patrolling this area for a long time. He would probably be the best person to speak with about it."

"OK, thanks," replied Conner.

Standing six feet three inches tall, Trooper Bruce appeared even larger wearing the distinctive drill instructor-style hat of the Wisconsin State Patrol. Walking over to meet him, Conner introduced himself.

"Excuse me, Trooper Bruce, my name is Conner Price and this is Don Golden. We are Special Agents with the Air Force Office of Special Investigations."

"Please, call me Taylor, said the trooper.

"Taylor, I understand you have been patrolling this area for quite some time?"

"I joined the sheriff's department here in 1935. I went overseas for a few years during the war and when I returned, I got on with the State Patrol. My first couple of years I was down south but I have been assigned to this area for the last six years."

"Can you tell us anything about the folks out in the woods that are scaring the ground search team?"

"I can tell you a little, but they live pretty deep in the woods and keep to themselves. There are plenty of rumors, but most of them are just that. I suppose you heard about Oddball Otto already?"

"Not yet," replied Conner

Rolling his eyes, Trooper Bruce explained, "Otto Bargenquast served in WW1 and lost his eye to a bayonet in the trenches of France. He has a lot of mental health issues. Shell shocked by the combat, they had to lock him up in a looney bin down in Milwaukee for a year. After they let him out, he came back up here and started causing problems all over the place. Drinking, fighting and just acting crazy all the time. The folks in Wausaukee started calling him Oddball Otto. He was too crazy to hold a job so he started burglarizing a bunch of homes. Eventually, the people ran him out of town and he took to living in the woods like an animal. Somewhere over the years he got mixed up with the group of folks that live out there. He was sort of their connection or go-between with town as he would barter for goods they needed. About four or five years ago something happened out there and they kicked him out apparently. He's been living in a shack up in Wausaukee last I heard."

"So, what happened this morning? Why did he run off when he saw you?" asked Don.

"First off, I have been after him for a few weeks now for breaking into cars. Not a major issue but he's been working hard to avoid me. But the larger issue is he knew I would put a stop to him leading the search party. He may have hoodwinked the game warden with his hunting guide story, but I know what kind of man he is and he was certainly up to no good."

"What do you think he was up to?" asked Conner.

"Well, at first, I thought he was trying to pull a fast one somehow to steal from the Air Force. But this morning, I talked with one of the people in my patrol district who mentioned they saw Otto walking into the woods two days ago carrying a white football helmet."

"What would he be doing with a football helmet?" asked Don.

"I didn't think much of it either, so I just dismissed it. But this morning, when I learned he was leading the ground search team that found the pilot's helmet it hit me. From a distance, an Air Force pilot's helmet looks a lot like a football helmet."

The potential realization hit both agents at the same time. With a sick feeling in his stomach, Conner asked "You think Otto planted that pilot's helmet somewhere where the search team would find it?"

"I don't know for sure, but yes, I think it's very possible."

"Have you told this to Major Gibson with the Air Police yet?"

"No. It occurred to me after I was out on the boat. When we got back a minute ago, I checked in with the radio operator but he couldn't reach the ground search team. Said they are out of range."

Looking at Don, Conner said, "That means Otto knows where the pilots are and is trying to intentionally lead us in the wrong direction. At least where Legend is as that was his helmet."

"Trooper Bruce, we need to locate Otto immediately. This is a life-or-death situation for those two pilots. Please radio the State Patrol headquarters and have a "be on the lookout" order issued to all cars. Don, you go tell Colonel Roberts what we have learned and have him pass it on to Major Gibson the next time he radios in. Let's meet back here in five minutes and Trooper Bruce can lead us to Wausaukee to where Otto stays."

CHAPTER 31

Sitting in the restaurant, Sandy could tell from the looks they were getting from the waitress that Otto was typically not a welcome customer.

"So, Otto, tell me about yourself. How did you come to get involved with the people in the woods? What do they call themselves again?"

"They just refer to themselves as the Clan or the Family."

"Were you a member of the Family?"

"I was for a very long time. But no more."

"How did you meet them?"

"After the war, I no longer fit in. Things just weren't right in my head. I moved into the woods to get away from the townspeople. As a child, we hunted and trapped our food so it was natural for me."

Otto continued, "One day, a teenage girl from the Family was out hunting and stepped in one of my traps. She was barefoot and the trap broke her ankle and cut her leg. I carried her several miles back to her people. The girl was Nanja, the granddaughter of the queen."

"A queen?" asked Sandy.

"Yes, she is the leader of the Family."

"Is her name Thordis?" asked Sandy, recalling the story she heard about the girl at the catholic chapel.

"Yes. She is Queen of Forest Egersund."

"What is considered Forest Egersund?" asked Sandy, now taking notes.

"A sacred place deep in the woods. You won't find it on a map."

"Where did the name Egersund come from?"

"That was the name of the small village where Queen Thordis lived as a child. It was near Peshtigo. Her father, Guenther, was the leader of their clan. In those days, the men ruled the family and the women were the subservient ones."

"You mean the women rule now and the men are subservient?" asked Sandy.

"That is what Odin commanded," replied Otto.

"Odin, the Norse God of War?" clarified Sandy.

"Yes. Odin instructed Guenther to sacrifice one of his daughters. Odin sent a Valkyrie to select the child and the Valkyrie chose young Thordis. But Thordis was her father's favorite and he wanted to save her for himself. Guenther lied to the Family about the prophecy and told them that her older sister Hanna had been the chosen one. But when he tried to sacrifice the wrong child, it angered Odin and he sent a wall of fire to destroy Egersund."

"Was this the same fire that destroyed Peshtigo and many other communities in 1871?" asked Sandy.

"Yes, Odin destroyed many to punish Guenther for his deceitfulness. But he spared Thordis along with her little brother and six other children. Odin appeared to her in a vision and instructed her to gather the children and take refuge in the well as the fire passed over them."

"That's amazing!" exclaimed Sandy as she wrote down the story on her notepad as fast as she could.

"The next day, men from Peshtigo found them alive in the well and took them to a boarding school. While at the school, Odin came to Thordis again in a series of three visions. She was told to gather the children and take them up to the woods. This would become known as the Forrest Egersund, after the town Odin destroyed."

"Did Odin tell Thordis in a vision that women would now be in charge?" asked Sandy, looking for a women's liberation angle to the story.

"Odin made her the Valkyrie on Earth and instructed her to grow the Family in the forest."

Noting that Thordis had adopted much of the story from the Catholic chapel, she had altered it to fit her own narrative. Not sure if Thordis was just a fraud, a crazy person, or both, the story was outlandish.

"How did she grow the family with only her little brother and six other children?" asked Sandy.

"The brother would eventually share his seed with each of the girls and the Family grew. Later Odin instructed them to gather seed from men outside of the family."

Sandy could not believe what she was hearing and struggled to hide her facial expressions. Otto was speaking in a matter-of-fact way about such astonishing things that she was afraid he would stop talking if he saw the shock on her face.

Sandy asked, "OK, so that was in the 1800s. When did the girl… Thordis, step on your trap?"

"I got wounded in the Argonne Forest back in October of 1918. I spent a couple of months in a field hospital in France, then another year in a veteran's hospital in Milwaukee. I guess it was probably 1920 when the girl stepped on my trap. I was born in 1900 so I would have been around twenty years old," said Otto.

"Was Thordis grateful when you brought her granddaughter back?"

"Yes. It fulfilled the prophecy."

"It was a prophecy for you to bring her granddaughter back injured?" asked Sandy.

"Yes. Just as Odin only had only one eye, Guenther also had one eye, losing the other in the Civil War. The prophecy foretold that after three generations, a one-eyed warrior would emerge and provide the seed for the family's next leader. Nanja was the third generation descended from Guenther and when I carried her back wearing an eye patch, all the people fell to their knees in praise."

Sandy asked, "So you and Nanja had a child?"

Taking the last bite of his free sandwich, Otto replied, "Yes, she has four children from my seed. The first three born were boys but Odin finally blessed us with a girl. Her name is Randalin and she will be the next Queen of Forest Egersund."

"How old is Randalin now?"

"She is seventeen years old now."

"I see. Will she become the queen when her great-grandmother passes away?

"That was the prophecy, but first she must conceive a child by an injured warrior sent from the heavens.

"Another injured warrior?" asked Sandy.

"That is what the prophecy said. The Family values bravery in battle above all else. It's the only way to enter Valhalla after death. If she is not with child by this warrior before her eighteenth birthday, she is not to be the chosen one."

"What will happen if this injured warrior who comes from the heavens does not emerge and impregnate Randalin before she turns eighteen?" asked Sandy, wondering if this story could possibly take any more turns.

"Then Thordis will have failed as the Valkyrie and Odin will destroy the Forest with fire, just as he did her father's village eighty-four years earlier. If she is not with child, the day before Randalin turns eighteen, Thordis will sacrifice her to appease Odin."

Sandy could not believe the story she was hearing. It was so bizarre that if even partially true it would be the story of the decade. Things such as ritual sacrifice, incestuous sexual abuse, a religious cult started by a mentally ill runaway child after surviving the Great Peshtigo fire, etc.

Even if the story was only something conjured up in the delusional mind of a one-eyed mountain man, it could still serve as a headline for the tabloid press. But what if the story was true? Was this young girl, Randalin, in danger of being sacrificed by her great-grandmother and her band of crazy inbred Vikings? Sandy simply had to know the truth…and hopefully land the story of her journalistic career.

Reaching across the table, she placed her hand on top of Ottos, to show support for him. A tactic she had used many times before to gain trust and evoke emotions in a person she was trying to manipulate.

"That is such a sad story, Otto. Is that what came between you and the Family? The prophecy about your daughter?"

Otto nodded slowly and looked down to avoid eye contact, which was another manipulative tactic employed by Sandy.

"I quarreled with Thordis on my daughter's thirteenth birthday. Randalin loved a boy and wanted to be promised to him. I, along with the boy's father, were in agreement. But Thordis was furious as she did not like the boy's father. That night Odin came to Thordis in a vision and told her the prophecy that an injured warrior would come before her eighteenth birthday. I questioned her prophecy because her visions from Odin seemed to come only at times of convenience. Nanja and I crafted a plan to take our daughter Randalin and flee the community in the dark of night. Thordis learned of our plan and I was banished from the community forever."

"That's so sad, Otto. You haven't seen your wife and daughter in five years?"

As a tear started to form in his eye, he said, "I have seen them. I have watched my daughter grow over the years by hiding in the woods. She will see her eighteenth year soon and she is still without child. I recently tried to return to the Family to protect her. Thordis had given me a series of tasks I must accomplish, but this morning I failed."

"What were the tasks?"

"I don't want to talk about that."

"How did you fail?"

"I have said enough for this day," replied Otto.

Not wanting to push her luck as Otto was the key to the story, Sandy changed her tactic.

Squeezing his hand one last time, she said, "I understand Otto. Do you think Queen Thordis would speak with me? Perhaps I could help?"

Looking up and into her eyes for the first time during the conversation, Otto said "I can take you to her."

CHAPTER 32

Casper had apparently drifted off or possibly lost consciousness while lying on the ground. He was awakened by four robed individuals opening the heavy door and walking in. The smallest of the four removed her robe. It was Nanja.

Entering the small partitioned section, she knelt down next to Casper and placed her hand on his forehead.

"You are very warm," she said.

"Please Nanja, can you call the police for us? I have a wife and a child."

"You are supposed to be here right now. It is the prophecy."

"Yes, I understand. I don't wish to leave. I would just like to contact the police so they can let my wife know I'm safe. I don't want her to worry. Can you help me do that?"

Smiling, she said, "I cannot. If Odin wishes her to know, he will give her the knowledge."

"What do you want from us? Why must we stay here?"

"It is the prophecy," repeated Nanja.

Trying not to show his frustration at her lack of answers, Casper said, "Can you please tell me about the prophecy so I understand?"

She replied, "My daughter Randalin is to be the next Queen of Forest Egersund. She must be with child before her eighteenth birthday, which is fast upon us. If she is not with child, she will be sacrificed to appease the Gods."

Hearing the word sacrificed didn't sit well with Casper. The situation just got more intense if that was even possible. Keeping his calm demeanor, he continued to ask probing questions to try and gain more intelligence about their situation.

"So, what does the prophecy say about me and my friend?"

"Odin came to my grandmother in a vision five years ago. He said a mighty warrior would be sent from Asgard just as you both have. The warrior would bless Randalin with a daughter, which would be half God and half human. She would be great and lead our people to Valhalla."

Trying to make sense of what she was saying, he asked her questions.

"What is Valhalla?"

"Valhalla is the hall of the slain. It is majestic and ruled over by the God Odin. Half of all warriors who die in combat, with honor, may go to Valhalla upon their death. There they will live with Odin and the Gods forever."

"You said the mighty warrior would come from Asgard. Where is Asgard?"

Surprised at his question, she said "Asgard is the center of the universe. It is inhabited by the Gods. You and your friend fell from the heavens. Are you not from Asgard?"

Not knowing how his answer would affect their safety, he avoided telling her he was not from there.

"How do you know we are mighty warriors?"

"You both wore a battle helmet like our Viking ancestors. Odin placed you upside down in the tree of knowledge as a symbol, just as he pierced your friend with a tree branch to represent a spear," she explained.

"I understand the helmet, but what do you mean about being upside down in a tree and pierced with a spear?"

Thinking the divine being was testing her faith and knowledge with his questions, she continued to answer them. She felt if Odin had sent him all the way from Asgard to give her a grandchild who would be a half God, he was truly worthy of her answers.

"The God Odin, eager to learn all forms of knowledge, performed the ultimate sacrifice. He plucked out his own eye, pierced himself with his own spear, and hung himself upside down in the sacred tree of knowledge for nine days."

Recalling portions of a lecture on Norse Mythology while attending the Military Academy at West Point, Casper was starting to understand his captors to some degree. They were obviously descendants of Scandinavian immigrants with a Viking heritage. The secluded people must have somehow been cut off from modern society and survived under the teachings of a deranged elder, probably the so-called Queen of Forest Egersund. Given his physical state, Casper believed his best option was to learn as much as he could about the clan to manipulate the situation for his benefit.

Casper asked, "Why did Odin believe his sacrifice would give him knowledge?"

Desiring to demonstrate her knowledge to the warrior god, she continued.

"Mimir was Odin's most trusted friend and advisor. During the war between the Gods, Mimir served as an advisor to the high God. Although he gave him excellent advice, the high God could not see it and believed he had been tricked. He cut off Mimir's head and sent it back to Asgard. Odin was able to preserve the head and revive it. Odin placed Mimir's head next to the Well of Knowledge as Mimir was the wisest of all the Gods. The well fed the roots to the Tree of Knowledge. It was Mimir who told Odin he could drink from the well and gain its knowledge, but he must first make a sacrifice as an offering. Odin plucked out one of his own eyes, pierced his body with a spear, and hung himself upside down in the tree as the sacrifice."

Starting to understand their belief system and how they fit into it, Casper attempted to manipulate the conversation to an advantage.

"Yes, I am from Asgard, as is my companion. My name is Ghost and my friend's name is Legend. Odin sent us here to gain more knowledge and we have already made our sacrifices. I hung in a tree of knowledge and my friend pierced himself with a branch to represent a spear. Odin said this sacrifice was more than enough and you would welcome us as guests."

Smiling, Nanja said "Yes, you are very welcome here. We are so proud to have you among us."

"Thank you. Please untie my hands so I may be more comfortable."

Nanja untied his hands as he requested then started to cry.

"Why do you cry, my child? You should be happy by our presence."

"I am very happy and my tears are of joy. We feared for a long time that you would not come to us, and my daughter would perish."

With his hands now free, Casper gently reached up and took ahold of Nanja's hand.

"Thank you, Nanja. We are very happy to be here as well. We have already been granted much knowledge since we arrived. Please untie my companion, Legend, as well."

Nanja smiled proudly and looked back toward her three robed companions.

"Untie the God called Legend," she commanded to the robed men.

Casper, wondering if he should push his luck or just allow the ruse to play out more. He chose the first.

"Now that I am enlightened

with more knowledge, it is very important I communicate with the local police department. You must help me get a message to them."

"If it is Odin's desire, it will surely be done. I will go tell our queen the good news and if she grants it, I will send one of my sons to find the people you speak of." While she spoke, Nanja pointed at three large robed men standing by the door, indicating they were her sons.

"Come children, let's go share the good news with the Family," said Nanja as they left the building.

Once they were gone, Casper whispered through the partition to Legend.

"Legend, are you awake? Did you hear that?"

Whispering his response, he said "Yeah, I heard it. Not sure I believe it, but I heard it."

"Did they untie your hand from that peg?"

"Yeah, I can't believe that worked."

"Well, it hasn't worked yet, but at least we have a chance now," replied Casper.

"Do they think they are Vikings? Is that what they were talking about?"

"I'm not sure but they seem to believe in the same Norse Gods that the Vikings did. I'm sure their belief system has evolved and been influenced based on the views of their delusional leader."

"Where did you learn about Norse Gods?" asked Legend.

"I had a lecture on it when I was at West Point. Didn't they cover that topic at the University of Florida?"

"If they did, I must have skipped that day. But now that I think about it, I did attend a lot of toga parties."

Laughing, Casper replied, "Toga parties are Greek, but you never cease to amuse me, Legend."

"So, they think we are Norse Gods? That could work in our favor. But what's the difference between Norse Gods and Greek Gods?

"Greek Gods are immortal. Norse Gods can be killed."

CHAPTER 33

Driving towards the forest, Sandy was feeling a bit uneasy. While determined to get her story, she was starting to feel vulnerable in the wilderness with the strange mountain man. While he appeared nice enough, he clearly had some psychological issues and a menacing-looking tomahawk. While the weapon was simply a utilitarian tool for a woodsman, it was still concerning.

"How much farther is it?" asked Sandy.

"We can park at the end of this farm access road and walk into the forest from there."

"How far will we have to walk?"

"If we walk fast, we can be there in two hours."

"Will we be back before dark?"

"It depends on how long you speak with Queen Thordis."

"What if it gets dark and we are still there?"

"Then we will walk back to the car in the dark," replied Otto.

Sandy parked the car at the end of the dirt road. She was feeling more and more uneasy about her decision and wished she had told someone where she was going and who she was with. As they walked into the thick woods, modern society quickly disappeared.

As Otto moved with ease through the thick terrain, it was obvious he was used to such a trek. Sandy, struggling to keep up with him, didn't ask to slow down as she was anxious to get to their destination and return to her vehicle before the sun went down. She stumbled occasionally on the uneven ground that was covered with brush and fallen logs. Her new, oversized hiking boots were stiff and not broken in, causing a friction rub on her heels after just a few minutes of hiking. While she knew a blister would soon develop, she ignored the pain for the sake of the story.

For the first thirty minutes, Sandy worked hard to memorize their route and remember how to get back to the car. After navigating over hills, through ravines, and over fallen logs, she was now completely disoriented. She was totally reliant on this strange man to get her back to civilization.

Coming to a small river that was about ten feet across, Otto stopped and looked up, sniffing the air like a wild animal. Holding that position, he slowly raised his arms to the sides and then moved them over his head, similar to a referee indicating a touchdown. With his eyes closed, he spoke softly to himself in a language unfamiliar to Sandy.

Growing more concerned by the second, she looked around for a direction to run in case things turned bad. Finding no one direction better than another, she looked back towards Otto who was looking up at a strange symbol hanging from a tree. It must have been one of the symbols that spooked the airmen on the search team. It consisted of several sticks tied into a triangle with sage and an animal skull fixed in the center. While similar to a Native American dream catcher, it had a heavier, more ominous feel about it.

After several minutes, Sandy didn't know if she should interrupt him or simply sneak off into the woods. Slowly backing away from him, she inadvertently stepped on a stick, making an audible snap under her boot. Coming out of his trance-like state, Otto slowly turned his head towards Sandy and said, "We must cross the river here."

Her heart pounding in her chest, she tried to hide her fear as best she could. Watching as Otto stepped from the moss-covered river bank into the water, she could see it was about mid-thigh deep on the man. Reluctantly following him, she was soon up to her waist in the cold water. While the river wasn't moving rapidly, the current was moving enough to push her about six feet to her left by the time she made it to the other side.

Struggling to climb from the river onto the slippery bank, Otto extended a tree branch for her to hold onto. Grasping it with both hands, the powerful man pulled her onto shore with ease. Without saying a word, he turned and continued on their journey.

As she followed him, she noticed the fringe on his mountain man clothing was dripping water, rapidly drying itself. The thin moccasins he wore were wet but would dry much faster than her hiking boots and thick socks which squished when she walked. As she continued to walk, the wet fabric of her socks clung to her feet, increasing the friction on her blistered heels with every step.

"How much farther do we need to go?"

The man didn't answer her or even acknowledge that she spoke.

"What was that symbol hanging in the tree back there? Where you praying to it?"

Still, not answering her, the man kept a steady pace moving through the forest.

After several more minutes of walking, Otto came to a small pile of rocks stacked strangely. It was obvious the formation was intentionally placed there as it could not have occurred in nature. To Sandy, it was reminiscent of the smaller version of the Stonehenge rock formation in England. Otto knelt down and twisted the rock that was resting on top of the formation, pointing it in a new direction. This must be some sort of rudimentary communication method thought Sandy.

As Otto continued on, Sandy tried to memorize the rock formation so she could draw it again later.

"What was that rock formation back there?" asked Sandy, not expecting an answer.

Suddenly Otto stopped in his tracks and held his hand up to Sandy, signaling her to stop. Crouching like an animal, Otto slowly drew the tomahawk from his belt.

Looking around the forest, Sandy didn't see or hear anything unusual. Whispering to Otto, she asked what was wrong. Not answering her, he just tightened his fist around the handle of his weapon.

"You are not welcome here!" came a deep voice from somewhere to the left.

"I am bringing this woman to Thordis," replied Otto, to the unseen voice.

Sandy looked in the direction of the voice as a large man dressed in animal skins stepped out from behind a tree. His appearance was terrifying with long braided hair and dark face paint across his eyes similar to a raccoon. He wore a headdress made out of a wolf's skull, similar to what a Native American warrior might wear. He held a huge knife and looked extremely menacing.

"You cannot bring this outsider to the Family…and you are no longer welcome either," said the large man.

"Koll, I am still your father," said Otto to Sandy's surprise.

"Thordis said you cannot return to the Family!" came a voice from their right.

Sandy looked towards the second voice and saw two more men dressed in similar animal skins and holding weapons.

"I tried to lead the outsiders away from here as she asked me to. I planted the helmet in a location that would lead them to the east. But this morning one of their warriors recognized me and I had to flee," said Otto.

Hearing this, Sandy's heart started beating even faster if that were possible. The three scary men challenging Otto was bad enough, but now she was convinced Otto was not being truthful. From the conversation she was witnessing, it seemed Otto was not asked to help by the police, rather he was leading the search team intentionally in the wrong direction.

"Thordis said you failed at your task," said the man he called Koll.

"Yes, but it was unavoidable. I am bringing this woman for Thordis to sacrifice as penance. This sacrifice will surely please Odin and he will smile upon us."

Hearing this, Sandy turned and started running. She didn't know where she was going or what direction she was headed, she just ran as fast and far as she could.

CHAPTER 34

The Wisconsin State Patrol car pulled out of the boat launch at Lake Noque-bay and started traveling north. Trooper Bruce had just been issued one of the new 1955 Chevy Highway Patrol cars with the new paint scheme of a blue hood and roof over a white car. A red dome light sat on the roof while a large chrome siren was mounted on top of the front right fender. A large State Patrol Logo painted on the doors ensured people knew it was a state trooper rather than local law enforcement.

"How far is it to Wausaukee?" asked Don, as the two special agents followed behind the trooper in the unmarked OSI car.

"I think it's about a twenty-minute drive," replied Conner.

"What do we do when we find Otto?"

"We make him tell us where the pilots are. Hopefully, they're still alive."

"What if he doesn't cooperate?"

"I don't expect him to cooperate…let's just cross that bridge when we get to it." replied Conner, knowing firsthand the hell a downed pilot goes through while waiting for rescue. In Conner's case, a rescue that would not come until after a year of captivity.

Don, not being one to step too far outside of official procedures, worried Conner would go rogue in an effort to save the missing pilots. While he could understand the need and desire, he was conflicted as the procedures were in place for a reason. Maybe he had been assigned at headquarters for too long…. but just maybe, Conner had been away from a proper command structure for too long.

Changing the topic, Don asked, "Where do you call home, Conner?"

"Home is where ever I hang my hat these days, but I grew up in Montana."

"I grew up in Maryland. Big family, seven kids in all. I'm the oldest. Dad is an attorney," said Don.

"You close with your family?" asked Conner.

"Pretty close, I guess. My father is pretty vocal about me not living up to my full potential, but I wouldn't say he is ashamed of me."

"You are a military officer and a federal agent. What more does he want from you?"

"He has had my entire life planned out since before I was born. I followed in his footsteps for college and attended Yale, his alma mater, for my undergraduate degree. While he expected me to continue with my education and attend law school, I wanted to serve my country."

Conner now understood Don a little better as well as his desire to follow protocol. My dad was a ranch hand and mom took in laundry to help pay the bills. I was raised in a small rural town in Montana with my older brothers Henry and Jack and our little sister Adeline."

"You all close?"

"I guess about normal. We all have jobs that require travel so we don't get together all that often."

"Oh? What do they do?" asked Don.

"Hank, or Henry as he likes to be called these days, is a movie stuntman in Hollywood. He works a lot of westerns and makes a career out of getting shot off horseback. Jack is on the rodeo circuit and travels all over the place. Adaline is a stewardess with American Airlines."

"You didn't get the horse-riding bug from your father like your two brothers?"

Smiling to himself, as he never realized the connection between his father and brothers until Don spelled it out for him. His brothers had followed their father's passion for riding horses and the cowboy life. Back in his day, dad served with a cavalry unit chasing the outlaw Poncho Villa around the Mexican border until he was reassigned to France during WW1. Serving in K Troop, 3rd Cavalry, he served as a Scout until he was wounded during the Meuse-Argonne Offensive.

"My brothers were several years older than me and spent a lot of time with our dad on the range. As I was younger, I had to stay home with mom a lot, and I guess I was resentful. I got into a lot of fights at school and looked for ways to rebel. When I was fourteen, I got a job and saved up to buy a military surplus Indian motorcycle. I guess it was my way of rejecting my dad and brothers by riding a mechanical horse. Funny, I never really thought about it in that light before."

Don now understood Conner a little better, and his desire to operate by his own set of rules.

As the conversation came to a lull, Conner looked out the window as the green Wisconsin scenery passed by. There was so much forest to search and if they couldn't get a clue to narrow it down, the pilots didn't stand a chance…if they were even still alive.

As the state patrol car pulled up to the abandoned railroad stop, Conner pulled the Bel Air up next to it so they could communicate through their open windows.

"He sometimes stays in that shack over there," said the trooper, pointing to the rickety structure.

"Do you think he is in there now?" asked Don.

"Only one way to find out. One of you guys should approach from the rear in case he sees us and tries to make a run for it. If he gets into the woods, you'll never catch him. That old man moves like a wolf in that terrain."

Don walked wide to get into position to cover the rear of the shack, being sure to avoid a direct line of fire in case Conner or the trooper need to take a shot for some reason.

Once in position, Conner and the trooper approached the front, staying about ten yards away.

"Otto! Are you in there?" shouted Trooper Bruce.

Hearing no response, the next course of action would be to approach the shack and pull back the curtain covering the doorway.

"Is he known to carry a gun?" asked Conner.

"Not to my knowledge but I'm not sure about it. I know he hunts with a bow and arrow and he always has that homemade tomahawk on him. It's your investigation Conner, you want to go through the door first?" asked the trooper.

Scratching his head, Conner looked up at the tall trooper and said, "Well, he is a civilian. Maybe you should go first," he said with a grin.

As the two men approached the front of the shack with their revolvers drawn, each one took a position on opposite sides of the doorway. Conner reached up and grabbed the tarp, yanking it down so the trooper could look into the small structure. Taking a step inside to clear the corners, he said "It's empty."

The small shack was spooky on the inside, with animal skulls and pelts on the walls and hanging from the ceiling. There were also a few odd symbols made out of antlers and sticks hanging from the ceiling.

"Those must be the kind of symbols the ground search team found in the woods," said Conner.

"They are pretty creepy," replied the trooper.

Conner reached down and picked up a fixed-blade knife with a tan, pressed leather handle. It had a five-inch blade and a tan sheath.

"This is a US Air Force model 499 survival knife made by the Ontario Knife Company. It's the new contract knife for our pilots and just came out this year. It's highly unlikely a civilian would have one of these."

"That as well as the helmet is enough evidence for me. What's that jar in the corner?" asked the trooper.

Conner bent down and picked up a glass mason jar filled with murky fluid. Bringing it over towards the doorway to get better light, they could see something inside of it. Holding it up to the light, they could see the jar contained what appeared to be a human eyeball.

"That must be from one of the missing pilots. I hope they were not alive when that was taken," said the trooper.

"We need to find Otto immediately. I need you to radio your headquarters and get more troopers and sheriff's deputies up here. I need to get to a phone and try and get more OSI agents as well," said Conner.

"There is a diner up the road a bit with a pay phone. I'll make the radio call and meet you up there in a few minutes. We can establish a plan from there," said Trooper Bruce.

"Sounds good," said Conner as he stepped out of the shack.

Yelling out to Don, he said, "We need to go!"

Informing Don about what they found in the shack while they drove, they arrived at the diner in just a few minutes.

As the two men entered the restaurant, Conner said "We should probably grab some food to go while we are here. I imagine it will be a long night and we won't have another chance for dinner. I'll order if you want to go make the call to your OSI District Headquarters and get us some more manpower up here."

"Sounds good," replied Don, as he walked to the pay phone in the back of the diner.

Conner walked up to the counter and took a seat. The waitress, noticing his badge and gun came over to take his order.

"Hi sweety, what can I get for you?"

"How is the special today?"

Looking over her shoulder towards the short order cook in the back, she looked back to Conner, rolled her eyes and said "If I were you, I would just go with a burger and fries."

Smiling, Conner said, "OK. I'll take three orders of burgers and fries to go, and three Coca-Cola's also.

The waitress yelled the order to the back, "Melvin, I need three number ones."

"Three number ones!" echoed the cook from the kitchen.

"I haven't seen you two here before. You aren't detectives from the sheriff's office. You boys FBI or something?" asked the waitress.

"Something like that," replied Conner.

"I read *True Crime* magazine every month. I love a good crime story," said the waitress, while squinting as she looked down at the badge clipped to Conner's belt.

Smiling, Conner said, "It says Special Agent, Air Force Office of Special Investigations."

"That sounds important," said the waitress, while giving Conner an overly seductive look.

"It pays the bills," he replied, while looking back to see if his partner was returning to the table to help him avoid an awkward conversation.

"You going to be in town long?"

"Not too long, we are just here looking for a man with the State Patrol. Trooper Bruce should be here momentarily."

"You looking for a military man on the run from something?

"No, we're looking to speak with a local man. A vagrant that hangs around some times. You see anyone like that recently?" asked Conner, just taking a chance that she may have seen him.

"Just Oddball Otto. He was in here a little while ago," said the waitress.

Looking up, Conner said, "When did you last see him?"

Based on the look she gave him; Conner could tell she was not surprised the police were looking for Otto.

"He had lunch here a little while ago."

"How long ago did he leave?"

"Oh, about ten minutes ago. We usually don't allow him in here as he can make a scene when he gets riled up. But this time he was with some lady so we let him be."

"What did this lady look like?" asked Conner.

"Well, she was about my height, and about thirty or so."

"Was she wearing overalls and a scarf in her hair?"

"Yeah, that's her. What did Otto do?"

"We just need to speak with him. Did you see which way they went when he left?"

"He and that lady left in her car. They drove away from Main Street."

Standing up, Conner placed some cash on the table and told the waitress they would need to skip dinner.

"Don! We need to go! I will meet you in the car!" Conner shouted to his partner in the back of the diner before leaving.

As Conner was opening his car door, Trooper Bruce was pulling in.

Conner walked over to the state patrol car and spoke with the trooper through his open window.

"Otto just left here ten minutes ago. He was with a female reporter and I think she is in danger. They are traveling in her 1955 Ford Fairlane with Illinois plate 257207. Please put that car out over the radio. As soon as Don gets out here, we need to start looking for it. It left here traveling away from Main Street."

Trooper Bruce started broadcasting the information over the radio as Don came jogging out of the diner with the three meals and Cokes in a bag.

"The waitress shoved this into my arms while I was coming out. What's going on?"

"I'll tell you while we drive. Get in," said Conner.

As Conner was about to pull out, Trooper Bruce shouted from his car window "I radioed to the sheriff's deputies to check the roads headed to the next towns. I'm headed towards the farm roads by the woods if you want to follow me."

"Sounds good!" shouted Conner as they drove from the diner.

"What's going on asked Don?"

"Otto was just at the diner with the reporter. They left just a few minutes before we arrived. I put out an all-points bulletin for her car. Sheriff deputies are checking the roads between here and the other towns and we are checking the roads leading to the woods."

"She has no idea what kind of danger she has gotten herself into," said Don.

"Hopefully we'll find her before she finds out."

After traveling down the unmarked dirt farm road for about ten minutes, the state patrol car slowed to a stop with the agents behind him. Trooper Bruce pointed out the driver-side window down a dirt access road that ended at the edge of the forest. Sitting at the end of the access road, about three hundred yards away, they could see a two-tone convertible parked at the trailhead.

Conner pulled onto the left side of the road and up next to the trooper so they could communicate through the passenger side window.

"Is that your reporter's car?"

"It looks like it. It's a brand-new Fairlane convertible with a white over-blue paint scheme. I can't imagine there would be more than one around here," said Conner.

"I'll call it in but it will be difficult for them to find us as the farm roads are not marked. We can go back to the paved road and wait for reinforcements or we can go it alone and hope they find us. Your call," said the trooper.

Conner looked over to the car then back to the trooper, "She is in danger and every second counts. Don and I will go down there and start searching while you go back to the paved road and get back up. Well see you in a little bit."

"Roger that, be safe and watch your backs. I'll get back as soon as possible," said the trooper.

Turning down the access road, Conner slowly crept up to the parked car in an effort to observe the surrounding area for possible clues or evidence. It would be an incredibly easy ambush site as the agents were surrounded by thick forest offering endless concealment opportunities.

Parking behind the Fairlane, they stepped out and walked up to the car. Checking the plate to verify it was correct, Conner looked into the windows for anything pertinent. Finding nothing, he searched around the immediate area. Pointing to the ground leading into the forest, Conner said "They entered here. You can see her small boot prints following behind his soft-soled moccasin prints."

"Well at least she was alive at this point and wasn't being carried or drug," said Don.

"Let's go after them. I just need to grab a bag out of my trunk," said Conner as he returned to his car.

Opening the trunk, Conner removed the pilot bag that he kept with him for emergencies. Placing it over his head and shoulder, the satchel hung beneath his left arm.

"Let's move out. Follow about ten paces behind me so we're not bunched up in case we get ambushed. Walk to the sides of their footprints. Try to keep quiet and stop and listen every so often. We will be able to hear much farther than we can see in this terrain," said Conner.

Drawing his five-shot Smith & Wesson revolver from its holster, Don followed him into the forest.

CHAPTER 35

Otto could hear Sandy turn and run away through the forest as his two youngest sons gave chase. He stayed to speak with his eldest child Koll, confident the two younger men would be able to retrieve his sacrificial offering.

"You look well son," he said to the thirty-year-old warrior.

"It has been a long-time father. I am surprised you are still alive after many years of living outside the forest."

Otto, being one of the only clan members with knowledge of the outside world, chose to allow his son to live in ignorant bliss. The outside world was cruel and he knew the Family would not easily survive if forced to assimilate.

"How are your sister and your mother?" asked Otto, not letting on that he had been watching over them from afar.

"Mother is good but I fear for Randalin."

"Why is that?"

"Her eighteenth birthday nears and she is still without child. A few weeks ago, a one-eyed warrior was sent to our village from Asgard. We believed he had been sent to us from Odin to give her the child the prophecy spoke of. But the man was a false prophet, sent by Loki, the God of Mischief, just to torment us. He fought with honor and was killed in battle. Thordis did not want the Valkyrie to take his soul to Valhalla so she had his head cut off.

Otto already had knowledge of the matter as he was the one who brought the one-eyed warrior to Thordis. He abducted the man from a boat on the lake, removed one of his eyes, and brought him to the queen so his daughter wouldn't be sacrificed. But when the man refused to impregnate her, Thordis had him killed.

Koll continued, "Odin was pleased we did not fall for the false prophets. Later he sent not one but two injured warriors from Asgard. One of them will provide the child for Randalin."

Otto was also aware of this as he was the one to bring the news of the pilots to Thordis. It was another attempt to keep his daughter from being sacrificed.

"I know of the injured warriors who fell from the heavens and they are in danger. Many soldiers are coming from outside the forest to kill them. Thordis asked me to lead them away by placing one of the God's helmets in a location that would take them in the wrong direction. I tried to do this but I failed because one of the soldiers recognized me."

"Thordis said you had failed at your task but she did not share with us the details."

"I was bringing the woman as an offering of the sacrifice for my failure. Has Randalin been impregnated yet?"

"Soon. But Thordis has yet to choose which of the two Gods is to be the father."

"Have they recovered from their wounds?"

"Not yet. One of the Gods has asked for us to send a messenger outside the forest to inform those that live there of their location. Thordis has forbidden this."

"That was wise. The soldiers from outside the forest are dangerous. I believe they will be coming towards the village soon. You should have the warriors prepare for this."

"Our warriors are ready to repel them," said the younger man.

"Be careful. Their weapons are powerful."

"If it is Odin's will, they will be defeated."

"You look, good son, as do your brothers. When you catch the woman, please tell Queen Thordis that I brought her as a sacrifice to the Gods. I will leave the forest now.

"This will be done, father. It was good to see you again. I'm glad you are well."

As Otto walked away from the forest, he was once again reminded he was a man without a land. With one foot in each world, he was accepted by the people of neither.

CHAPTER 36

Not knowing if she was going in the right direction, Sandy ran as fast as she could, forgetting all about the pain from the hiking boots. As she ran, she jumped over fallen logs and ducked under tree branches blocking her path. While she was not acclimated to hiking, as a trained dancer she was very fit and had significant leg strength. Much smaller than the men pursuing her, she was able to take advantage of running through smaller openings in the thick forest.

After running as fast as she could for several minutes, she was getting winded. Glancing behind her, she could see at least one of the men was still chasing after her and about thirty yards away. Motivated to keep running, she pressed on until she approached a drop-off of about six feet with a small stream at the bottom. Jumping down, she landed hard and fell forward. As she caught herself with her open hands, she felt a sharp pain in her left palm.

Looking down, Sandy could see a sharp piece of wood protruding through the back of her hand. When she extended her arms in front of her body to prevent her face from hitting the ground, her palm landed on a tree branch that was sticking straight up from the muddy river bank. The sharp piece of wood was immovable and must have been attached to a larger tree that was buried under the mud. Refusing to panic, Sandy used her right hand to grasp her left wrist and pull upwards, painfully sliding her hand up and off of the six-inch wood spike that had impaled her.

Assuming her pursuer would have closed the distance, Sandy chose to hide rather than attempt to keep running. After dropping down the six-foot bank, she knew she would have temporarily dropped out of view. Moving backward through the stream she had landed in, she concealed herself as much as possible under the bank she had jumped from. Kneeling down, the water came to chest height and she forced her upper body into some thick brush as far as she could. Praying she was concealed enough, she tried to control her breathing so as to not be heard.

She could hear the footsteps of the large man just a few feet above her on the bank. Hoping the sound of the moving river concealed her heavy breathing, she flinched as the man dropped down right in front of her. Luckily, he was facing away from her. Standing in the stream just a few feet away, he appeared huge. He stood well over six feet with very broad shoulders. He wore a vest made out of buckskin and his arms were exposed. There were several designs and symbols tattooed on his arms and he was holding a weapon that resembled a tomahawk or battle ax.

After standing still for several seconds to observe the area, the man turned to the right and started walking with the flow of the steam. Sandy imagined he was searching for her footprints leading out of the water in order to follow her trail. She was concerned he would eventually turn and come back once he did not find any. She wasn't sure if she should remain hidden or attempt to run in the other direction. What if the other men were also in the area now and not just this one man?

Sitting still for several minutes, partially submerged in the cold water, she finally got her breathing under control. Quietly trying to push her upper body further into the prickly brush to conceal herself, the pain in her heels and left hand started to take over her thoughts. She could slowly open and close her hand so she assumed the branch had penetrated between the bones. The soft tissue injury was severe and incredibly painful. While she couldn't visibly examine the wound given her location, she knew it was bleeding heavily. Reaching up with her right hand she removed the boy scout bandana from her hair and wound it tightly around her left hand in an attempt to stop the bleeding and protect the wound. Using her teeth, she pulled the makeshift bandage tight.

Her next focus was on her feet. She could feel painful blisters already forming on her heels due to running in the stiff, new footwear. The fast sprint didn't help the situation any. S

he was trying to decide if it would be better to take off her boots and run in her socks, risking stepping on a sharp branch like the one that penetrated her hand, or continuing with the heavy, painful boots. Neither choice was appealing.

Hearing the sounds of an animal call above her position on the upper bank, she held still. While the sound was guttural and didn't sound human, she feared it was actually one of the mountain people communicating with the others. Moments later she heard a return animal call from down the river in the direction of the man that was chasing her walked. She was now convinced it was the men communicating with one another. But how many were there? Other than Otto, she had seen at least three others. They were so accustomed to blending into their environment, there could have been a whole tribe for all she knew. One thing was certain, she was not about to be sacrificed to appease anybody.

Looking around for an item she could use as a weapon; all she could find were small rocks and sticks where she was concealed. Her Gun! In all of the excitement, she had completely forgotten she had taken the small pistol out of her suitcase and placed it in the chest pocket of her overalls. Slowly moving her right hand up from holding pressure on her wounded left-hand, she reached into the pocket and grasped the small Colt.

While the little pistol in her hand was comforting, she wished it was a larger caliber and held more bullets. While six rounds of .25ACP were usually enough to convince a person who didn't wish to be shot to turn and run, it was very lacking in power for a determined predator who was motivated by a religious belief. Especially when the predators were the size of the men chasing her. Still, she was very happy she had the foresight to bring it along.

The small nickel-plated gun with ivory grips was very attractive for a lady, but it also reflected the sun and didn't blend well with the natural environment she was trying to hide in. Knowing this, she kept the pistol low and behind the brush, careful not to let it submerge in the water.

Calculating her odds, Sandy decided she would have a better chance of waiting until dark before slipping out of her concealed position. Hungry, injured, and lost in the woods, she preferred finding her way in the dark over facing her pursuers.

CHAPTER 37

Kneeling to examine the footprints, Conner was having a difficult time following the path taken by Sandy and Otto. Leaves and other debris made tracking the prints slow going. After tracking for about one hundred yards into the forest, Conner reached into his satchel and removed his compass. Having a general idea of the direction they were headed; he would have a rough idea of where to proceed if and when he lost the track. The reverse bearing would also help him navigate his way back to the car.

Off in the distance, he could hear the sound of air chopping in the sky. The pilots must have determined the bullet holes in the helicopter weren't critical. The helicopter would be a significant aid in the search as it could fly much lower and slower than the fixed-wing aircraft that had been conducting the air search to this point. A relatively new contraption, Conner was still amazed the machines could stay in the air.

After about forty-five minutes of following the prints, Conner lost the track after crossing a stream. While checking the compass once again to make sure he was staying on course, he caught a glimpse of movement to his left in his peripheral vision. He was pretty sure he saw something tall move behind a tree about thirty yards away. It was too tall to be a deer and too stealthy to be a bear.

Looking back at Don, Conner used hand signals to communicate. He first pointed to his own eyes, indicating that he saw something. Next, he pointed at the large tree to his left. Once Don nodded his head indicating he understood, the two separated and started moving around the tree in opposite directions from one another. As they did this, a large man dressed in animal skins with a head dressing made from the skull of a wolf, stepped out from behind the tree.

"Drop the knife!" shouted Conner, as the large man was holding a huge blade honed from a piece of metal.

The man's response was a blood-curdling scream as he charged forward while raising the weapon over his head.

Backpedaling to create distance, Conner fired all five rounds of his .38 caliber revolver in rapid succession. The large man fell to a knee momentarily but stood back up and continued his forward momentum. Tripping over a log as he backed away from the threat, Conner found himself on his back with an empty weapon. Rapidly trying to access his satchel to get to his personally owned .45acp, he heard several more rounds fired as Don emptied his revolver into the large man's back.

Conner saw him wince in pain as he stopped moving towards him and slowly turned to face Don. Don was frantically dumping the five spent shells out of his revolver and trying to load fresh ammo as the man stepped towards him. Conner was finally able to retrieve the .45 from his satchel when the large man fell to his knees, but still clutching the large blade.

"Drop the knife!" shouted Don.

The blade finally dropped from the man's hand as his fingers relaxed. The massive warrior fell forward onto his face without trying to catch himself.

"Holy crap!" said Don, as he closed the reloaded cylinder back into his revolver.

"Check your six o'clock!" shouted Conner, while getting back on his feet. "He may not be alone."

After searching for additional threats, the two agents didn't observe any. Off in the distance, they could hear a voice shouting.

"Agent Golden! Agent Price!"

It must have been Trooper Bruce finally catching up to them and hearing the gunfire.

"Over here!" shouted Conner.

They waited as the trooper came through the brush with two Manitowoc Sheriff's deputies.

As the uniformed men approached, Conner told them what had happened. One of the deputies rolled the man over while the other provided cover.

"This guy is dead," said the deputy.

"He didn't die fast enough," replied Don, still breathing fast from the adrenaline rush.

"I wish OSI didn't make us carry these small five-shot .38's," said Conner, as he returned his personally owned pistol to his satchel and retrieved his empty revolver from the ground. Reloading the weapon, he secured it back in its holster.

"That was too close for comfort. Thanks, Don," said Conner.

Looking down at the huge man covered in animal skins and strange tattoos, Trooper Bruce said "We only have a little bit of daylight left. I suggest we mark this location and drag this guy out of here. We can restart the search at first light with more personnel."

Looking off into the forest, Conner hated the thought of abandoning the search while Sandy was still at risk. But he knew it would be both futile and dangerous to continue in the dark.

"You're right. We'll need to get a lot more people out here to conduct the search properly. I want to start again at first light."

"Will do," said one of the deputies.

"Ok, well I guess we can't leave this guy here overnight. Let's start dragging," said Trooper Bruce.

Lifting the large man, it was apparent he weighed well over two hundred pounds. After carrying him about a hundred yards through the rough terrain, they had to sit him down to rest. While catching his breath, Conner examined the many odd tattoos and brands on his skin. The tattoos were almost blue in color and must have been made with some sort of ink produced from indigenous plants or berries.

"You guys ready to go again?" asked Trooper Bruce.

"Yeah, I guess so," said Conner. "But this guy is bleeding all over us."

"Well maybe that's because you pumped so many holes into him." said one of the deputies, indicating their actions were overkill.

"If I had more bullets in my gun he would have more holes in him," said Conner, not caring what the deputy thought of the matter.

Just as it was starting to get dark, the men were finally approaching the clearing where the vehicles were parked. Conner was happy to see an Air Force jeep and a large M35 truck along with several local and state police vehicles.

"Everyone OK?" asked Major Gibson who was standing next to the jeep.

"Well, other than this guy, we are still missing that female reporter and the hunting guide. We found a human eyeball in a jar back at Otto's shack. I'm concerned it belongs to one of our missing pilots."

Major Gibson looked down at the huge body they carried out of the woods. "I sure as hell hope there are not too many more of them out there."

"Yeah, I think you better arm your search party," said Conner.

"I have a few more guys driving up from Truax AFB tonight. I will have them bring some carbines and shotguns. Also, we finally got the helicopter up and running. They just completed their test flight. Now that we have that the search should move much faster."

"Agreed," said Conner. "I want to get started first thing in the morning as that reporter is in danger."

"It's probably too late for her," replied Major Gibson.

"It's probably too late for our pilots as well, but we need to try," said Conner.

A flash from a camera off to the side got the men's attention.

"Good job boys, glad you are safe!" said the sheriff who was running for reelection.

"Agent's Price and Golden, this is Sheriff Weber," said Trooper Bruce.

"Nice to meet you sheriff," said Conner.

"Mind if we get a photo?" asked the sheriff, signaling his aid to take a picture of him with the search party.

"Actually sheriff, we try to keep a low profile as we may have to go undercover in our next assignment, you understand," said Conner, avoiding being used as a pawn for local politics.

"Oh, sure, I completely understand," said the sheriff. "What can I do to help?"

"Glad you asked, sheriff," said Conner. If you could leave a couple of men here tonight to watch the reporter's car, that would be helpful. I don't want Otto to slip away during the night. Also, do you have a medical examiner in Marinette?"

"Sure, I can leave a couple of guys to watch the car. We do have an appointed coroner in the county.

"Does the coroner have a medical background?" asked Conner.

"He is a volunteer fireman as well as my son-in-law," said the sheriff.

"Would it be possible for me to attend the coroner's examination?"

"Sure. Do you want to do it tonight so you can partake in the search in the morning?

"That would be wonderful, thank you."

"OK, we can load the body up and head over to Marinette now."

CHAPTER 38

Hearing his friend's cough moving deeper into his lungs, Casper was concerned that infection was setting in.

"How are you doing over there?"

"I'm doing fine," replied Legend.

"I'm not asking for a tough guy response. I legitimately need to know your medical status as it relates to our situation."

"OK, I think my injury is causing an infection. I have a fever, chills, cold sweats, sore throat and my cough is worsening. It burns when I urinate and my injury is incredibly painful."

"Can you walk if we get a chance to escape?"

"I will certainly try but I wouldn't say it is a realistic option at this point. How are you doing?"

"I'm starting to get some of the feeling back in my legs. Our best shot is to continue to manipulate them and try to get a message to the police."

As the two pilots whispered through the partition, they heard people approaching from outside.

The heavy door opened and Nanja entered with two large men in hooded robes. The men carried a large animal skin and placed it on the floor next to Casper.

"Thordis will see you," said Nanja, as the men picked him up and placed him on the animal skin.

As the makeshift litter was lifted, Casper could feel pain in his left leg once again. He was pleased he was starting to feel his lower extremities as his paralysis may not be permanent, yet the fracture in his leg was becoming much more painful.

Leaving the building, Casper tried to look around at his surroundings to identify anything useful. It was getting dark so visibility was limited. Looking up, he could see stars, indicating the tree canopy was not as thick over the center of the village. That was important if he were to have the opportunity to signal aircraft somehow.

They approached a structure that was more elaborate than the others. It was built into the ground like a partial basement. The upper walls and roof extended only a couple of feet above ground level, to allow natural light to enter through the small windows. A stone staircase led below ground to the front door. Nanja entered the door first, then instructed the men to follow while carrying Casper.

The scent inside the room was strong with burning incense and sage. The smells were so thick it was uncomfortable for the pilot to breathe. In the center of the room, there was a large wooden chair facing a large dark curtain. The men placed the animal skin on the chair and positioned Casper into a painful seated position. Using strips of leather, the men secured his arms and waist to the chair, holding him upright. Once he was secure, Nanja instructed the two men to leave the room. After they left, she lit two torches and placed them to the left and right of the curtain.

Nanja spoke softly to someone behind the curtain before turning and leaving the room as well. The curtain was then slowly pulled back by an elderly woman who was waiting on the other side. She was slender and probably around seventy years old. Dressed in a white tunic, possibly made of rabbit skin, her hair was long and gray. Two braids extending over each shoulder. Casper assumed this to be Gyda, Nanja's mother.

Behind her, sitting on a chair facing Casper was an even older woman who had to be Queen Thordis. Also dressed in white animal skins, she wore a crown made of woven sticks. Her chair was fashioned out of one of the ejection seats from the P-89C and adorned with dozens of animal bones and antlers into some sort of macabre throne.

Sitting on a pedestal beside her was a severed human head, with one eye missing.

Once the curtain was fully drawn open, Gyda turned to face Thordis, knelt down, and placed her forehead onto the floor in what appeared to be a subservient, praise position.

Clearly spooked by the bizarre ritual, Casper fought to maintain his composure and continue the ruse that he was in fact sent by Odin.

The old woman spoke first, in a quiet raspy voice.

"I am Odin's Valkyrie on Earth. Queen of Forest Egersund."

Speaking with confidence, Casper replied "I know who you are Thordis...and I also know you Gyda. Please rise and sit beside your mother."

Gyda looked up with a sense of shock on her face. She was both honored and surprised that this divine being knew both her name and that she was the eldest daughter of Thordis. Unaware that he had elicited the personal information from Nanja, this affirmed for her that he was truly sent by Odin. She slowly rose and took a seat on the floor next to her mother as instructed.

Casper continued, "My name is Ghost. I have been sent by Odin from Asgard. You have done well Thordis and Odin is very pleased. I have gained the knowledge I was seeking and I must now speak with others to fulfill Odin's prophecy. Please send someone to find a police officer and bring him to me. This is commanded by Odin."

With a confused look on her face, Thordis looked over to the severed head sitting next to her and started speaking to it in a low whisper.

Casper interjected, "Who is this you speak to? Surely you do not believe it to be the great Mimir?"

Thordis appeared taken back. It was clear to Casper that the old woman was deranged, probably from a lifetime of living as a social outcast in addition to her advanced age. His only hope was to manipulate the situation.

The confused woman replied, "He represents Mimir and provides me guidance. He is called Warden. He was brought to me by my great granddaughter's father, Otto."

"Does he speak to you also Gyda?" asked Casper, in an attempt to sow distrust between the two old women.

"No, Warden only speaks to Queen Thordis."

"Yes, I know," said Casper. "That was foretold to me by Odin before he sent me here. He said you are special and will lead the group going forward. The head, I mean Warden, does not speak the truth and Odin protects you from hearing his poisonous lies."

Looking up, Gyda asked, "Is this true?"

"I am queen!" shouted Thordis in a voice as loud as she could muster.

This tactic helped Casper understand the dynamic between the two women. While Thordis was certainly insane in her own right, she was sane enough to use her position of power to manipulate and control her clan as a false profit.

"Thordis. you have served Odin well but now it is time for you to rest. You will go to Valhalla soon. Gyda, it is now your time to lead. You must send a person to bring a policeman here and your clan will be blessed by Odin."

"Stop talking!" shouted Thordis, fearing the loss of control.

"Thordis, if you truly follow Odin, you know my words are true."

Angry, the elderly woman got herself so worked up that it triggered a coughing fit.

"Enough," she said between coughs, "Take him back."

Gyda, unsure what to do, slowly stood up. Was this God from Asgard telling the truth? Was she now the true leader of the clan? She knew her mother was cruel and deceitful, having visions from Odin only at the most opportune times. But after a lifetime of living in fear at the hand of an abusive, dominant mother, she didn't disobey her easily.

"Gyda! Have him returned at once!" commanded the queen.

Gyda slowly walked past Casper while he continued to make soft, compassionate eye contact with her. She slowly walked up the stairs and moments later, returned with the robed men who took him back to his quarters.

CHAPTER 39

Just after Nanja and the men took Casper to see Thordis, Legend heard the
door open, followed by soft footsteps. Looking up, he saw a teenage girl
peering sheepishly around his partition. Wanting to continue his partners
ruse, Legend attempted to speak as if he were also a divine being. He had
recently watched the hit biblical movie, *the Robe,* at the base movie theater.
Using Hollywood as a lead, he spoke.

"Fear not child, please show yourself?"

The teenager slowly walked around the partition. Lowering her hood,
Legend could see she had been crying.

"Please, kneel beside me and hold my hand," he instructed, in an
attempt to gain her confidence through a personal moment.

The teenager did as instructed, but kept her eyes directed downward
as if she was not worthy.

Taking a gamble that the girl was Randalin based on her age, he asked
"Are you the great-granddaughter of Queen Thordis?"

This caused the girl to look up, momentarily, with a surprised look on
her face, before once again diverting her eyes.

"Yes, I am," said the trembling voice.

"Randalin, why are you afraid?"

The girl was shocked that the divine being knew her name.

"I ask for mercy. I have faltered in my faith."

"Please look at me child," said Legend, wanting to establish a personal bond with her.

As she looked up, he gently wiped a tear from her cheek.

"What have you done Randalin?"

"Thordis has said the prophecy was that I would be granted a child by a great warrior who fell from the heavens. I am to be pledged to either you or your companion. But I am unclean and not worthy of your seed."

Trying to think of how he could use this information to his advantage, he asked her open-ended questions just as he heard Casper do with her mother.

"Who is this man you have laid with?"

Crying, she said, "His name is Anders."

"Do you wish to be with him?"

She began to cry harder while squeezing his hand.

"I have always felt like I belonged to him. Since we were young. Now I am with his child."

This was a shocking turn of events and one that would need to be calculated well.

"Fear not Randalin. It was meant to be. This was foretold by Odin before I left Asgard. Does Thordis know you are with his child?"

Nodding her head while she cried, she said, "Thordis commanded me not to tell anyone else."

"Does Anders know you are with his child?"

"Yes, but Thordis ordered him to be sacrificed to Odin to keep our secret. I helped him escape last night before he was executed. The queen is furious with me. She said I am to lay with you or your companion so she can tell the Family that the child is half God and that her prophecy was correct."

"Listen to me carefully. Your child will be a great leader but you need to protect it from Thordis. You must flee and go find a policeman outside of this community. Tell them about me and my friend and bring them here. This is important. Can you do that?"

"Yes, I will try," she said.

"No. You must not only try, you must succeed. It is the will of Odin. Do you understand?"

"Yes, I will do as you have instructed."

"Good. Go now child," said Legend,

Randalin stood up, now emboldened with the new knowledge. In just moments, her entire life had changed. With a smile now on her face, she exited the room thinking about how she would complete her task. She would need to slip away in the dark and try to locate the outside world that she had only heard of in stories.

Smiling and crying tears of joy, the naïve young girl left the hut to return to her home. Turning the corner, she abruptly came face to face with her mother and two of her brothers. Nanja was not pleased as she had eavesdropped on the conversation from outside the window.

"You have brought shame to our family. You have disobeyed the prophecy and lay with Anders," said Nanja.

"Mother, the God they call Legend said this was meant to be. My child will be a great leader and it is Odin's will. Queen Thordis knows of this and she is trying to deceive the family. You know this to be correct mother," said Randalin in a pleading voice.

Not sure how to respond to her daughter as she believed what she was saying to be true. However, Queen Thordis ru led with an iron fist and one did not go against her easily. Just five years earlier her daughter desired to be joined by Anders and it resulted in getting her husband Otto banished and the boy's father sacrificed.

Not knowing what else to do, she instructed her sons, "Take her to Thordis."

CHAPTER 40

It was dark in the forest and Sandy had been trying to sit still for several hours. Shivering from being submerged in the cold water, she placed her bottom lip between her teeth to prevent them from chattering. Listening intently for the sounds of the men chasing her, the trickling sound of the stream made it challenging. Finally convinced that it was sufficiently dark and enough time had passed, she attempted to make a run for it.

It was difficult for her to get out of the concealed location as her muscles had stiffened in the cramped position. Her lower body was numb from the cold water. Taking her time to avoid any unnecessary splashing or rustling of brush, she made it to a standing position. Her legs were both asleep, and she had to stand still for several minutes to allow the blood to start flowing and the feeling to return. With her left hand bandaged in her scarf and her right hand clutching her pistol, she didn't have a free hand to help stabilize herself.

Hiding in the dark for hours on end, she had ample time to get lost in her thoughts. Reconsidering if her career choice as an investigative journalist was worth all the risks, she envisioned how her life would be if she were a simple housewife. Just days ago, such a thought would have been outlandish to her. But now, after meeting Conner and having a near-death experience, maybe married life wasn't so bad after all. Perhaps Conner was right. Maybe she was missing the bigger picture? Who was Sandy Jane Elliot really? Had she spent so much of her life trying to prove everyone wrong that she never noticed when they were right?

Her thoughts also went back to her father. While she loved the man dearly, she also despised him for the occupation that he seemed to choose over his family. Working for the OSS and later the CIA, he was gone often and missed much of her childhood. While she never knew exactly what he did for the government, she knew his work was highly important. She was proud of him yet she could never bring herself to tell him. As a strong-willed, emotional teenager, she intentionally made things difficult for the man. Now that he was missing in action, she regretted how she treated him when she was young.

Sandy tried to take a step to test if the feeling had sufficiently returned to her legs. A sharp sensation of pins and needles quickly let her know she had to wait another minute before trying to move. Her thoughts returned to her father. He had gone missing when she was seventeen and the CIA placed her into protective custody because of some classified threat. Like an emotional teenager, she rebelled against the authority figures in her life and as soon as she was able, she refused the protection.

A realization occurred to her when she thought back to her childhood about her father, she pictured him looking like Conner Price. That made her realize all the similarities between the two men. From the occupation to the personality to the intellectual confidence, Conner must have been what her father was like when not viewed through the eyes of an emotional bratty child. Perhaps that was what drew her to Conner. While he frustrated her, she felt safe and comfortable with him. Either way, she very much missed her father...and she missed Conner.

Taking another test step, she could tell the feeling had returned to her legs. As she started to walk, she was quickly reminded of the intense pain from the blisters on her heels. Her water-logged boots only increased the friction. It was clear she would need to remove her boots if she intended to trek miles in the woods. Once out of the water and onto the other side of the river bank, she knelt down and slowly removed each boot and each soaked sock. The relief was almost instantaneous as the pressure was removed from the blistered raw skin on her heels. Sinking her boots in the river to conceal them, she tucked her socks into a pocket so she could use them later as a bandage. She would simply have to be careful as she walked. Keeping her feet close to the ground, she preferred stubbing her toes over stepping on sharp objects. It would be slow going in the dark, but at least she would make some degree of progress.

Returning her pistol into the chest pocket of her overalls, she would now have a free hand as she began her journey. Walking slowly, she held her hands out in front of her to feel for tree branches that could poke her in the face. Every few feet she would encounter a new obstacle or tree and would have to negotiate around by feel alone. It would be a long night at this pace and if she was unable to make enough distance in the dark, she may need to hide once again when the sun came up.

As she slowly moved through the terrain, she could hear the sounds of animals howling in the distance. Wondering if they were the wolves, coyotes, or humans communicating like animals, she couldn't decide which was more frightening. Encountering a large fallen log blocking her path, she attempted to climb over it in the dark. Placing her bare foot down on the other side, the slippery moss-covered surface failed to provide adequate traction. When she placed her weight onto her foot, she slipped and fell to the ground. The impact, as well as trying to stop the fall with her injured hand, was incredibly painful.

Sandy lay on the ground, sobbing quietly, as her hand throbbed painfully with each beat of her heart. While she was raised a Christian, she abandoned organized religion when her father disappeared. It had been years since she prayed. She knew that in times of extreme stress or fear, such as during war, all people will believe in a higher power. She could clearly hear her father's voice saying "there are no atheists in a foxhole".

CHAPTER 41

The forty-five-minute drive in the dark from the search site to the coroner in Marinette offered plenty of time for Conner to process all of the information. He focused on the many aspects of the investigation, from the search for the pilots to the man he had just shot, and especially, if Sandy was safe. If she was still alive, it would likely be a very long night for her. His mind kept wandering off of the investigation and onto the conversations they had shared. He enjoyed spending time with her and it made him second-guess his career choices. Could he be someone who could settle down in a little home with a white picket fence? While the mundane life had never appealed to him before, maybe he was the one missing the bigger picture.

As the ambulance he was following pulled up to the Marinette General Hospital, Conner parked in the adjacent parking lot. After retrieving the investigative camera and crime scene kit from the trunk, he followed the two men pushing the gurney. Once inside the hospital, they traveled through a labyrinth of hallways until they came to an empty examination room. After removing the body from the bag, they placed it on a table for the coroner.

Moments later, the sheriff entered the room with a younger man Conner assumed to be his son-in-law.

"Agent Price, this is our County Coroner, Noah Fleming."

Shaking the man's hand, Conner said, "Thanks for doing this at such a late hour. I really appreciate it."

"I'm happy to help," said the man in an unconvincing tone. It was apparent his father-in-law had insisted he come in at the late hour in an effort to accommodate the Air Force and possibly gain some political points.

"But I'm not exactly sure what you want me to look for. The man was clearly killed by law enforcement and the death was witnessed by two of you."

Conner, assuming the man lacked the training of a modern forensic pathologist, knew he would need to conduct the examination himself. He just needed the man to be present from a jurisdictional perspective. As the man appointed by the elected sheriff, he had the legal authority to conduct the exam.

Conner explained, "A couple of reasons actually. First is because it was an officer-involved shooting. The Air Force OSI will be conducting its own investigation in addition to the one the sheriff's office will do. You know how the feds are, they want everything documented in triplicate. The second thing is this man's body may hold clues."

"Clues to what?" asked the sheriff.

"Well, I'm not exactly sure just yet. But I know if we put him in the ground without examining him, when we do have questions, it will be too late to get the answers."

"Do you mind?" asked Conner, indicating he wanted to examine the corps.

"No. Go ahead and do what you need to do," replied the coroner.

"Sheriff, was that a public library I saw across the street?" asked Conner.

"Yeah."

"If one of your deputies has an after-hours key, we could really use a book to help us decipher the meaning of his tattoos. Any books on Vikings, Norse Gods, Mythology, etcetera."

"OK," said the sheriff as he turned to give a command to a deputy that was waiting in the hallway.

"Let's start by photographing and removing his clothing and placing them in a paper bag. That way we can send them to the crime lab for analysis."

"Crime lab?" asked the sheriff. "That sounds expensive. I'm not sure we have the budget for that sort of expense."

"Not to worry, the FBI crime lab will do it for us. But I'm pretty sure Wisconsin also has one now, probably down in Madison. Most states operate a crime lab nowadays. If there is an expense, the Air Force will pick up the tab."

Examining the clothing, it was something you would expect to see a hundred years ago on a mountain man. The jacket and leggings were made of buckskin, soft suede leather from the hide of a deer. The clothing was trimmed with a fringe, a functional item that allowed the garment to shed moisture and dry faster. The fringe acted as a series of wicks to disperse the water. They also served as camouflage, breaking up the outline of a human form, allowing the wearer to better blend into the environment.

Looking at the clothing, sheriff said "It looks like he copied his look from that Disney series I watched with my grandson a few weeks ago."

"*Davy Crocket and the Wild Frontier,*" chimed in the coroner.

"I think this guy was probably sporting this look long before Walt Disney made that mini-series," commented Conner, while examining the man's moccasin footwear.

Conner removed his camera and connected the cumbersome flash device. "That's a pretty fancy camera you have there," said the sheriff.

Showing it to the men, Conner said, "It's a Brownie Flash Six-20." The square metal camera body used 620-size film and featured an optical vision finder and even had a built-in close-up lens.

After photographing the body clothed, they removed the garments for processing. Now that the body was naked, Conner asked the coroner to complete a sketch, identifying the exact locations of all of the bullet wounds.

The coroner noted six bullet wounds on the anterior side of the body. Three in the upper chest cavity and three in the abdomen.

"I thought you shot him with a five-shot revolver. Did you reload and shoot him again?" asked the sheriff.

"Looking down at the wounds, Conner said, "The larger hole in the right side of his abdomen is an exit wound. That was one of Agent Goldens bullets that didn't hit bone and penetrated out the front. Good thing I was on the ground when he fired or that round could have hit me as well.

Looking at the wounds in the chest, one of the bullets was directly over the location of the man's heart. Examining the wound, the sheriff said, "This round right here was a kill shot. Why did agent Golden shoot him in the back after that?"

Continuing to take photographs, Conner explained, "The entire situation lasted about three seconds. While my bullet to the heart may have eventually been fatal, the man didn't stop his aggressive action until he had lost enough blood to cause him to lose consciousness. The man was still approaching me with a huge knife and I was on the ground with an unloaded weapon. I thank God that Don shot the man. In doing so, he saved my life."

"That makes sense," said the sheriff.

"There are really only three things that will stop aggressive activity in a gunfight. The first is a central nervous system hit (brain and spinal cord) that turns off the subject's ability to fight. The second is exsanguination (the loss of blood). When a person loses enough blood and can no longer pump oxygenated blood to the brain, they lose consciousness. The third is psychological. Most sane people will stop aggressive activity due to pain or fear of death. That's why many people fall to the ground with a non-life-threatening bullet wound. If the person is intoxicated, on drugs, experiencing adrenalin or some sort of psychological driving force, they will continue to fight until the body can no longer function."

The three men worked together to roll the large man over onto his stomach. Conner took more photographs while the coroner sketched the posterior of the body. "I see four hits. Two in the upper back, one in the back of the right upper arm, and one in the low back, which likely penetrated out the front of the abdomen. One of his five rounds must have missed."

"Well, that's nine out of ten shots that hit their target during a highly dynamic situation. I would say that is pretty good shooting," said the sheriff.

"Yeah, thank God for accuracy. I would be a little happier with more power and higher capacity weapon. A Government model 1911 chambered in .45ACP has much more power and carries two more bullets. While the Air Force has plenty of them in inventory, the OSI wants us to be like our FBI counterparts and carry the .38 special."

Pulling out a tape measure, Conner unrolled it and laid it on the table next to the dead man. Seventy-six inches noted the coroner on his notepad. Doing the math in his head, Conner said, "That makes him six feet three inches tall. I would estimate his body weight at around two-hundred ten pounds. Age would likely be in the late twenties."

Examining the man's hands, Conner said, "His hands are heavily calloused from manual labor. His nails are long and filthy. They appear to have been trimmed with a knife or an uneven cutting tool leaving a jagged edge."

Examining the teeth, he stated for the coroner, "There is no evidence of any professional dental work. Three molars are missing on the right side. It looks to be the result of old trauma."

Stepping back and looking at the body in its entirety, Conner opined, "This guy has led a hard life. Is it possible he spent his entire life in those woods?"

"I'm certain of it," said the sheriff. "That clan of mountain people has lived back in those woods for as long as anyone can remember."

"That's incredible," said Conner, amazed at how this could be possible in the year 1955.

The men were interrupted by a knock on the exam room door. The sheriff opened the door and accepted a stack of books the deputy had collected from the library. Searching the titles, the sheriff held up the book "*Norse Mythology, the Religion of Our Fathers*, published in the year 1875.

"This one has some drawings of symbols similar to the tattoos and brands on the body," said the sheriff.

"Sounds good," said Conner, while taking close-up photographs. "See if you can find a match or something close."

Placing the open book on a tray next to the exam table, it displayed a chart of symbols called "*the Rune.*"

As the sheriff scanned the seventy-five-year-old textbook, he paraphrased what he had read.

"This mythological language is called the Rune and was translated by the Norse God Odin. Odin stabbed himself with a spear and hung upside down in a tree for nine days in order to gain the knowledge of the Rune alphabet."

The sheriff continued, "These symbols not only represent letters, but also have deeper meaning and were even thought to possess metaphysical or magical powers. These symbols were carved into trees, stones and even marked the graves of heroes."

Looking up from the book, the sheriff said "I guess this guy was magic."

"Well, he sure as hell wasn't bulletproof," said Conner, while continuing to take close up photographs.

"I think the strange symbols the Air Force search team encountered in the woods were some bastardized variations of these symbols," said the sheriff.

"I agree," said Conner. "What are these three symbols that are tattooed on the man's right cheek?"

Scanning the book, the sheriff said, "The first one appears to represent heritage. Maybe he is a descendant of the group's leader or something. The second symbol means protection and the third means torch."

"What about this tree symbol on his left arm? It appears to be a brand rather than a tattoo."

Turning a few pages, the sheriff said, "That appears to represent the tree of life, called Yggdrasil. It is the tree that Odin hung upside down in to gain the knowledge of the Rune."

Using rubbing alcohol and a rag, Conner scrubbed the man's chest to remove the dried blood from around the bullet wounds. Under the blood was a large tattoo that looked like three animal horns intertwined. "What about this one?" asked Conner.

Turning a few more pages, the sheriff said, "That is the Triple Horn of Odin. They are drinking horns apparently. It goes on to say it represents the three times Odin drank from the well of knowledge."

"OK, now for the interesting one," said Conner, as he held up the dead man's right arm bearing what looked like a Nazi Swastika tattoo.

"According to this book, that symbol goes back a couple thousand years and represents strength, order, prosperity and good luck."

"Interesting, I guess Hitler stole the symbol from the Vikings. That makes sense now that I think about it as the Germanic people are descendants of them."

The association between Vikings and Nazi Germany transported Conner back to his prisoner-of-war experience ten years earlier. Every night he would go to sleep listening to the sound of the German commandant's record player broadcast across the camp on loudspeakers. He would always play the same song, "*Ride of the Valkyries*" by the German composer Richard Wagner. The famous song, composed in 1854, was a favorite among German military officers.

"Conner? Conner? You still with us?" asked the coroner.

"Yeah, sorry...my mind wandered to another place for a second. What was your question?"

"Why do you think the tattoos are blue and not green?"

"I suppose it is due to whatever material they used for ink. What does the book say about it?"

Looking up from the book one more time, the sheriff said, "It says they used wood ash to make the ink."

"Well, they are a resilient bunch, that's for sure. If things don't go well tomorrow you may have a few more of these guys on tables around here. We are going to locate our two pilots and that reporter; and these people can't avoid it any longer. One way or another, this clan is going to join the twentieth century.

CHAPTER 42

The sun was just starting to shine through the trees as the search teams assembled. Looking at his watch, it was five thirty. Now that the size of the search team had grown considerably, Major Gibson stood on a Jeep to elevate himself over the crowd while he conducted the initial day's brief.

Today there were more than eighty men in attendance from the Air Force, National Guard and multiple law enforcement agencies. The abduction of the reporter and the officer involved shooting the night before had dictated the increased presence. The fact that the area to be searched was greatly narrowed down and the addition of the helicopter had increased the odds of a successful mission.

Today's search team was equipped differently than the day prior. This morning, every man was armed. Many of the civilian law enforcement officers carried shotguns and revolvers while the Air Force Policemen carried M1 Carbines.

"Can I have your attention!" shouted Major Gibson. While it was phrased as a question, his tone indicated it was an order.

"This morning we will have four separate ground search teams. Each team will consist of ten men from multiple agencies. The ranking civilian law enforcement officer in each team will have jurisdiction over law enforcement matters while the ranking Air Force member will have jurisdiction over the search and rescue operation. Each team will have both a radio operator and a medic assigned. Each team leader has a detailed map indicating your predesignated search patterns. Stay on course unless directed by the command post of an updated search grid."

"I will be operating in the airborne search team. Now that we have a helicopter, we will be more effective as we can fly much lower and slower than the fixed-wing aircraft we were using previously. The odds are finally moving in our favor. Are there any questions?"

Hearing none, Major Gibson directed each team to the awaiting trucks to transport them to their designated search zone.

Don looked over to Conner and asked if they should tag along with one of the search teams.

"That's up to you. I want to get on board that helicopter to see how that crazy thing stays in the air," replied Conner, when actually he felt riding on the helicopter was his best chance to find Sandy.

"Should I go with you?"

"Your call, but it may serve you well to hang back at the command post and get some face time with Colonel Roberts. I think he is finally starting to warm up to OSI."

"That's actually a pretty good idea," said Don.

"OK, I am going to go take a look at that aircraft."

The helicopter was an amazing invention and had drastically changed aviation over the past few years. The USAF purchased fifty helicopters two years earlier during the Korean War. These helicopters had been used with great success as an air ambulance, transporting wounded soldiers directly from combat zones to a Mobile Army Surgical Hospitals (M.A.S.H.). This new style of aircraft was saving lives that otherwise would have perished on the frozen foreign soil. The aviator in Conner simply had to know more.

The Sikorsky H-19 Chickasaw was a multi-purpose helicopter and could actually serve as a troop transport. This helicopter was in the process of changing Army doctrine regarding battlefield troop deployment as it was large enough to carry soldiers into battle. This gave the US and its allies a significant advantage in combat mobility. The silver helicopter had a thick yellow stripe painted on it and the black letters spelled out the word RESCUE across the side. Walking up to the two pilots standing beside it, Conner introduced himself.

"Good morning, I'm Conner Price."

Shaking hands with the pilots, they introduced themselves as Captain Brad Pfeffer and Lieutenant Dave Wheaton.

"Are you the OSI Agent that shot the crazy mountain man last night?" asked Wheaton.

"Yeah, one of them at least. I was hoping to catch a ride with you this morning on the search. Do you have any extra room?"

"That would be up to Major Gibson. We just fly the thing; he is in charge of the search mission."

"OK, I will check with him. How many passengers does this thing hold and what is its range?"

Patting the side of his aircraft, Captain Pfeffer said, "This thing is a beast. Beside the two of us, we can carry ten troops or eight stretchers. She has a cruising speed of 85mph and has a range of 450 miles. Of course, that range is in ideal weather conditions with only the pilots on board."

"This thing is amazing."

Looking at the heavy-duty winch fixed to the left side of the aircraft, Conner asked about its capabilities.

Captain Pfeffer replied, "It is a mechanical hoist that can lower a cable down as far as one hundred and fifty feet. It's great for lowering people down or picking them up in locations where we can't land this thing. We can use it for plucking a man off of a ship at sea, from the side of a cliff or like today, from a forest with a heavy tree canopy."

"This thing will change aviation for sure. I wish we had this beast during WW2. It's the perfect machine for picking up pilots shot down behind enemy lines, especially ones that went down in the ocean."

The thought transported him back to the day he was shot down. Most Americans back home never really understood the danger that combat pilots faced in WW2. The statistics were daunting with fifty-one percent of aircrew being killed in action, twelve percent being wounded and thirteen percent becoming a prisoner of war. Only twenty-four percent of aircrew members would survive the war unscathed.

Conner snapped back to the real world as Captain Pfeffer was explaining how the rotor and stabilizer worked. Unlike a fixed wing pilot, a helicopter pilot uses both his hands and feet to control the aircraft.

"I guess you need to be pretty coordinated to fly one of these," said Conner joking.

Captain Pfeffer replied, "Do you know why an airplane pilot is usually smiling and a helicopter pilot is scowling? Because a helicopter doesn't want to fly."

"I don't follow."

"A fixed wing pilot can add thrust, and eventually the plane will achieve lift all by itself. It obeys commands like go left, go right, go up or down. You can even take your hand completely off the control yolk and the plane will pretty much continue to do what you last told it to. A helicopter is an entirely different animal. Flying it is like rubbing your head while patting your stomach. You always need to be doing something with your hands and feet to stay airborne. You can never remove your right hand from the control."

Thinking about what the helicopter pilot said, Conner smiled and said, "Well you better spit your gum out before I climb aboard this thing. On that note, what damage did those bullets do?"

"We went over this thing with a fine-toothed comb. We found two bullet entrance holes on the side of the passenger compartment. One of the bullets was stopped inside by a box of sea rations and the other one exited through the other side without hitting anything critical. We did a test flight last night and all systems were a go."

"Good enough for me, let me go find Major Gibson."

Conner walked over to the command post where the major was looking over maps with Colonel Roberts.

"Morning Conner," said Major Gibson.

"Morning Bob, Colonel," replied Conner. "Do you think you have an extra seat in the helicopter for me this morning?"

Scratching his head, Major Gibson ran over the assignments in his head. "It seats ten but we need to carry two stretchers for the downed pilots. Besides myself, I need a radio operator, two medics, and a spot for that reporter if we can find her. I was bringing a couple of my Air Policemen for manpower and security. If you don't mind helping out, should we need it, I can swap you for one of my MP's."

"Happy to help with whatever tasks you need, major," replied Conner.

"Sounds good. We will be taking off in half an hour. I just want to give the ground search teams a few minutes to get into place. That way we don't waste fuel and cut our air time short before they are ready to go."

"Perfect, thank you."

"How are you doing after shooting that guy last night?" asked the colonel.

"I'm doing ok. It's still hard to believe it even happened. He came right at me while both of us had him at gunpoint. A man that size with a crazy religious ideology is hard to stop. He soaked up those .38 special rounds like a sponge."

"How many did he take?" asked Major Gibson.

"We fired ten rounds and scored nine hits between the two of us. One of my first rounds struck him in the heart but it still took several seconds for him to lose enough blood to drop the knife and lose consciousness. If your ground teams encounter a group of these warriors, they will have a fight on their hands."

"Let's just hope it doesn't come to that," said Colonel Roberts.

"Unfortunately, if your missing pilots are still alive, they are likely being held by this group. We know Otto planted Legend's helmet to lead us in the wrong direction and we found a new issue pilot survival knife in his shack. We were attacked when we were following his tracks into the forest. I think it's obvious that they have come into contact with at least one of your men. And let's just pray the eyeball I found didn't belong to one of the pilots."

Conner could see the emotion in Colonel Roberts' face. It was apparent he was thinking about men he had lost under his command.

"Whether alive or not, we are going to bring those boy's home…and I don't care how many of these bastards we have to put in the ground to do it," said the Colonel.

CHAPTER 43

As the sunlight was shining through the forest, Sandy was both relieved as well as terrified. She was happy as she could now see while navigating the rough terrain, yet feared she would be seen by the men pursuing her. Her bare feet were bloodied and in pain as she had spent the night stepping on and kicking rocks and sticks in the dark. Now that she could see the morning sun, she was able to get her bearings. Knowing that the sun rises in the east and sets in the west, she determined she had been traveling to the northeast. While she didn't have a planned destination or knowledge of how far she would need to travel, she pressed on. Looking for a road or some form of civilization, she was just happy to be gaining distance from her pursuers her.

The more sunlight penetrated through the trees, the faster she was able to move. Ignoring her growing thirst and hunger, she was determined to make it to safety. As she came over a ridge, the terrain on the other side was less dense and extended on a downward slope. Grateful she would be able to move faster, Sandy paused briefly next to a thick tree to observe the area in front of her before exposing herself.

As she scanned the trees, she observed two strange symbols hanging from branches. These symbols, formed out of sticks and animal antlers, reminded her of some evil warning from a Brothers Grimm fairytale. She was certain these were the same types of symbols that the airman had encountered during their search for the missing pilots.

This reminded her that there was a military search party in the woods. While she had no clue if they were even operating in the same forest as her, at least there was a potential for rescue. She would love nothing more than to see Special Agent Conner Price walking through the forest and calling her name. She smiled to herself, imagining how that could be the perfect ending to the novel she would someday write. She also thought to herself, that could be the perfect next chapter in her own life's story.

Taking a seat on a large rock, she took the opportunity to examine her feet now that she had some light to see by. In addition to the large blisters on her heels, she had several painful cuts and abrasions from traveling in the dark. Pulling her socks out of her pockets, they were still damp with river water. Using them for protection, she put the socks back on her feet but rolled them back down over themselves so it did not cover the blisters on her heels. This also doubled the layer on the bottom of her feet. While it offered only limited protection, it was psychologically comforting as she didn't know how far she would need to travel. She wanted to make better time now that she could see where she was going.

Off to her left, she could hear the sound of something crashing through the forest. Lying flat on the ground to conceal herself behind some brush, she waited and watched. Moments later, she saw a teenage boy staggering through the brush. He appeared injured but was still moving with a sense of urgency while looking over his shoulder. Dressed in buckskins and moccasins, he was holding a hand over a belly wound that was bleeding heavily. Looking back as he staggered, his foot caught an exposed tree root causing him to fall. He lay on the ground, wincing in pain, just ten yards from where she was hiding.

While Sandy didn't consider the boy to be a threat, she was more concerned about what he was running from. Reaching into her chest pocket, she withdrew her small pistol and held it at the ready just in case. Looking in the direction of where the boy came, she saw a tall figure stepping out from behind a tree. While she wasn't sure, he could easily have been one of the men chasing her last night. While he was incredibly large, he moved through the woods with stealth. She could see him approaching, but had yet to hear him make a sound.

She could see the fear in the young man's eyes as he attempted to get up and continue running. Once he got back onto his unstable legs, the man pursuing him was closing in and walking at a steady pace about twenty yards away. Pulling a tomahawk from his belt, the large man threw it with great force at the injured boy. Spinning as it traveled through the air, the weapon glanced off the boy's shoulder, leaving a deep gash and knocking him back onto the ground. After striking the boy, the weapon landed on the ground just a few yards from Sandy's hiding place.

The large man walked past the boy lying on the ground to retrieve his tomahawk. Sandy quietly thumbed off the safety of her pistol and took aim at the man in the event she was spotted. He bent over and picked up the weapon, before turning back towards the boy.

"Uncle, please! You don't have to do this," said the boy.

"You disgraced yourself and angered the Gods. Thordis has commanded your sacrifice."

"I love her and she is pregnant with my child," said the boy.

"You have damned us all by your actions. By running away, you have lost even more honor. The Valkyrie will never allow you to enter Valhalla now."

The large man raised the tomahawk over his head in preparation to take the life of his own nephew.

Bang! A single round from Sandys pistol struck the large man in his muscled upper back.

Turning around in both shock and anger, the large man was trying to determine what had happened.

The small caliber round had not incapacitated the large man as she had hoped. Standing up from her concealed position, she prepared to fire additional rounds before trying to run from the new threat.

The man started walking towards her as his fist tightened on the handle of his weapon. Sandy, worried her underpowered pistol would not cause much internal damage to the man's body, took careful aim at his head. Bang! Bang! Bang!

Sandy watched in disbelief as the small bullets ripped jagged lacerations in the flesh of the man's forehead, but seemed to deflect off the thick, angled frontal bone of his skull. As the man raised his tomahawk over his head to strike her, she took careful aim for his left eye and fired once more.

The round struck its target, causing him to stop in his tracks. She knew the best chance of penetrating the skull and striking the man's brain was through the eye socket. While the large man didn't fall from the wound, it was apparent the internal trauma stopped his aggressive actions. He stood there with a blank look on his face as the weapon fell from his relaxed hand.

With only a single bullet left, Sandy slowly backed away from the man. She watched as the injured boy struggled to get to his feet once again before walking over to his now catatonic uncle. Reaching down, the boy picked up the tomahawk and placed his other hand on the older man's shoulder.

"You shall see Valhalla, uncle," said the teen, before striking the large man in the right temple with the tomahawk. Sandy watched in shock as the lifeless body collapsed to the ground.

Evaluating if the wounded boy was a threat to her or not, her instinct told her he wasn't.

"Thank you for helping me, my name is Anders," said the teen.

"I'm Sandy. Do you know how to get to civilization?"

"What is that?" he asked.

Trying to think in terms the sheltered teen may understand, she said, "Is there a community outside of yours that is forbidden?"

Still confused by the question, Anders said, "We may go anywhere in Forest Egersund."

"How do you know where the forest ends?"

"The markings in the trees tell us."

Sandy was starting to piece together some of how the strange community functioned. The strange markings hanging in the trees were not an evil warning to outsiders, but a warning to the members of the Family. Thordis had used them as a fear tactic to prevent her group from communicating with outsiders and learning the truth.

Looking for more information, Sandy asked "What happens if you cross the boundary of the forest?"

"It is forbidden."

"Yes, I know that. But what is the consequence if you do?"

"There was only one-man Odin allowed to cross the boundary to the outside world."

"Is that Otto?" asked Sandy.

With a surprised look on his face, he said, "Yes, Otto. Do you know of him?"

Not sure how much truth she should share at this point, she said, "I spoke with him yesterday."

"Yesterday? He still lives?" asked Anders.

"Yes, he lives. Did you think otherwise?"

"I was not sure. He left when I was a child. I didn't think he could survive long outside the chosen forest."

Switching gears, Sandy started questioning the boy on why his uncle was trying to kill him.

"You called that man uncle. Why was he trying to kill you?"

Anders looked down towards the ground, the reason was obviously very emotional to the young man. "I fell in love with a girl named Randalin. I had always loved her. She is Otto's daughter and is in line to inherit the kingdom. The prophecy stated that she would bear the child of an injured warrior who descents from Asgard."

"Where is this Asgard?" asked Sandy.

"It is the place where the Gods live."

Anders continued, "If this warrior does not impregnate Randalin by her eighteenth year, she was to be sacrificed to Odin. As her birth year was approaching, we feared she would be killed by her great grand-mother, Thordis."

Starting to understand, she asked, "You slept with Randalin and gave her a child to prevent her from being sacrificed?"

Nodding, he said "Yes. We have always loved each other. In our thir-teenth year of life, we wanted to be joined together forever. My father and her father, Otto, were supportive of the union but Thordis forbade the marriage. Both our families objected to her decision, which caused a split in the community. But that night, Thordis had a vision from Odin. The Gods called for my father to be sacrificed and Otto to be banished from the forest. Odin also shared a prophecy that Randalin would be impregnated by a wounded warrior from Asgard before her eighteenth year. Their offspring would be a half God and lead our clan in the future."

Sandy was not surprised at the convenient timing of the vision, as the crazy charlatan they call their queen would seemingly do anything to protect her façade, even commit ritualized murder. This is an amazing story thought Sandy and would make a great novel in its own right. Snapping back into reality, she remembered she would need to survive the ordeal in order to accept her Pulitzer Prize.

Anders continued, "A few months ago, an injured warrior came from outside our forest to impregnate her. But we learned that the man was not really sent from Asgard. He was just an outsider taken from his boat by order of Thordis to deceive us. She had the man's eye gouged out and told us it was a sign from Odin. The marriage was not consummated as the man fought to his death trying to escape. Thordis had his head cut off and keeps it with her for counsel, just as Odin kept the head of Mimir."

Anders continued, "Randalin felt that if I gave her a child, the people would believe that the outsider had fathered it before he was beheaded. But Randalin became afraid of the wrath of Odin and confessed our plot to her great grandmother. Thordis ordered her to remain silent about being preg-nant and also ordered my sacrifice. Randalin helped me escape just before I was to be put to death. This man on the ground is my uncle. He was sent to track me down and sacrifice me in order to save our community from Odin's fiery wrath."

"Do you know the name of the outsider that was beheaded?" asked Sandy.

"She calls him Warden," said Anders.

Sandy couldn't imagine how this story could get more bizarre. She asked, "How will Thordis explain to the people when Randalin starts to show she is pregnant?"

Looking down in shame, he replied, "We should never have doubted the prophecy. Just as Thordis has foretold, a few days ago Odin sent not one, but two great warriors down from Asgard. Both were injured as the prophecy indicated. One hung upside down in a tree just as Odin had and the other impaled himself with a spear. One of these God's was intended to impregnate Randalin…but she is already with my child…I have damned my people to death."

Trying to piece the puzzle together, she asked, "Did these men fall from the sky?"

"Yes."

Knowing these two men were the missing pilots who had ejected from their airplane, Sandy asked, "Are these men still alive?

"Yes, but they are hurt badly. The fall from the heavens was great."

The conversation was interrupted by a strange sound coming from the distance. The chopping sound seemed to be getting closer as both of them looked up to the sky through an opening in the tree canopy. Moments later, they saw what Anders believed to be a silver beast flying overhead.

CHAPTER 44

Randalin sat alone on the wooden chair waiting to speak with Queen Thordis. She had been waiting all night for this conversation and dreading every minute of it. When she confessed her pregnancy to her great grand-mother days earlier, the queen's reaction was to sacrifice the boy she loved and the father of her unborn child. Now that she had helped him escape and told the God they call Legend of her pregnancy, Thordis would be even angrier.

Randalin was disappointed in her mother. Nanja knew that Thordis was an evil and controlling leader. Many in the clan believed her visions from Odin only came when it was essential for her to maintain power or get her way. Her mother had witnessed first-hand how the queen operates, especially after she banished the man she was joined to. The fact that her mother had turned her own daughter in was not a surprise, but disappointing all the same.

She could hear a door opening on the other side of the curtain. Moments later, her grandmother Gyda walked around the curtain. The old woman avoided making eye contact with her while she prepared the room for the queen's presentation. After lighting the incense and sage, she lit the torches that sat on each end of the curtain. Gyda glanced up just one time and Randalin could see the old woman had been crying.

Her grandmother was nothing like her great-grandmother. Gyda was a soft-spoken woman with a kind and gentle demeanor. This was not a good attribute among a warrior clan that desired to emulate their Viking ancestors. Thordis was controlling and abusive of her daughter, and kept her subservient her entire life. The blessings of the queen passed over Gyda to her daughter Nanja. And now, it appeared Randalin was about to lose whatever favor she had with the queen as well.

As the curtain was pulled back, exposing Thordis sitting on her new throne, both Gyda and Randalin dropped to their knees and placed their foreheads against the ground. Expecting Thordis to tell her to rise and have a seat, the instruction never came. Randalin was to remain in the subservient position during the entire conversation.

"You have failed me yet again Randalin. First by letting yourself be deflowered by that unworthy boy. Then by defying my order to have him sacrificed to Odin. I know you aided his escape, but not to worry, I have dispatched his uncle to complete the ceremony to the Gods. His head will be brought back to us soon enough, and shall be by your side during your own ceremony."

Randalin, with her forehead still pressed against the ground, wept aloud at the thought of the boy she loved being beheaded by his uncle.

"Please spare him! I will do whatever you ask of me, but please allow him to live," pleaded Randalin.

"It is too late for that...and it is too late for you. You have spoken our secrets to that false profit you call Legend. Both of you, as well as the one they call Ghost will be sacrificed when the sun is highest in the sky. Your sins have caused Odin to forsake us all. Our only chance is to offer this great sacrifice to the Gods and pray they spare us from a fiery destruction."

Randalin glanced over to Gyda in a plea for help with her eyes. Gyda, who was looking over to her grandchild, closed her eyes and returned her forehead to the floor in shame. She was ashamed that she was not strong enough to intervene. She had been subservient her entire life and had never been able to stand up to her mother. But was it time for a change? Was the one they call Ghost, correct? Had she been called upon by Odin to lead the Family?

Raising the courage to finally speak up, Gyda pleaded, "Queen Thordis, I beg you for mercy. Please spare this young child."

Shocked at the insubordination, Thordis didn't know how to respond.

As the three sat in silence for over a minute, Gyda made another plea for mercy, "Mother, please spare this child. I know you can find it in your heart. She is of your blood…She is of our blood."

Finding her response in anger, Thordis replied, "She shall not be spared, and you Gyda, will perform the ceremony for your petulance."

Randalin wept, while glancing over to her grandmother. Gyda, ashamed she was not strong enough to protect her granddaughter, closed her eyes and kept her head pressed against the floor and wept.

CHAPTER 45

Hearing hammering outside, Casper was awakened from his sleep. It was daylight and the sun was shining in through the window. Taking an assessment of his physical condition, he could feel his lower body once again. There was pain in his left leg and his lower back every time he tried to move.

Thinking about his interaction with Thordis the night before, he worried he had pushed too hard. While he felt he was successful in driving a wedge between the two older women, he wasn't sure Gyda had the fortitude to take control of the community. At least while he was gone, Legend was able to have a conversation with Randalin and she agreed to go get help. Now they just had to stall for time until she returned. Hopefully Legend's condition would hold out as he had been coughing terribly during the night.

"Legend. Legend! Can you hear me?" asked Casper, after not getting a response from his friend and partner. Fearing the infection was progressing, he knew time was not on their side. Hoping that the ruse they were using to manipulate their captors would be successful, it may not work fast enough.

Casper heard the sound of people approaching and unlocking the door. Hopeful it was someone there to rescue them. He was disappointed when two large hooded men entered the room carrying the buckskin, they used as a litter. They moved past Casper to Legends partition.

"How is he doing?" asked Casper.

The men did not respond.

"Can I speak with Nanja?"

Still not responding, the men carrying Legend passed him and continued out of the room. He wondered where they were taking him and if he was still alive. About ten minutes later, the two men returned and placed the buckskin on the ground next to Casper. After placing him on top of it, they lifted him up and carried him outside as well. The sun was bright overhead, making it difficult for him to see. The movement caused excruciating pain in his back and leg, so much so that it was difficult to breathe. Trying hard not to scream, he fought through the urge by clenching his teeth and balling his fists.

As the men placed him on the ground, they lifted him to a sitting position and sat him with a hard surface against his back. It was a six-foot tall log that had been stuck in the ground like a totem pole. They tied leather straps around his neck and waist, both to hold him in the seated position but also to restrain him. Once again, his wrists were bound together. This new development led Casper to believe they were no longer being considered divine beings sent from Asgard. It looked like he had pushed his ruse too far and angered Thordis who feared the potential loss of control.

Once he was secured, the men moved away, allowing Casper to see his surroundings. There were two similar poles planted in the ground in the form of a triangle. Casper was fastened to one while Legend and Randalin were fastened to the others. All three were secured in a fashion to face inward at each other. Legend's body hung limp as he was unconscious. While Casper worried about his friend's condition, he thought it may be for the best that he was not awake to experience what was to come.

The young girl looked down at the ground and wept. Casper recognized her as the girl who helped Nanja bathe him after he was captured. He assumed things had not gone well overnight. She must have been caught trying to leave and get help after speaking with Legend.

"Randalin," said Casper, trying to get the girls attention.

She looked up with a defeated look on her young face.

"What do they intend to do with us?"

"When the sun is highest in the sky, they will sacrifice us to Odin."

Looking up to check the sun's position in the sky, he estimated it was around 10 o'clock. They probably had about two hours left for the rescue team to find them. A true optimist, Casper was starting to lose hope for the first time since ejecting from his jet.

"Why are they sacrificing us if we are divine beings sent from Asgard?"

Randalin replied, "Thordis has said you are a false profit spreading lies."

"Do you think I am a false profit?"

"I believe you were sent to help me. Thordis is afraid of losing power and has said many false things to the clan. I no longer believe she is speaking with the Gods."

"Randalin, do you believe I possess knowledge greater than Thordis?"

"Yes, of course I believe that. Thordis changes what the Gods tell her when it is convenient for her."

"Do the people know this?"

"Yes, many speak of it in private but they fear her wrath. When someone challenges her rule, they are sacrificed to the Gods."

Well, that's more effective than having a civil debate thought Casper.

"Randalin, listen to me and I will tell you what I believe. I will share with you the path to the afterlife."

Looking up with an amazed look on her face, she asked, "You can take me to Valhalla?"

"Yes, but things are not as you have been told all your life. There is only one God and through him is the path to eternal life.

"Only one God?"

"Yes. One God created the heavens and the earth. Two thousand years ago, he sent his son, Jesus, not to condemn the world, but to seek and save the lost. Jesus died for our sins and rose from the dead three days later, enabling us to move from physical death to eternal life in Heaven."

Randalin looked at him with a confused but hopeful look on her face. She asked, "So even a person like myself, who has lied and been deceitful, can still get to Valhalla?"

"Yes, that is correct," said Casper, not having the time to explain the intricacies of Christianity to her as the sun was rising in the sky.

"But I will die soon. Is it not too late for me?"

"It is not too late for you. Jesus died while nailed to a wooded post. He was positioned between two others who were also nailed to wooden posts. These two others were both sinner and thieves. One of the thieves beside Jesus realized the error of his ways, trusted in God, repented and was promised by Jesus: "Truly. I say to you, today you will be with me in paradise."

Casper continued, "Eternal life in heaven is possible for all. You don't need a Valkyrie to fly over a battlefield and select you. All you need to do is ask him into your heart through prayer and accept him as your lord and savior."

"This is all I must do?" asked Randalin.

"Would you like to pray with me?" asked Casper.

Crying, the young girl nodded her head as she wept.

As the two prayed together, she felt a warm calm come over her. She was no longer afraid as Casper ended the prayer with amen. When he opened his eyes back up and looked at the young girl, she looked like she was at peace.

Smiling and looking up to the heavens, she asked, "Does the one God have Valkyries that fly in the sky?"

Not sure what she was asking, he replied, "There are beings called angels. Sometimes they are known to fly."

Randalin smiled and said, "I can hear their wings as they approach."

Confused by her remark, he stopped talking and listened intently to his surroundings. He could also hear the angels in the distance, but the sound of the angels' wings he heard belonged to the rotor of a USAF rescue helicopter.

CHAPTER 46

"That's not a beast, it's a helicopter! They are here to help us!" said Sandy, as she waved her hands above her head in hopes they would see her through the trees. The helicopter was just above the treetops, about one hundred-fifty feet in the air. The only thing she had to waive was her scarf that was tied around her hand covering her wound. As she tried to remove it, she felt pain as the blood had clotted, sticking the fabric to her skin.

Having a single bullet left, she wondered if the men in the helicopter could hear the small caliber pistol over the sound of the engine. While she was certain they would not be able to, she had to try. Raising the small nickel-plated weapon over her head, she fired her single round into a safe direction. The helicopter was so loud she could barely hear the report of the pistol. There was no way the men in the helicopter could have heard it.

Sitting in the open doorway of the H-19 Chickasaw, Conner was still amazed at the aerodynamics of such an aircraft. The ability to hover over a single area was not a possibility when he was flying in the war. His thoughts were put on hold as he saw a flash come from the forest floor.

Looking down, he was trying to determine where it had come from. The tree canopy was thick and he was trying to look at the areas between the trees. Tapping the knee of Major Gibson, who was sitting next to him, Conner pointed to his own eyes, then to the area beneath them, to indicate he saw something. He then motioned to bring the helicopter back around to that area. Major Gibson stood up and spoke to the pilot, who slowly brought the helicopter back around.

"There it is again!" shouted Conner. Unable to be heard over the sound of the helicopter, he pointed down with his finger. As the powerful wash of the helicopter rotor blew the leaves and tree branches, Conner was able to see through the canopy momentarily. He felt a huge sense of relief when he saw Sandy, waving at the helicopter and holding something shiny and reflective in her hand.

Unbuckling himself from his seat, Conner stepped over to the hoist and placed his leg inside one of the straps. Looking back at the major, he indicated he wanted to be lowered down on the cable. The major shook his head no, preferring to contact the ground teams and have them move to the area to investigate.

Conner looked over at the major and forcefully pointed downward, indicating he wanted to be lowered immediately.

Reluctantly, the major reached over and took hold of the winch controls and started to lower Conner down on the cable. Not sure of what was waiting for him on the ground, Conner drew the government model 1911 pistol from his waistband and held it at the ready. As he slowly penetrated the tree canopy, he could see Sandy standing next to the body of a large, seemingly incapacitated mountain man. A few yards away was a smaller man dressed in buckskins, on his knees with his forehead pressed to the ground.

Not sure what the threat was, Conner kept his pistol at the ready and he was slowly lowered towards the ground.

Sandy, elated that a rescuer was being lowered down to her, averted her eyes as the powerful wash of the helicopter was blowing debris around violently. Shielding her eyes as she looked up, she was amazed to see her hero, Special Agent Conner Price, dangling before her. As soon as his feet hit the ground, she hugged him tightly. While her embrace was certainly welcome, Conner was still unsure of the threat on the ground.

Sandy, aware of Conner's concern, pointed to Anders and said, "Conner, he helped me and he is wounded."

"We'll take care of him," yelled Conner over the sound of the helicopter.

Pointing to the direction the boy came from, Sandy continued, "He came from that direction. That's where the downed pilots are. They are injured and are being held captive at the village."

"OK! Tell that to Major Gibson as soon as you get up to the helicopter. He will radio the ground teams."

Conner placed the harness around Sandy and instructed her how to hold on. When she was ready to go, he looked up to the helicopter and signaled to raise the hoist. As the slack in the cable started to get taken up, Sandy pulled Conner close to her, kissing him on the lips. Looking into each other's eyes, she was slowly lifted away from him on a slow ride up to the waiting helicopter.

Conner, torn between watching the beautiful woman ascend and securing the scene, he knew he had to turn his attention to the wounded boy on the ground. As he tried to talk to the boy, it was clear he thought Conner and the helicopter were some sort of magic beasts. He was terrified and the noise and wind from the machine were a new experience for him. Conner examined the wound on the boy's shoulder, then forcefully rolled him over and found a stab wound in his abdomen.

It took about five minutes for Sandy to be raised up to the helicopter and the medic to be lowered to the ground. To Conner, it felt like an hour, as he tried to hold pressure on the boy's wound without any medical supplies. Once the medic made it to the ground, he started to provide care to Anders. Conner took the opportunity to go examine the large corps left on the ground. Very similar to the man he killed the night before, this man had the same basic tattoos and brands. Conner reached down and picked up the bloody tomahawk that was lying next to him. Placing it in his own belt, he returned to help the medic try and get Anders into the harness.

The boy was scared and violently resisted having the harness placed around him. The frustrated medic yelled to Conner over the sound of the helicopter, "He's bleeding out! If we don't get him up there now, he is going to die!" Hearing this, Conner made a fist and punched Anders hard in the face, knocking him unconscious.

"Well, that's one way to do it!" shouted the surprised medic at the actions of the special agent. The two men then worked to place the limp body into the harness. Once Anders was secured, the medic motioned for the men in the helicopter to hoist him up. Once he was being lifted off the ground, the medic asked about the dead body.

"That guy is dead. We don't have time right now to load him up. Just remember where it is and we'll send the ground team over or come back later. Right now, we need to go rescue the wounded pilots, that's the top priority!"

"Roger that!" the medic yelled in reply.

Waiting for the cable to return, Conner pulled out his military compass and took a bearing of the direction Sandy said the boy came from. That would give them a better chance of locating the village and the pilots once they were back in the air and the forest blended together.

When the cable was finally lowered once again, both Conner and the medic placed one leg into the harness and held onto the cable with both hands. The medic gave the signal to hoist them up and the two were slowly lifted off the ground.

CHAPTER 47

Pulling the compass from its pouch, Master Sergeant Tratnyek placed it on top of the map that was resting on the ground. Ensuring the bearing was correct, he marked their location on the map in pencil. Folding the map, he secured it along with the compass back in its pouch. The thirty-nine-year-old combat veteran was highly experienced at land navigation and had earned the Silver Star medal for his expertise as a pathfinder on D-Day.

Joining the army after graduating high school, he would experience far more action during his career than most men. Serving as a Pathfinder during WW2, he parachuted behind enemy lines to mark the drop zones for the paratroopers during the allied invasion of Normandy. He went on to serve in the Battle of the Bulge where he received a second Silver Star and a Purple Heart. Transferring to the Air Force when it became a separate service in 1947, he was assigned as an Air Policeman. He would be wounded a second time while searching for a downed pilot during the Korean War when one of his troops stepped on a landmine.

"Break time is over, prepare to move out!" he shouted to the other nine men in his search team. Other than Tratnyek, the team consisted of a radio operator, a medic, five Air Policemen, a Wisconsin State Trooper and a Marinette County Sheriff's Deputy.

"Airman Sian!"

"Yes Sergeant?"

"I want you on point. Now that we are crossing some of these strange symbols in the trees, I want an experienced man up there."

"Roger that!" said the young Airman First Class. At only twenty-two years old, he wasn't much older than the rest of the flight, but he had completed a tour of duty in Korea. That combat tour provided a wealth of experience that could not easily be taught at the Air Base Defense School at Parks AFB, California.

"Sergeant Tratnyek!" shouted the radio operator who was kneeling about fifteen yards away. He was listening to the handset and writing down notes from the command post. "Roger that Command Post, Search Team One out."

Hanging up the headset, the airman looked up to the sergeant who was now standing over him.

"That was command post. They found the reporter and another injured mountain man. Another one of those mountain men was killed in the process. They have intelligence that the two downed pilots are alive but injured. They are being held captive by that cult in their village. While they don't have the exact location, they have a general direction. Here are the new coordinates they want us to move towards," said the radio operator while handing the notepad to the sergeant.

Looking at the new coordinates, MSgt Tratnyek retrieved the map from its pouch just to ensure he understood the new terrain ahead of him. Putting the map back in its pouch, he issued new orders to his team.

"OK men, listen up! We have new orders. The downed pilots are believed to be alive and injured. They are being held captive by more of these crazy bastards. Our guys had to kill another one of them today. We are moving in a new direction, twenty-three degrees west of our current course. We are moving towards the general direction of the village. Expect hostile actions. I want three Air Policemen in the front and two in the back for rear security. I want civilian law enforcement, the medic and radio operator in the middle of the pack. Everybody, cover your zones and watch your fields of fire. Airman Sian, adjust your bearing and take point. Are there any questions?"

Nobody had any questions. They all understood their orders and what they needed to do. While the situation was intimidating for the young airmen, they all had faith in their sergeant. If anyone could bring them home safely, it was Master Sergeant. Tratnyek.

"Good, let's move out."

After traveling just two hundred yards in the new direction, Airman Sian stopped walking and held up one arm while opening his fist, the hand signal for halt. Next, he took a knee and examined the path in front of him as it just didn't seem right. The ground had more leaves covering it than other areas. Using the barrel of his carbine, he gently pushed away some of the leaves, revealing a tarp underneath. Slowly lifting the tarp, he discovered it concealed a five-foot-deep pit, intended to be a boobytrap. At the bottom of the pit were several sharpened spikes pointing upward. The intent was for a person or animal to step on the leaves and fall into the concealed pit, impaling themselves on the spikes.

Slowly moving back to the second airman in the patrol, he whispered, "Booby trap in front of us. I am hearing movement in the trees to our left. Pass it back."

Acknowledging the message, the second airman slowly stood up in order to pass on the message to the next man when an arrow came whistling from somewhere to their left, striking him in the upper back.

"Contact Left!" shouted Airman Sian, as he dropped into the prone position and aimed his carbine towards the woods.

The rest of the airmen dropped into tactical positions as well, while the trooper and sheriff's deputy remained standing and instinctively went for their sidearms. Two more arrows whistled through the air, both striking the deputy in his chest, just as his revolver cleared its holster.

The state trooper fired several rounds into the forest at the direction the arrow came from. Standing upright while frantically working to reload his revolver, he made an easy target as another arrow came from the woods, striking him in the abdomen.

After taking three casualties in just seconds, Master Sergeant Tratnyek kept his calm. Knowing they were sitting ducks for the concealed enemy and would be picked off one by one, he issued bold and decisive orders.

"Rear element cover fire! Forward element assault! On me, move out!"

This tactic caught the ambush party off guard as they had not anticipated such a bold move. The members of the clan were masters of camouflage and had worked diligently at selecting locations to assault the infiltrators with arrows. When the outsiders charged their locations, rapidly closing the distance for archery, the clan members were forced to leave their concealed locations and draw their tomahawks and knives. This exposed them to a hail of gunfire from the cover element.

Six members of the ambush team fell to the ground after sustaining multiple bullet wounds each from a devastating wall of gunfire. Two members turned and ran away while the last three stood to fight the charging airmen.

Airman Sian led the charge and was several feet in front of Master Sergeant Tratnyek. As he ran towards a huge warrior dressed in wolf skin garb, he felt his boot catch on a tripwire tied between two trees. Falling to the ground, he placed his left hand out in front of him to break his fall while holding his carbine in his right hand. When he hit the ground, he heard a loud snap and felt immense pain in his left arm. He had fallen into a concealed bear trap that had snapped shut on his forearm. The heavy spring caused the sharp metal teeth to clamp down violently and crush his soft tissue and likely break the bones.

Trying to stand up, he was unable as the bear trap was chained to a spike in the ground. Airman Sian struggled to bring his carbine up to a firing position as the large warrior was approaching and ready to strike him with a tomahawk. Lifting the carbine one handed and pointing in the general direction, he pulled the trigger. Bang! Bang! Click! The first two rounds struck the large warrior in the soft tissue of his legs before the carbine malfunctioned.

Trying to clear the jam one handed, there was no way he would be able to get his gun back into the fight in time.

Bang! Bang! Bang! Airman Sian watched as an explosion of crimson erupted from the warrior's chest as three .30 caliber bullets penetrated this thorax. Looking up from the ground, he saw Master Sergeant Tratnyek run past him with smoke coming from the barrel of his gun. He watched as the seasoned veteran, engaging the last two warriors while on the move, dropping each with a three-round burst from his carbine.

As the Master Sergeant scanned the forest for additional threats, he took a knee and inserted a fresh fifteen round magazine into his weapon.

"Sian! Are you hit?" asked the sergeant while scanning the area in front of him.

"I'm caught in a bear trap!" replied the airman.

"Say again?" asked the sergeant for clarification, his ears ringing from the gunfire.

"I think I'm caught in a bear trap," said the airman in a surprisingly calm voice.

Looking over his shoulder, the sergeant was surprised to see the airman on the ground with an actual metal bear trap clamped around his forearm.

"Medic!" shouted the sergeant.

"I have wounded back here! Just do what you can!" replied the medic.

Evaluating the situation and concerned the enemy could make a counter attack, Tratnyek shouted "Fall back into a defensive circle!"

He then walked backwards to Airman Sian's position, keeping his weapon pointed in the direction the attackers fled. Kneeling down to the trapped airman, he instructed him to keep watch while he released him from the trap.

He considered placing a tourniquet on the arm before releasing the trap as there was considerable soft tissue damage and lacerations. As he didn't observe any arterial bleeding, he decided against it. Placing his carbine on the ground next to him, he used both hands to pry the trap open, allowing the airman to pull out his wounded appendage.

Picking his carbine back up, he instructed the wounded airman to fall back to the defensive position. Following him, Tratnyek walked backwards while providing cover. Once back in the group, he took a fast count of his men and resources. The deputy and one of the air policemen had been killed in the action. The trooper was in critical condition and Airman Sian had an injured arm. The medic was frantically working to save the trooper while another airman bandaged up Sian's arm.

"Everyone top off your weapons with a fresh magazine! Keep your bodies low and your eyes open. Call out anything that looks suspicious. Radioman, get Command Post on the line.

Master Sergeant Tratnyek low crawled over to the medic who was working on the trooper. The trooper was young, the same age as his young air policemen. He was conscious and in severe pain. Losing blood internally from the deep penetrating abdominal wound, he was apologizing to the Master Sergeant.

"What are you sorry for son, you did just fine."

"I stood there and shot while I should have hit the deck like the military guys."

"You did just as you were trained to do, son. You were brave and you held your ground. Civilian law enforcement training is just different than military training. You did fine and I think you might have got one of them. I would be happy to serve with you anytime. Now just lay back and let the medic fix you up."

The radio operator crawled over to the Master Sergeant and handed him the handset.

"Command Post is on the line."

Speaking into the receiver, he said, "Command Post from Ground Search Team One."

"Go ahead for Command Post," came the reply.

"We have been engaged by hostile forces in an ambush style assault. We have repelled the assault for now but have sustained casualties. I have two dead and two wounded. There are about a dozen dead or wounded enemy combatants near our position. Ground Search Team One is no longer able to continue with the primary mission. Repeat, Ground Search Team One is no longer able to continue with the mission. I have one critical that needs immediate medical evacuation."

"We copy your radio traffic Ground Search Team One. Acknowledge you have wounded that require medical evacuation. Acknowledge you are no longer able to continue the primary mission. We will divert Ground Search Team Four and Air Search Team One to your location. Hold tight, help is on the way."

"Roger that. Ground Search Team One to all other Ground Search Teams, the area is heavily booby trapped. We have encountered metal bear traps and punji stick pits. Proceed with extreme caution. Ground Search Team One out."

CHAPTER 48

The sun was high in the sky and Casper knew his time had run out. About twenty members of the clan had gathered in a circle to attend the sacrificial ceremony. Counting seventeen women and only three men, he wondered why the disproportionate numbers.

"Why are there so few men in the clan?" he asked Randalin.

"There have been outsiders in the woods recently. Yesterday one of our warriors was killed. He was one of my brothers. Today many more outsiders are in our woods and a war party was sent to protect the clan. They have not yet returned. That is where most of the men are."

Casper was hopeful that it was the search party that had killed the warrior yesterday. That would mean they were getting closer. Hearing the helicopter in the distance earlier was a great feeling, however, he didn't think he had much time left before the sacrifice.

Looking over his shoulder, Casper watched two of the large men leave the area and walk to the underground structure where he met Thordis. Disappearing down the stairs, they returned a few minutes later, carrying an elaborate chair holding the queen. Once they returned to the area where the sacrifice was to take place, they sat her down so she could oversee the process. Casper could hear the sound of the helicopter once again. Closing his eyes, he said a prayer that the rescue team would find them before it was too late.

Casper watched as one of the men returned and placed a small table next to the queen. The other man placed the severed human head she called Warden on the table. Next, Gayda walked up to the queen and placed a crown made out of twigs upon the queen's head. When she did this, all the people in the clan fell to their knees and placed their foreheads on the ground.

Casper could tell Gyda was upset and had been crying. He assumed his ruse had caused an internal conflict between the two old women.

Thordis looked up to the sky and spoke to the heavens, "Odin, your chosen child has forsaken us. She has been deceitful and bears the child of a mortal. She has damned us all. Because of her actions, the warriors that fell from Asgard have proven to be false profits and spread lies to destroy us. Please accept our sacrifice and spare us from the storm of fire."

Hearing the helicopter once again, Casper had to stall for time. He spoke aloud to the group.

"Listen to me! I come from Asgard and I have been sent by Odin to enlighten you all. Your queen is no longer Thordis, but Gyda is to wear the crown now. This has been commanded!"

"Do not listen to him! He speaks lies!" shouted Thordis.

"I speak the truth! Listen to your hearts and you shall know I am correct. Raise your heads from the ground and look at me. Thordis is no longer your queen!"

"Silence!" shouted the queen. "I am the ruler of Forest Egersund. Gyda, I command you to take the ceremonial blade and complete the sacrifice."

Gyda, slowly picking up the blade from the table, had a look of defeat on her face.

Hearing the sound of the helicopter getting closer, Casper used it to his advantage.

"Do you all hear the sound of Odin's Valkyrie? It will appear in the form of a metal dragon. If you do not obey me, it will strike you all down."

Casper could see several of the clan members starting to lift their heads, both looking up at him and to the sky.

"Kill him now!" screamed the queen, as loud as her old voice could carry.

As Gyda looked down at the knife in her hand, she hesitated. Just then, the silver H-19 Chickasaw helicopter passed overhead striking fear in the people.

Taking advantage of the situation, Casper yelled, "All hail Queen Gyda! The Valkyrie has spoken and she is the new leader! Gyda, Odin commands you to place the crown upon your own head."

One by one, the clan members started to chant "Hail Queen Gyda" along with Casper.

As more of the family was chanting her name, she became emboldened for the first time in her life. Gyda placed the sacrificial knife back on the table and reached up to remove the crown from her mother. Lifting it off of the old woman's head, the meek woman looked up at the family members cheering for her. Feeling love for the first time in many years, she smiled as she placed the crown upon her own head.

As the people cheered for their new queen, Casper saw movement behind her. He watched in horror as Thordis quietly stood up from her chair, behind Gyda. Surprised that the old woman was able to stand, he tried to shout a warning but he was not heard over the loud celebratory chanting of the clan and the growing sound of the helicopter. He watched in horror as a bony hand holding the sacrificial blade reached around Gyda and in a single movement, sliced her neck wide open.

Gyda, reached up to her neck in an attempt to put pressure on the fatal wound. It was a futile attempt as both the trachea and one of the carotid arteries had been severed. She fell to her knees with a look of panic on her face. Standing behind her, Thordis lifted the crown from her head just before the lifeless body fell to the ground.

The clan members also watched in horror, many of them dropping to their knees and once again placing their foreheads to the ground to show subservience to Queen Thordis.

The old woman was surprisingly tall and far more mobile than anyone was led to believe. She replaced the crown back upon her head while staring down at Casper. She slowly walked past him over to her great granddaughter Randalin. Standing behind where she was tied to the post, she held the bloody sacrificial knife up while looking Casper in the eyes.

"Her deceit put her here. But your blasphemy is far worse. You will watch as she is sacrificed to the Gods by having her throat slit, but your sacrifice will be far slower…and much more painful."

CHAPTER 49

After Conner and the medic carefully crawled back into the helicopter from the hoist cable, Conner took a seat in the open doorway on the left side of the aircraft next to Sandy. While one medic was working on Anders, the second medic started examining Sandy. Conner pulled the tomahawk from his belt and handed it to Major Gibson to inspect.

Major Gibson took the ax and looked at it briefly before setting it down on the floor of the helicopter. He then looked at Conner and yelled, "Ground Search Team One has been engaged! They have casualties. We need to go pick them up!"

Conner gave a thumbs up, but kept a watchful eye on the terrain below to look for the village the pilots were supposedly held at. As the tree canopy passed by a few feet beneath them at fifty miles per hour, Conner saw a brief opening in the trees and what looked like a village of sorts. Slapping Major Gibson on the leg to get his attention, he then pointed down and signaled for the helicopter to swing back around.

After instructing the pilots, the large helicopter made a wide, slow turn, trying to make its way back to the location indicated. After searching for a couple of minutes, they finally came to a hover over an opening in the trees. Looking down about one-hundred and twenty feet below, they could see several people gathered in the center of the village, who appeared to be on their knees in a prayer position. They were all in a circle facing three wooden poles that had been stuck in the ground. Conner could see a person tied to each of the poles. He thought to himself two of the people tied to the poles must be the missing pilots. He then watched in horror as a woman stood and slit the throat of another woman.

Jumping out onto the cable, Conner yelled to lower him as he drew his pistol from his waistband. Major Gibson grabbed the control to the winch and started to lower the cable. As it would take about ninety seconds for Conner to reach the ground. Maj. Gibson instructed one of the air policemen to shoot the woman with the knife. The motion of the helicopter made it difficult for the airman to hold his sights on the woman, in addition, Conner was dangling on the cable below like a pendulum continuously obscuring the target.

Conner, watching the macabre scene unfold beneath him, pointed his pistol at the woman holding the knife. He watched as she walked over and stood behind a girl who was tied to one of the poles. Assuming she was going to slit her throat next, Conner tried to aim at the woman but due to the constant swing of the cable and the strong winds from the helicopter's rotor, he couldn't keep the front site on his target and he didn't want to risk hitting the girl.

Lying on the vibrating floor of the helicopter, Anders regained consciousness. Scared and in pain from his wounds, he noticed the strange people that abducted him were all looking out the open door on the left side of the strange machine. Desperate to escape his captors, he noticed his uncle's tomahawk resting on the floor near him. Slowly reaching over, he picked up the weapon while everyone was distracted. Struggling to get to his knees, then into a wobbly standing position, he moved to attack his captors while their backs were turned.

Captain Pfeffer, while holding the helicopter as steady as possible, looked over his right shoulder into the troop compartment located behind and below the cockpit. Seeing the buckskin clad teenager getting to his feet with a weapon in his hand, he tried to yell a warning but he couldn't be heard over the sound of the helicopter. Having no other option to prevent the imminent attack, he used the pilots' controls to tilt the helicopter to the right.

Sandy, looking up just as Anders was raising the weapon over his head, screamed while holding her uninjured hand up to protect herself. Just as this happened, the helicopter tilted hard to the right, causing the young warrior to fall backwards and out of the open door on the other side of the aircraft.

Conner, dangling on the cable, had steadied his aim enough to risk taking a shot. Just before pulling the trigger, he was yanked upwards several feet due to the hard actions of the helicopter. He watched in shock as Anders body fell past him in the air, hitting the ground hard just feet from where Thordis was standing. Looking back up to the helicopter then back to the ground, he thought to himself, there is no way that just happened.

Captain Casper also watched in shock and amazement as a body fell from the helicopter landing just behind Thordis. Assuming it was one of the aircraft crewmembers who fell out by accident, he was wondering why the man was dressed in buckskin like the villagers. Another confusing factor was the man dressed in civilian attire descending from the Air Force helicopter on the cable holding a pistol.

The villagers, fearful that the dragon sent by Odin was spitting out members of their clan, jumped to their feet and fled into the forest screaming in fear.

As Conner's feet were almost on the ground from being lowered on the slow cable, he watched the woman with the knife reach around the young girl's throat who was tied to the post. Just as she was about to sacrifice the girl, a tomahawk came spinning through the air from the woods behind her. Lodging into the back of her skull, the weapon ended the long rule of the sinister queen.

Finally on the ground, Connor rapidly worked to remove himself from the harness and watched as Oddball Otto walked out of the forest. It was his tomahawk that had killed the old woman and saved his daughters girl.

Knowing he was a dangerous man; Conner yelled for him to stop and raise his hands. Otto stopped walking and slowly raised his hands over his head. Moments later, Conner was relieved to see the Air Force Policemen from Ground Search Team Two entering the village from the woods. Signaling them to take Otto into custody, he was finally able to turn his attention back to the pilots.

Trying to decipher what had taken place in the village was no easy task. Walking over to the conscious naked man tied to the pole, he yelled over the sound of the helicopter, "What is your name?"

The man replied "Captain Glen Casper, United States Air Force."

Kneeling next to the man while untying him, Conner said, "Glad to meet you Ghost, your wife Becca sent me to bring you home."

CHAPTER 50

The next twenty-four hours was a flurry of activity as dozens of federal, state and local government personnel arrived at the village to conduct their portion of the investigation. Special Agents wearing black business suits from both the FBI and OSI, collected evidence, took photographs and interviewed all the involved parties. Social services from Marinette and the adjoining counties were trying to figure out what to do with the surviving villagers and how to get them to assimilate into modern society. Most would be taken to the county insane asylum until they were deemed non-threatening.

There were numerous investigations that would need to be conducted from the lengthy history of crimes committed by the cult, to the abductions of the pilots, and for all the deaths that occurred over the past couple of days. The Wisconsin Department of Natural Resources dispatched several Conservation Wardens to collect the severed head of their fallen brother as well as clear the woods of all the booby traps left by the cult.

The dead were processed and transported to Marinette as additional medical examiners were brought in to assist the local coroner. The wounded, consisting of the two pilots, the trooper, Airman Sian, Sandy, and two of the village warriors that survived the gun fight, were taken to the Marinette hospital for stabilization. The next day the three Air Force members would be transferred to the base hospital at Truax AFB.

Conner, wanting to go visit Sandy at the hospital, had to remain at the village to assist with the investigation. By the time he was able to get to the hospital that night it was well past visiting hours.

The next morning, Conner walked into the Marinette Memorial Hospital wearing agent attire. Stopping into the men's room, he used the mirror to check his hair and adjust his tie. He had strong feelings for Sandy and he wasn't sure what to do about it. He hadn't seen her since she kissed him the day before. He wore his suit today, primarily because he wanted to look good when he visited her.

Walking out of the restroom into the lobby of the hospital, the first thing Conner noticed was a small gift shop near the entrance. Not wanting to show up empty handed, he walked in and purchased a bouquet of flowers in a vase. Once he had it in hand, he felt a little silly, like a high school boy going to pick up his prom date.

Walking up to the nurse's station, he checked with the charge nurse. Smiling, he looked down at the nameplate on the desk and said, "Good morning, nurse Potter, is it?"

Smiling back, she said, "Yes, but we are pretty informal in these parts. You can call me Trish."

"Well, good morning, Trish. My name is Special Agent Conner Price. I'm looking to speak with a female that was brought in yesterday. Her name is Sandra Elliot." He said while showing her his law enforcement credentials.

"Oh yes, she left last night. The doctor tried to get her to stay for observation but she said she had a story to write. I guess she is a reporter or something."

"Something like that. What was the extent of her injuries?"

Nurse Potter flipped through some papers on the desk before finding the right chart. Summarizing as she read, she said "She was dehydrated, had cuts and blisters on both feet, dozens of bug bites and a severe puncture wound to the left hand. It looks like she experienced psychological trauma as well but refused to speak with the psychologist. After she received an IV and had her physical wounds treated, she left."

Disappointed that he missed her, he thanked the nurse and placed the flowers on the desk. "Here, these are for you," he said. As he was walking away, the nurse called out to him.

"Oh, Agent Price?"

Turning back to the nurse, he replied "Yes ma'am."

"There is a note for you. I guess she knew you would be coming by and left this for you. It has your name on it."

Thanking the nurse, he took the note and returned to his car to read it in private. Once back in the driver's seat, he turned on the ignition and adjusted the air conditioning. Opening the note, it said.

Dear Conner,

I assumed you would come check on me. Actually, I was hoping you would. I'm so sorry I missed you but I needed to get my story to the editor. I can't thank you enough for rescuing me, and for the special conversations we shared. Thoughts of you have occupied my mind over the past few days, especially when I was alone and scared in the forest. I dreamed of you saving me, and when I saw you coming down through the trees, I couldn't believe my eyes.

You have made me re-evaluate myself, as well as what I want out of life. For that I cannot thank you enough. You are very special to me and hopefully our paths will cross again one day.

Love,

Sandy

CHAPTER 51

"I don't even know what to say," said Special Agent Johnson, after listening to the telephonic briefing from Conner.

"Yeah, it's pretty bizarre that's for sure. It's been a long week."

"How are you doing with shooting that guy?"

"I'm doing fine. It was Agent Goldens first time killing a man but he seems to be doing alright. The Internal Affairs agents are here at Truax AFB now. I gave my statement to them a little while ago."

"When do you plan on coming back to Ohio?"

"I need to wrap up a few loose ends here. I will probably head back tonight or in the morning. Is that alright?"

"Sure, that's fine. Do what you need to do and I'll see you when you get back."

"Thanks."

"Oh, and Conner, wear a suit when you out-brief that colonel."

Laughing, he said "Will do boss," and hung up the phone.

Looking in the mirror, he adjusted his tie and put on his suit jacket. Picking up Sandy's note from the hotel dresser, he looked at it one more time. He had probably read it a dozen times over the last twenty-four hours.

Tucking it away into the breast pocket of his jacket, he left the room enroute to the base hospital.

Located only two blocks from the visiting officers' quarters, he decided to walk rather than drive. He had a lot on his mind and the walk would give him a few minutes to think. Like Sandy, he was re-evaluating what he wanted out of life. Although he was used to the fast-paced life of Project Blue Book, he was lonely. It would be nice to have someone to share things with.

Inside the base hospital, he walked up to the military nurse's station. An Air Force captain wearing the new WAF silver tan uniform, asked if she could help him. Looking down at her nametag, he replied, "Good morning, Captain Brase. Did I pronounce that right?"

Smiling, she said "Pretty close, but you can call me Jen," in a flirtatious way while making eye contact.

Smiling back, he showed her his credentials and said "I'm Special Agent Price. I'm looking to speak with the two pilots that were brought in from Marinette."

"They are in rooms 202 and 203."

"How are they doing?" asked Conner.

The nurse smiled and said, "Surprisingly well for all they have been through. Legend is conscious now and already trying to flirt with all of my junior nurses. Captain Casper is doing better. He does have a broken vertebrae in his back but the doctors think the paralysis is only temporary. He's already getting some feeling back now that the swelling has been reduced. He will need a surgery on his back and another to repair his leg, but he should recover."

"That is good news. Can I see them?"

Smiling, she said, "You're are OSI, how could I stop you?"

Conner laughed and said, "I try to play by the rules as much as possible."

Walking down the hallway, he stopped and looked into room 202. Conner laughed as he saw four nurses crowded around the hospital bed as

Lieutenant Kelly "Legend" Jensen told the harrowing story of his captivity. Shaking his head, Conner moved on to room 203.

Looking inside the room, he could see Mrs. Casper standing next to the bed, holding her husband's hand. Not wanting to interrupt, he turned to walk away.

"Agent Price?" the female voice called his name from inside the room.

Conner stopped walking and turned around as Mrs. Casper walked out into the hallway with tears of joy in her eyes.

"Yes ma'am?"

Smiling. the woman reached up and gave him a tight hug, holding it for several seconds.

"Thank you so much for bringing him home to us."

Not finding the words to respond to her during their emotional embrace, he said "It was my pleasure ma'am. There were a lot of men involved in the rescue."

"I'm sure there were Conner. But it was you that God selected to bring him home to me. I don't know why, but he chose you. I think this experience was meant for you as much as it was for my husband."

"Well, I'm not sure about that but God does work in mysterious ways."

"That he does. I am going to go get a cup of coffee. Glen would love to speak with you so I will leave you two alone."

Conner stepped into the hospital room and closed the door behind him so they would have some privacy. As he walked over to the bed, Casper said, "My wife wants to name our child after you if it's a boy."

Laughing, Conner said "I can think of better names," as he pulled up a chair and sat next to him.

"She can be a pretty stubborn woman when her mind is made up."

"I can see that. So, how are you doing?" asked Conner, getting the topic back on the wounded pilot.

"Well, the pain meds are great and my prognosis looks good, so I have that going for me. But I'm more worried about that young village girl, Randalin."

"Yeah, that's an incredible story, but one that I think will have a happy ending. She has been medically cleared and is in fact pregnant. I hear she will be taken to the Shrine of Our Lady of Good Help, in Champion Wisconsin. They will give her a place to stay while she has the baby, then help her assimilate to the world. Her great grandmother Thordis was taken there as a child after surviving the great Peshtigo fire. She ran away and started that cult in the woods."

"That's incredible. If I read this story in a novel, I would be certain it was fiction," said Casper.

"Well, you just might see that book someday."

"What do you mean?"

Not wanting to hijack the conversation with his feelings for Sandy, Conner just said, "It's an amazing story, one that needs to be told."

"Were you able to determine who the severed head belonged to. The one she called Warden?"

"Yes. Two weeks before you crashed, Thordis was worried that she would be exposed as a fraud if Randalin didn't get pregnant by the great warrior from Asgard. She had a former villager named Otto abduct a man from a boat, gouge out his eye and bring him back in order to explain Randalin's pregnancy. The man they abducted was a Wisconsin Conservation Warden. Apparently, he refused and fought to the death. Thordis had his head cut off and told the people it was like the head of Mimir that Odin had in Norse mythology. That's why she called him Warden…she thought it was his first name."

"What will happen to the surviving villagers?"

"That's a local matter, but most of the male warriors were killed in the assault on the search party. Most of the others have been rounded up and the state is trying to determine how dangerous they are and what to do with them. Their entire belief system has advanced hundreds of years overnight. It will be challenging for many to assimilate."

Changing the topic, Casper said, "Colonel Roberts and I had a long conversation last night."

Smiling, Conner asked if the old man talked him into accepting his promotion to major and staying in the Air Force.

"Well, yes, that did happen, but that's not what I'm getting at."

"No?"

"We talked about you. He told me that you used to be a fighter pilot and got shot down during the war. You were also taken captive and injured. He said your injuries ended your flying career."

Nodding, Conner said, "Yes, that's all true."

"I don't think it was a coincidence that you were the one who found me."

"I don't follow."

"You were a fighter pilot whose injuries ended his flying career. You were able to stay in the Air Force by finding a new path that was meaningful to you. For you, it was investigations. While I will survive my injuries, it is all but certain I will never fly again. I feel that I am destined to be a minister. Colonel Roberts said he would try and help me stay in the service and change careers to be a chaplain."

Casper continued, "I'm a man of faith, and over the last few days my faith was tested many times. I prayed to God while I was captive, and he sent you to find me. He answered my prayers with you."

Conner didn't know how to respond to the man, but felt a tear of emotion start to form in his eye. Not one to allow himself to show emotion, he tried to cut the conversation short.

"I'm glad you are doing well, Ghost. I need to run; I have to out brief Colonel Roberts before I head back to Wright-Patterson AFB."

As Conner turned to walk away, Casper called to him.

"Conner. I think God chose you to save me. But I also think it was to save you as well. I don't understand why or how, but I get the feeling you are supposed to move forward from the past."

Conner turned and looked back at the man in the bed, still not sure what to say.

"Thanks Glen," said Conner while coming to attention and rendering a salute.

Casper returned the salute and smiled as Conner left the room.

CHAPTER 52

Once Conner was out of the room, he wiped the tear from his eye. The message from Casper hit home and he felt it was time to re-evaluate his life. Leaving the base hospital, he started to walk the two blocks to the headquarters building where he would say goodbye to Colonel Roberts. As he was walking down the sidewalk of the main boulevard, a sedan pulled over to the curb in front of him.

Seeing that Don was driving, Conner got into the passenger seat.

"You forget to say goodbye?" asked Don.

Smiling, Conner said, "No, I just stopped by the hospital to check on the pilots. Now I'm headed over to say goodbye to Colonel Roberts and I was going to stop by to see you last."

"I'm heading over to see Roberts myself. Did you see this morning's paper?" asked Don as he handed him a copy.

Opening the paper, Conner read the headline, *American Heroes—Air Force Pilots and the men who saved them.*

"Well, that was fast." said Conner, amazed at her tenacity. "I'm kind of surprised at the headline though. I figured she would have gone for something involving UFO's, religious cults or the like."

"Yeah, I'm guessing your influence played a big part in how she framed her story."

"I don't follow."

"While she addressed the facts of the story, she emphasized the heroics of the pilots and the rescue team. I think you helped her see the bigger picture," said Don.

As Conner thought about his words, Don handed him an envelope from FBI Headquarters.

"What is this?"

"It's a classified report containing the information you requested on Mrs. Sandra Jane Elliott."

"Anything interesting?"

"Her birth name was LaFawn Aescht. Her mother died when she was fourteen. Her father was a German immigrant as a child who later became a Navy officer. When WW2 broke out, he joined the Office of Strategic Services (OSS) and then the Central Intelligence Agency after the war. He was leading a clandestine operation that was helping the war effort at the start of the Korean War. He was recruiting and training a network of Chinese expatriates that could serve as a guerilla force to destabilize the government. He went missing in 1950 and is believed to be a Prisoner of War somewhere in China. Apparently, there was a threat against his family that generated the name change. Her new name, Sandra Jane Elliot, was assigned by the CIA and she was initially under their protection. Being headstrong, she eventually refused the protection and wanted to live life on her terms. Obviously, that info is classified."

"Well, that explains a few things. Her journalism tradecraft had the telltale signs of an inexperienced counterintelligence officer." Conner had to smile, surprised that she had inner demons she was struggling with herself. Maybe she was deeper than he gave her credit for.

"She doesn't know the details about her father, just that he went missing."

"Her car was owned by a company in London. Was that connected to the agency?"

"Yeah, the Dewey Chemical Company is a shell corporation operated by the British Military Intelligence Section Six (MI-6). Even though she is no longer under CIA protection, they have insisted on a few safety measures to serve as tripwires to detect foreign intelligence interests. When we ran her plate, it flagged the system at the CIA."

As the two agents arrived at the Truax AFB Headquarters building, they parked the car and walked inside. Entering the large lobby, they were greeted by Major Gibson and Master Sergeant Tratnyek, who were just leaving. The four men stopped to greet each other and shake hands in passing.

While Conner was shaking Tratnyek's hand, he said "I hear you gave them one hell of a fight out there."

"It was a team effort and my cops stepped up to the plate. I'm pretty proud of them."

"I hear you have quite the combat history in WW2 and Korea. Are you about ready to retire now?"

"Soon, I have one last deployment before I'm done. I'm headed to Indochina in a couple of weeks. The French are pulling out of a little country called South Vietnam. We are helping them establish their own Air Force to defend against communist aggression."

"You don't think you have seen enough action yet?"

"It's not a direct-action mission. We are just advisors. My combat days are behind me.

"Let's hope so, but things have a way of escalating when you are around. You were just on a simple search and rescue mission and ended up leading an infantry charge in the woods."

Master Sergeant Tratnyek laughed at the comment.

"Well good luck and stay safe," said Conner as he and Don continued on to Colonel Roberts's office.

As the agents entered the command section, they checked in with the receptionist.

After identifying themselves, they asked if the colonel was available.

The Staff Sergeant working the desk asked, "Is he expecting you?"

Don replied, "We don't have an appointment, but I think he was expecting to hear from us this morning."

The Staff Sergeant picked up his telephone and had a short conversation while looking at the men in civilian attire. After hanging up, he said, "Colonel Roberts said to send you back to his office."

"Thanks, we know the way," said Don.

As the two men came to the end of the hall, they noticed the colonel's door was open.

"Please come in gentlemen, and have a seat," said the colonel.

"Thank you," replied Don, while Conner closed the door behind them for privacy.

"So, when do you head back to Wright-Patterson?" asked the colonel.

While Conner had hoped to stay another day or two to visit with Sandy, that was not meant to be. "I will be heading back later today."

"Well, Conner, it's been great serving with you. I know you OSI guys operate in your own world, but if there is anything I can ever do for you, please don't hesitate to ask."

"Thank you, sir, that means a lot," said Conner, actually being sincere. "I heard you had a conversation with Captain Casper last night. He and his wife think I was sent here by a divine power."

"Yes, he is a man of faith. But you have to admit, a lot of strange coincidences lined up for you to get here. The connection with Project Blue Book, your history as a downed pilot, prisoner of war and a man whose injuries closed one door but opened another."

"Well, you seemed to have convinced him to remain in the Air Force and accept his promotion. That's a start."

"Yeah, it will be an uphill battle, but he has character and we need more like him."

"Agreed," said Conner.

The colonel pointed to the newspaper sitting on his desk and said, "I see your reporter friend had a busy night. She must have gone right to the editor after leaving the hospital."

"I haven't read it yet; did she say anything about Project Blue Book or UFOs?"

"No, but I think she has a thing for you. She made the Air Force look very good this time, especially you."

"Did she mention me by name?" asked Conner, concerned about the publicity.

"Not by name, but it was clear she was talking about you. I think you have a fan." said the colonel.

While Conner was disappointed that she left without saying goodbye, it made him feel good that she hadn't already forgotten about him.

"Well, the entire story was pretty crazy. Just the fact that four generations of that family could survive in the woods all those years," said Conner.

"I just can't help but be amazed at the coincidence. I know Thordis was crazy and made up all of her prophecies, but that was bizarre," said the colonel.

"What coincidence is that?" asked Conner.

"The prophecy that her great grand-daughter, Randalin would be impregnated by a wounded warrior, who fell from the heavens, before her eighteenth birthday.

"I don't follow," replied Conner.

"I was told that Randalin secretly got pregnant a few weeks before her eighteenth birthday, but the boy, Anders, was not a mighty warrior who fell from the heavens. But at the end, he was. He was injured, and fell from a helicopter with a tomahawk in his hand. The injured warrior did fall from the heavens after all…and she was pregnant with his child before her eighteenth birthday. The prophecy actually did come true."

Both Conner and Don were in shock by this revelation. In all of the excitement, that fact had slipped past them. It was an amazing coincidence, one that sent chills up the seasoned investigators back.

CHAPTER 53

Three days had passed since he had been kissed by Sandy and he couldn't get her out of his thoughts. The special moments he shared with her was burned into his mind, as were the soft touch of her lips. Sitting in the Bel Air outside the OSI Project Blue Book office at Wright Patterson AFB, Conner was lost in his thoughts.

He was brought back to the real world when the 1948 Ford Super Deluxe pulled into the empty parking space to his right. He had to smile when he made eye contact with Special Agent Tucker, who was just returning from his Blue Book assignment in Kentucky with no air conditioning. As the two agents got out of their cars to return to the office after several days on the road, they greeted each other.

"How was Kentucky?" asked Conner, with a smirk on his face.

"It was hot Conner, very hot," said Tucker.

Laughing, Conner said, "I'm glad you got assigned that one. My investigation got regional headlines, but yours kept it off of the national news. I think you are a celebrity now Tuck."

"Yeah, it was something alright," said Tucker.

"So, what was the deal down there?"

Laughing, he said, "They are calling it the Hopkinsville Goblin Case in the newspapers. It was a bizarre mixture of the effects of excitement and the misidentification of natural phenomena."

"OK, that's a nice official Blue Book resolution, but what really happened down there?"

Laughing, Tucker related, "Apparently twelve small aliens from a UFO were attacking a farm house and a group of five human adults and seven children held them off with gunfire for a period of four hours."

"That's awesome!" said Conner, enjoying hearing that another agent had to deal with local antics as well.

Tucker continued, "After investigating, it turned out the group consisted of carnival workers and pretty intoxicated ones at that. There was a comet that night which got them freaked out. Since they were just carney's passing through, they were unfamiliar with the wildlife in the area. The supposed two-foot-tall aliens they saw were actually just a few great horned owls who were defending their nearby nest. Being nocturnal, their eyes glow at night, and since they fly, the carneys thought they were levitating. They all got themselves worked up into an excited frenzy and started seeing them all over the place, in windows, doorways, on the roof, and behind furniture. They shot the hell out of the house for four hours."

Laughing, Conner said "I think my investigation was pretty good also, but I'm glad your story stole the headlines."

As both agents walked into the office, Jan, the receptionist, smiled and said, "Tucker, the boss wants to see you first…and he is not happy about the press coverage."

Tucker rolled his eyes while Conner laughed.

"Don't get too relaxed Conner, you are on deck for a butt chewing next."

As Tucker walked back to brief the boss, Jan wanted to talk with Conner.

"I know you just got back last night, but I need you to do something."

"What's that?"

"Please don't say no, this is very important to me."

"It sounds like I should run while I have the chance."

"My cousin is in town and she is expecting you to have dinner with her at 7pm."

"I just got back last night, and I have been on the road for a long time. I'm not really in the mood for going on a blind date."

"I don't ask you for much Conner."

"What?" he said laughing. "You ask me for stuff all the time!"

"Well, this will be the last time, I promise. It's important."

Conner just gave her a blank stare and didn't respond.

"Good," she said. "My cousin Kaylin will meet you at the officer's club formal dining room tonight at 7pm. She will be in a white dress...and CONNER, wear a suit."

CHAPTER 54

The formal dining room at the officer's club provided an elegant ambiance, with white tablecloths and polished silver. While Conner felt out of place in such a formal venue, it was impossible to tell as he was trained to blend into any environment. Looking down at his watch, it was ten minutes past seven o'clock. Maybe she won't show up, he thought to himself, wondering if he would still get credit for the date.

Thinking about the appropriate amount of time to wait before leaving, he looked over to the formal bar across the dining room. His eyes rested on the back of a beautiful woman walking away from him to order a drink. She was wearing a long white dress that accentuated her feminine figure and high heels. Conner thought to himself, she walks with the gate of a trained dancer, much like Sandy did. While it couldn't be her, Conner still looked for the bandaged left hand, but hers was concealed by long white gloves that were in style with the fashionable ladies.

"Excuse me, sir, are you Special Agent Price?"

Conner looked up to the waiter wearing formal attire, "Yes, that's me."

"I have a message for you, sir," as he handed him a folded piece of paper.

Opening the message, Conner noticed it was a handwritten note on Air Force OSI letterhead. It was from Jan.

"Conner, my cousin is not really in town tonight. Your date is with the woman in white sitting at the bar."

Looking back up, Conner could now see Sandy's eyes looking back at him from the reflection in the mirror behind the bar. It was reminiscent of the day they met one another. They both smiled, knowing that their next adventure was just beginning.

2-24-24

Halacopters sp. 236